DECEMBER
BOYS

Also by Joe Clifford

The Jay Porter Novels
Lamentation

Nonseries
Wake the Undertaker

Memoir
Junkie Love

Anthologies
Choice Cuts
Trouble in the Heartland (editor)

DECEMBER BOYS

A JAY PORTER NOVEL

JOE CLIFFORD

Oceanview Publishing
Longboat Key, Florida

ISBN 978-1-60809-171-3

Published in the United States of America by Oceanview Publishing
Longboat Key, Florida

www.oceanviewpub.com

10 9 8 7 6 5 4 3 2 1

PRINTED IN THE UNITED STATES OF AMERICA

For my sons, Holden and Jackson Kerouac

ACKNOWLEDGMENTS

THANKS TO MY lovely wife, Justine, who gave me the space, time, and feedback to make my deadline—in between giving birth to our second son. You are an amazing woman, and I am a better man for having you in my life.

Thanks to my sister Melissa and my brother Josh (I wish Mom had lived to see this), and to my other brother Jason, my inspiration for Jay Porter.

Thanks to my first line of defense, my beta readers Tom Pitts and Jimmy Soyka. Without your valuable insights, this book doesn't get written.

Thanks to my East Coast experts on diversion programs and juvenile detention centers (Scott Hartan) and alcohol-related matters (Josh Karaczewski); and my Midwest connection for all things rock 'n' roll (Blair Hook). Special thanks to Micah Schnabel and Two Cow Garage for use of their lyrics. Your music provided the soundtrack to this book.

Thanks to the crime writing community at large. Whether we've spoken at length at conferences or communicated briefly via social media, you are why I do this. I do feel the need to highlight a few of the main offenders. David Corbett, Hilary Davidson, Todd Robinson, Brian Panowich, Benoit Lelièvre, and Lynne Barrett—in one way or another you all helped to get me started, egged me on, or kept me going. Thanks for your tireless support.

And, last, thanks to my agent, Elizabeth Kracht, for finding my *Lamentation* novels a home; and to David, Lisa, Emily, Lee, Pat and Bob, and everyone else on the Oceanview team. Your faith in me means the world. I look forward to working together for years to come.

Oh you December boys got it bad /
Songs of losers and dreamers can be such a drag /
Birthdays and graduations through a telephone /
Another son of a son of a rolling stone / . . .
Now, there's gonna come a time when your little
world's coming apart /
'Cause this whole world is just dying to break
your heart . . .

—"Jackson, Don't You Worry," Two Cow Garage

DECEMBER BOYS

CHAPTER ONE

I SAT IN my idling truck outside the abandoned construction site, staring up at the towering specter of Lamentation Mountain. A cold rain fell, assaulting the roof of my ride. The thaw of spring would be here soon but for now temperatures hovered near freezing as one late-season storm rolled in after the next. Gusts picked up and whistled through the ravine. Even though I now lived on the other side of New Hampshire, I couldn't get far enough away. The range's black shadow hung over everything.

The rusted sign read "Property of Lombardi Construction: Trespassers Will Be Prosecuted." Thick chains wrapped around quarry gates to keep out vandals, an unnecessary precaution. Even criminals weren't trekking this far into the cuts to haul sixteen tons on to the back of a pickup. Someone would fetch the Bobcats and front loaders once the weather turned warmer and hardware could be wrenched free from the frozen earth, retrieved for scrap and sold. Or maybe not. The discarded metal might be worth more as a tax write-off.

I reached inside my glove compartment, bypassing Marlboros for a map.

Cold rain turned to sleet, which turned to freezing rain, icy pellets beating a steady pattern. Out the cracked windshield, which I hadn't gotten around to getting fixed since an accident last winter, I gazed across the gravel pit and up the steep, rocky banks of the culvert. One wrong turn and I'd ended up here. Just my luck. Perfect way to end the day.

I popped a piece of Nicorette gum through the foil, and unfurled the gas station map to find out where the hell I was. I couldn't read the tiny intersecting street names in between the bug-eaten holes and too-many folds. I wished I'd remembered my cell. Not that it would've helped. Tower service this far north was spotty. And forget GPS. I knew my wife would be pissed when she couldn't reach me, and my boss wasn't going to be any happier since my unexpected detour had put me behind schedule. I'd wasted an entire afternoon. I had to sign off on the Olisky file today. The last thing I needed was being reminded of the worst year of my life.

I pushed the map from the console, turned off the shoulder, and steered back onto the road. Exiting the property, I passed an empty guard station. Little wooden shack buried beneath a mound of snow. I hadn't noticed it on the way in. The shack had a newer, more recent sign affixed. Fresher rivets, shiny metal plate. All very official looking. One word in sleek red writing: Tomassi. I'd gone to school with a Louie Tomassi. Only reason the name registered at all.

With darkness descending, I was running out of time. The Oliskys lived half an hour south of Plasterville in Libby Brook, another faceless farming town tucked down meandering country roads, all of which were named some variation after Saint Thomas—Saint Thomas Place. Saint Thomas Route. Saint Thomas Way. Temps turned colder. Freezing rain bulleted the windshield. I had a brutal time deciphering signs. Out on the western front, landmarks were few and far between, occasional farmhouses cropping up in between a whole lot of nothing.

Took me over an hour to find the place. By the time I did, a wintery slice of silver moon peeked over the tops of tall pines, glinting down the backs of ice-slicked rock. When I stepped from the cab, crisp country air stabbed my lungs. I retrieved my little briefcase that held the Olisky report and my thermos with the coffee that had long run cold.

I committed the two silos and broken-down plow in an adjacent field to memory, in case I ever had reason to come out this way again. I doubted I ever would.

I introduced myself to the skinny teenager who answered the door, explaining who I was, who I worked for, and what I was doing there. He said his name was Brian and little else. Jittery fella. Tall but lanky, wispy almost. Like one good gust and he'd be carried away on the breeze forever.

The kid craned his head past me, running the length of bowed planks on the rickety, old porch. I didn't know what he was searching for. Nothing out there in the darkness but an Amish swing that had seen better days, a couple gallons of paint stowed beneath the seat. In the soft porch light, I could see where someone had started sanding the exterior but hadn't finished the job.

"My mother's not home," Brian Olisky said.

"You mind if I ask you a few questions about the car accident?" I cinched my winter coat tighter and blew on my hands, a not-too-subtle hint for an invitation inside. It was witch-tit cold out there. When that display didn't elicit the desired response, I stomped my feet for emphasis.

"It's my mom's policy."

"I know that, Brian. But you were in the car with her."

Like I hadn't bothered to read who the policyholder was? The kid was sixteen years old. Who knew why he was so twitchy and anxious? He'd probably been jacking it before I showed up. The boy wasn't biting, though, staring back at me through oversized glasses. Damn things bigger than his head. There wasn't much I could do. DeSouza got pissy anytime a policyholder complained about rude behavior, reminding me that, above all, "insurance is a service industry." But I also knew my boss would crawl up my ass if I'd wasted an entire day tooling around the sticks without closing the book.

"My mom isn't here," Brian repeated.

"Yeah. I heard you the first time." I flipped open the report, pretending to verify the name and address. Which was for the kid's benefit. I knew I had the right house. Wasn't a neighbor in either direction for miles, and he'd already told me his goddamn name. I clicked my pen, my money move. The sooner I got the information I needed, the sooner I could get on the road and get home. I hated missing my son's bedtime. Most mornings I was out the door before Aiden woke. If I got in too late, I wouldn't be able to see him at all. Spending more time with my son was half the reason I'd signed up for this stupid job in the first place.

"Just you and your mom living here?"

Brian shuffled his feet, antsy to be rid of me. I stared into the woodsy, rustic home, one of those old farmhouses that has been in the family for generations. No way the Oliskys could afford it otherwise. I knew the husband was out of the picture, and I'd seen Donna's paystubs. The interior was stuffed with cheap rocking chairs no one sits in, moth-eaten afghans no one wears, folksy advice stitched on wall-hung tapestry that no one follows.

"Can you come back later?" Brian said.

I shut the folder and stowed the pen, hoping to set Brian at ease. I didn't want to play the heavy. Standing there like some authoritative agency, I felt like Rob Turley, this guy I knew in high school who'd become our hometown's sheriff. Before my junkie brother Chris died last year, Turley had jailed him plenty over the years. Every time Turley would greet me in his uniform, a hitch in his step and stars on his shoulder, I could see through the act. You go from getting wasted together at reservoir parties to checking off boxes on application forms, deciding someone else's fate. Drop the officious pretense, be a regular guy, which was what I was anyway.

"Listen, man," I said, catching Brian's eye. "I just have a few questions on the claim. Straightforward stuff. Five minutes, tops." I thumbed behind me into the dark and cold. "This would be a lot easier to do inside. What do you say? Be a pal?"

The boy opened the door to let me in. Inside the mudroom, I wiped my shoes on the mat, removed my Patriots knit cap, and winced a smile. A grandfather clock stood proudly against oatmeal-colored walls, but the pendulum didn't swing.

I began to peel off my winter coat but stopped short. The drafty farmhouse wasn't much warmer inside. Heating these old homes wasn't cheap. Oil could run a couple grand, easy. I checked the roof beams. I'd spent a lot of time inside ancient Colonials like this when I was working my old job in estate clearing back in Ashton. Most were built in the 1700s, and the construction business had come a long way since the Revolutionary War. Overhauling an entire heating system could drain your bank account. Best bet was shoring up leaks.

"Y'know," I said, "You and your mom should insulate the ceilings." I pointed toward the rafters. "Wouldn't be too expensive. Build a fake ceiling, stuff a little fiberglass padding up there. You're bleeding money. Heat rises—"

"Um, so you want to ask me questions about the crash?"

"Right." I dropped my briefcase on a kitchen table littered with shopping flyers and red-letter final notices. I popped the top and pulled my file. "What day was the accident?"

Brian motioned at the chart in my hands. "Isn't it in your report?"

"Yes. It is. Just need to hear it from you."

"Last Monday." He squinted an eye. "About . . . one thirty?"

"Your mom picked you up from school?"

He nodded.

"What class?"

"Huh?"

"I'm assuming school doesn't end at one o'clock."

"Oh. Yeah. After lunch, so, um, trigonometry."

"You good at that stuff?"

"What? Trig? Yeah. I guess."

"I couldn't get past counting on my fingers." I wiggled my digits for a punchline. He didn't laugh. "Your mom picked you up from math class to bring you to the doctor?"

"Mmm hmm."

"What's wrong?"

"With what?"

"You said you were on your way to the doctor? Were you sick?"

"Oh, yeah. No. Just a checkup, I guess."

"You guess?"

"There's only one in town," Brian said.

"One what?"

"Doctor. Barth. Saint Thomas Court."

"I know. I talked to him."

In addition to Brian's mother Donna, I'd spoken with her co-workers at We Copy, visited the accident site and service garage that was handling repairs, and I'd conversed with the doctor's office. The boy was the last item on my checklist. I knew DeSouza wasn't going to be happy losing five grand, Blue Book value same as repairs, but that's why people have insurance.

"Then he told you I saw him?" Brian exhaled, a clumsy sound caught between nervous laugh and hiccup. "Why are you even here, man? I don't know what you need me for. If you already talked to Dr. Barth—"

"I told you. Standard inquiry. Your mom hit a telephone pole?"

Brian nodded, jamming trembling hands in pockets. My bullshit meter began creeping toward red. Just a feeling I had. Something about the kid's agitation and skittishness. I now saw his lip looked a little puffy, swollen, as if it had smacked off a dash on impact. How fast had Mom been going?

I glanced down at the report, pretending to read, peering up, looking him in the eye long enough to make him uncomfortable. Give him time and enough rope . . .

Brian's breathing sped up.

I snapped the folder shut. What did I care if this kid was covering for Mom's lead foot? Not like I got paid extra for the personality profile. Judging by the dilapidated, sad state of the house, the Oliskys could use the money. Let them come out a few bucks ahead. Good for them. My day was done.

Turning to go, I saw the photographs on the mantel and immediately recognized the wrestling poses, the staged yearbook kind, singlets and ear guards, grappling tigers ready to pounce. Before the bottom fell out of his life, my brother Chris had been a wrestling superstar for the Ashton Redcoats. Atop the fireplace more action shots from actual meets closed around an unlit candle in the center. Like a shrine.

I stepped past Brian into the small room.

"Hey! You can't be in there."

At the mantel, I picked up a gleaming gold trophy. Same heft as when my brother dominated the ranks, emotions ambushing me.

I inspected one of the photographs. The wrestler in the picture had the same features and facial expressions as Brian. Not like a brother. I mean, identical. Still slender, but tougher, more sinewy, ferocious. And without the glasses.

I turned over my shoulder. With closed folder, I gestured between them, Brian and the boy in the photos. "You wrestle?" He didn't strike me as the type.

He shook his head. "That's my brother, Craig."

I squinted to read the inscription on the wrestling trophy. Craig Olisky. First Place. New Hampshire Regionals.

I went down the line studying the fierce gaze in the snapshots. Cheering crowds, championship ceremonies. Remarkable, the resemblance.

"You look like twins," I said.

"We are. Were, I mean."

"You were twins?" I didn't catch the implication.

"He's dead."

I stopped touching Craig's photos, as if my fingerprints disgraced memories. "I'm sorry," I said, both for the violation and the loss.

"Painkillers and alcohol," Brian offered without provocation. "My dad moved out after that. Craig was his boy, y'know? It's just me and my mom now." He tried to smile. "Sometimes I think she got the short end."

Ten minutes earlier, I'd manipulated my way inside this kid's house. Now I couldn't get out of there fast enough.

"Hard to compete with a superstar," he said.

When he said that bit about superstars, something stirred inside, a realization: I'd never seen my brother wrestle. Chris had been ten years older, putting me at seven or so during his heyday, but still old enough to make a meet. I remembered my mother trying to get me to go see him, and me putting up a fight, refusing, throwing tantrums. I never saw a match. The thing that had made my brother special, what he had been best at in this entire world—the one thing he had to be proud of. Not a single meet. Years later, I'd talk about Chris' accomplishments as if they'd been my own, but at the time I'd been jealous. Pure and simple. Chris was such the star, garnering so much attention, even as a boy I was envious of him. Funny, given how pathetic my brother ended up.

"I did it," Brian said.

"Huh?"

"The accident," he said. "I was driving the car. My mother was at work."

I stared, dumbfounded. We were on two separate trains of thought, and circling back to the same conversation took me a moment.

"I'm not on the policy because it's too expensive to add me, and since my dad left, we don't have the money. I had that stupid doctor's appointment. My mom couldn't get off work. We're going to England. I mean, I'm supposed to go to England. With the marching band. I play bass drum. I'll never get to see Europe otherwise. I had to get all these shots for the trip, my mom worries a lot, and the deadline's coming up, and she has all these Christian CDs in the car. Holy roller Jesus crap—"

"Jesus?"

"I wanted to hear the radio, man," Brian said, "but nothing would come in. I had some mp3s in my backpack that my friend Jon gave me. But the backpack was crammed with textbooks and pens and earbuds. I couldn't find anything. I took my eye off the road for a second—not even a second, I swear. I hit the telephone pole."

I didn't know what to say.

"I called my mom. Her friend from work drove her over. When

the cops showed up, my mom said she was driving. Am I going to get in trouble?"

I shrugged.

"I don't care." Brian Olisky let go a terrific sigh, and a big smile crept over his face, like he'd heard a dirty joke in church and was fighting to suppress the giggles.

"Thanks," he said.

"For what?"

"I don't like lying. It was bothering the hell out of me."

My attention returned to the wrestling photographs on the mantel.

What's harder? Competing with a superstar? Or carrying the burden of being the last man standing?

CHAPTER TWO

Driving those country roads home, the bright, clean moonlight illuminating a path back to my wife so she could tear me a new one for being late and forgetting my cell phone, again, I couldn't help but think about my brother.

Once upon a time Chris had been bound for greatness. A shot at the Olympics. Representing America. Who knew how far he could've gone? Or maybe it was all revisionist, pipe dreaming. Even before our parents died in that car accident, Chris was a mess. Short fuse. Screws loose. A socket wrench short of a toolbox. Once he got hooked on dope, all bets were off, all hope abandoned. A bottom-feeding parasite, he lived a hard existence that stole whatever remained of the brother I'd known growing up. Small-town gossip tarnished his legacy, vicious rumors that refused to go away. I never bought into any of that garbage. Not even when Chris claimed those rumors were true. By that point he couldn't tell the difference between fantasy and reality. Which made sorting out the last few weeks of his life so difficult.

Last December, my brother and a scumbag pal, Pete, had been rooting around on a discarded computer, trying to secure personal information. They were running a credit card scam, check fraud, identity theft, whatever people like him did to cheat the system. They'd uncovered dirty laundry on this family up here, the Lombardis. Incriminating pictures of the father, Gerry.

It was hard to trust Chris, especially where the Lombardis were concerned. Long before the drugs, my brother was obsessed with that family, animosity stemming from his days wrestling for Gerry Lombardi in high school. Gerry's sons, Adam and Michael, so successful with their respective construction and political careers, didn't help matters; jealousy ate away at my brother. I saw the pictures. Hard to tell one way or the other, but after my brother got his hands on that computer, weird things began to happen. I spotted cars following me. My apartment was broken into. They found Pete's naked body behind the old Travel Center Truck Stop. Chris lost what was left of his mind attempting to implicate Gerry, his sons, the whole town of Ashton in one big conspiratorial cover-up. And I'll admit it. I followed him down that rabbit hole. I was so desperate to believe in my big brother again. I ended up on my knees right there with him, scouring the dingy floor for clues, another crackhead searching for crumbs in the carpet. Once Chris died, I knew I'd never get definitive answers. When so much remains open-ended, you can't shut lids or get any closure. I'd grown to hate the Lombardi family, too.

I popped another piece of gum, chomping to suck every drop of precious nicotine, going at it so hard I was in danger of ripping out a filling. I could feel it again, the pressure in my chest, rib cage seizing up, organs and lungs on lockdown, the inability to catch my breath. I'd been having these attacks for the past year, and the pills the shrink gave me ran out a while ago.

Fuck it. I dug around my glove compartment for my stashed pack of Marlboros. The cigarette was stale as shit, like breathing cinder ash and dry rot, but damn it tasted good.

By the time I pulled into my driveway, I'd burned through my last five emergency butts, but at least the shortness of breath had subsided. I fished the wintergreen mints from my center console and ground my molars, searching for the spark. A quick brush with my finger, hot breath in my palm, and I was good to go.

I hopped down from the cab, staring at soft soles on hard ice, missing the sound my old boots made crunching snow.

"Where have you been?" Jenny asked soon as I walked in the door. Our fat cat, Beatrice, rubbed her girth against my pant leg, leaving behind tufts of white fur, mewling for more.

"Work." I shook Beatrice off.

Jenny deadpanned, unsatisfied with my answer. I could feel her frustration bore a hole through the back of my head as I stepped around her for a beer. When I turned, she had her arms folded in a fighting stance, giving me the death stare.

"I had to sign off on a claim in the sticks." I bent in the fridge and snagged the lone beer from the top shelf.

"This is why you can't forget your cell. What's the point of having a cell phone if you aren't going to remember to take it with you?"

I slammed the door shut. "What's the point of a cell, period? Jesus, Jenny. Does someone need to be accessible twenty-four hours a day?"

"When someone's a father and a husband? Yes!" She wrinkled her nose. "Have you been smoking?"

I didn't bother to deny it. Even with these last six months of patches and gum, I knew I was still impervious to the smell of cigarettes. To a nonsmoker like Jenny, I'm sure I stank like a skunk in the cabbage patch.

"I thought you decided you were going to quit."

"*I* decided? Y'know, I'm a grown man, and if I want to have a cigarette after a shit day of work—"

"Keep your voice down. You're going to wake Aiden."

I popped the top from my brew and took a slug. "Where is my son?"

"Sleeping!"

We stood in the middle of the kitchen, staring each other down, high noon at eight thirty on a Friday night. Seemed all we ever did these days was fight. If we were talking at all.

Jenny blinked first. "What's going on, Jay?"

I exhaled and dropped in a chair, guzzling half the beer in a single swig. I'd been geared up to go the moment I stuck my key in the hole. "DeSouza had me check on an accident. Sixteen-year-old kid cracked up his mom's car. I saw some high school wrestling pics at their house. Turns out his brother died."

"In the accident?"

"No, just . . . died." I took another pull. "Drugs."

I didn't need to make the connection for her. My wife came behind my chair and slung her arms over me, hugging me tight.

"Maybe you should see Dr. Shapiro-Weiss again."

"Insurance won't cover any more visits, you know that." Our HMO's mental health policy was a joke.

"Then we pay out of pocket."

"Yeah? With what money?" Even with the steady paycheck of NorthEastern Insurance, we weren't exactly killing it financially.

"We'll find a way. We always do."

I hopped up and went to the fridge for another beer. I swung open the door. All out. I checked the pantry, top shelf, bottom, everywhere in between. "Where's the beer?"

"How should I know? You're the one who drinks it. You need to talk to someone. You can't keep this stuff bottled up. You have to find a way to deal with it."

"It?" I spun around. "And where does 'it' go after I'm done dealing with 'it,' huh?"

"You know what I mean."

"Yeah. I do. And there is no 'it.' 'It' is my watching my brother die in front of my eyes. 'It' is never getting to say goodbye or I'm sorry your life turned out to be such shit and that I couldn't do more to fix it when there was still time. Therapy, sharing, all that self-help garbage is hippy bullshit. No reconciliation. No peace. No justice." I grit my jaw. "That smug mutherfucker Lombardi might as well have pulled the trigger himself."

"Lombardi? Gerry Lombardi is dead. He's been dead almost as long as your brother. I wish he'd gone to prison too for what he did to those kids. But God took care of that—"

"I'm not talking about just Gerry. I mean Adam. Michael. That whole goddamn family—"

"That whole family? Jay, you sound like—" She pulled up short.

"Say it."

Jenny shook her head. "What are you so angry for? You act like you've got it so bad. You don't. You have a wife and son who love you, a steady job—"

"Steady job?"

"It's nothing to sneeze at. In this economy? Marjorie's husband Bob—"

"Bob? Who the hell is Bob? Who the hell is Marjorie?"

"The woman I work with at the bar? Do you listen when I talk? Marjorie's husband Bob has been out of work since last October."

"Why do I give a shit about some woman at a bar or her husband?"

"*I* work at a bar."

"My point! Same lousy job you had when I got this one. What's changed? Nothing!"

"I'm sorry you hate your job so much. I never told you—"

"What? To take it? Bullshit."

"I never said you had to take that job."

"No, you never did. Just like you never said I had to quit smoking cigarettes."

"You want to get lung cancer? Talk out a hole in your throat? Keep smoking! If you don't care enough to want to see your son—"

I stabbed a finger at her. "See! That!"

"What?"

"That. What you did there. 'If I want to see my son.' No, you didn't say I had to take the job. But I still had to do what you wanted all the same—"

"That's not fair."

"You made it clear that if I wanted us to be a family, I had to do the things *you* decided were best."

"I never once said that."

"You didn't have to. You threatened to move to Rutland. You threatened to take *my son* away because I wasn't making enough money—"

"It was never about the money!"

"Whenever someone says 'it's not about the money,' it's always about the money."

"Not true. I just thought you could be doing so much more than clearing out junk from dead people's houses."

"It's called 'estate clearing.' It's a legitimate career. Lots of people do it."

Jenny tilted her head, a card player's tell that I was pushing logic to its limit.

"Doesn't matter what it's called. I was happy."

"When have you ever been happy, Jay?"

"Thanks for telling me how I feel."

"Don't play that game. Like I'm some shrew of a wife, harping about what you can and can't do. You make me sound like one of those women who trapped you into getting married."

I returned a blank stare.

"Fuck you, Jay. You *asked*. You practically begged!"

"I wanted to get married! I love you. I want to be with you and Aiden. But this?" I tugged at the tie, freeing myself from the noose, and chucked it to the ground.

"I can't do this anymore," she said. "Watching you skulk around, refusing to talk or get help. Even when you're here, you're not here. You're emotionally unavailable—"

"'Emotionally unavailable'? Where do you come up with this shit? What's that even mean? Emotionally unavailable."

"It means when you are married to someone, you don't get to hoist burdens on your shoulders and act like carrying them around alone is heroic. Needing help doesn't make you weak—"

"Actually, that's the very definition of—"

"It makes you human."

"You sound like one of those posters DeSouza has hanging in the office. Fucking Teamwork. Fucking Inspiration. Fucking birds flying together because they believe in themselves and not because flight is the result of millions of years of evolution—"

"If you hate it so much—leave!"

"Just the job?"

That was the big blow I had in my bag, the one I'd been waiting to use. Leveling it now was a cheap shot, but I'd take it. Let the possibility serve as warning to back the fuck off. I never intended to leave, and, Christ, I felt like an asshole when I saw Jenny's eyes tear up. I knew I had gone too far. Even as I'd been throwing my tie to the ground, pitching a fit like a toddler who wasn't getting his way, I felt ridiculous. But I couldn't stop.

And that remorse only grew worse when I looked over and saw

Aiden standing there in his PJ bottoms, little boy potbelly, wide-eyed and terrified. He ran to his mother's side, like his father was some monster. My son didn't even look at me. Neither would my wife. I couldn't talk my way out of this now.

CHAPTER THREE

When I landed the job at NEI, I got health insurance for the first time in my adult life. Which included mental health visits. I didn't go for that touchy-feely crap, but I'd been having these fits, shortness of breath, vertigo, like my heart was about to seize up. I went to the clinic for a checkup, but everything checked out. The doctor said they were panic attacks, even though I'd never been accused of that before. Jenny urged me to see a psychiatrist. Even without her prodding, I knew Chris' death had messed me up enough that I could use professional help. So I signed on. Three trips to a shrink. That's all our HMO covered. Who the hell can sort out the shit I'd endured with my brother in three fifty-minute sessions?

Chris' death last winter had officially been ruled "suicide by cop" after he ran out of an old farmhouse, waving a gun around, leaving the police no other choice. But everyone knew the real reason he died: drugs. My brother had been an addict most of his life. His reason for living. And, in the end, his reason for dying.

Last spring I'd met with Dr. Louise Shapiro-Weiss over in Longmont. For three weeks, I spilled my guts in that tiny office, serenaded by gurgling waterfalls and raindrops dribbling over smooth stones, the calming, tranquil soundtrack designed to quell my looney tunes. The longer I listened to myself drone on, the more I wanted to rip that babbling brook from the socket and smash it against the wall.

I knew I sounded as nutty as my brother, outlining secret back-room meetings, collusion to conceal true agendas. When I got to the part about the hit man pretending to be a detective in order to bury my brother beneath the ice of Echo Lake, our time was up. And not a moment too soon. I was surprised the doctor didn't recommend I be committed. Instead, she wrote me a script for a sedative and wished me luck.

Some secrets are better left undisturbed. After Chris died, old man Lombardi kicked it. Heart attack fetching the morning paper. So what difference did it make now? Maybe my wife was right and I needed to suck it up, pay out of pocket, and see the doctor again. Desperate times and measures. I had to try something because what I was doing sure wasn't working.

I needed a drink. I didn't feel like driving in circles or sitting at a roadside bar alone. My buddy Charlie still lived in Ashton. Outside of Charlie, I didn't have many friends. I knew where I'd find him. Same place he was every night. Glued to a stool, getting soused at the Dubliner. My old hometown pub was over an hour away because of the long detour around Lamentation Mountain, which wasn't actually a single mountain but an entire range of them. What else could I do? A man without a country, I hit the 135 and headed east.

Couples fight, I told myself. She'll put Aiden back to bed, make herself some tea. We'll both take time to calm down. I'll call her later and apologize for being a jerk. Wouldn't be the first time. Sure as hell wouldn't be the last.

I felt for my cell, cursing when I realized I'd forgotten it. Again.

* * *

"Look what the canary dragged in," Charlie said, sizing up the target on the dartboard.

"You mean cat, you stupid fuck." The man standing beside him drained the dregs of a beer and set the empty pint glass down on a half wall.

A group huddled around my friend, anxiously awaiting the outcome of the next throw.

"Cat. Canary," Charlie said. "Who gives a shit? When I nail this bullseye, Danny Boy, you are going to owe me a beer."

On the television set above the bar, a newscaster reported on the Sox down in Fort Myers. Winter ball wrapping up, spring training around the corner, hope springs eternal.

Charlie lobbed a wobbly dart. A brief cheer erupted, drowned out by a chorus of boos when the fluttering shot missed its mark by six inches. Charlie dropped his head in exaggerated defeat. Another buddy clapped his back, whispering condolence, as someone else plucked the trio of darts from the board.

"I'm out," Charlie said, fetching his empty pint off the half wall. He slung an arm around my shoulder, pulling me across the floor toward the tiki smoking porch outside.

Liam, the owner of the Dubliner, was setting up his guitar and mic stand at the dark end of the bar. Liam's band, The January Men, used to play here on weekends. They'd broken up. Now he took the stage to sing his sad Irish songs alone, brushing strings, whispering lyrics. No one seemed to notice. I'd always thought his band sucked—they were too loud, never in sync, and you couldn't hear what anyone was saying when they were bleating away—but it still beat this sad bastard music. At least when the band was together, everyone bashing on his instrument, it could be a good time. By the end of the night, the crowd would join in, whole bar screaming along, wasted. Sometimes a girl would take her shirt off. There's comfort in numbers. Or maybe being with a group of other maniacs just hides the crazy.

"Hey!" Danny Boy called after Charlie. "Where's my beer?"

"Put it on my tab," Charlie hollered back. "Rita!" He held up his empty glass and pointed outside. "And one for my good friend, Jay Porter, hotshot investigator up from the big city."

Rita, the barmaid and Liam's wife, rolled her eyes.

"Don't be an asshole," I said.

"What?" Charlie said. "A little patience never killed anyone. Fisher tells me it's just a matter of time until you get the call up to the big leagues down in Concord."

Fisher was Charlie's friend who'd helped land me the job at NorthEastern. Like Charlie, Fisher had been around last winter when all that shit was happening with my brother. I didn't blame Fisher for the job turning out so awful. But he wasn't off the hook either. I'd been sold a bill of goods—namely that I'd be working out of Concord. Instead I got stuck in the outpost of Plasterville, which was actually further north than Ashton—I'd done the math—adding to the sense that I'd somehow taken a step back.

Charlie cinched the drawstring of his parka, Nanook peeking out the head hole. "Fisher swears it's gonna happen. Just have to pay your dues."

"Yeah. I've heard that one, too. And I think I've paid enough."

We grabbed a couple stools beneath the thatched overhang, icicles jagging down with menace. Rita popped out the back door and set a pair of frothing pints in front of us. She shook her head like we were nuts to be out there in that arctic blast. But if this was where you lived and you wanted a cigarette, what were you supposed to do? I remembered my dad describing the good old days, going to see a movie and people smoking in the lobby, buying popcorn and Jujubes, blazing up right in the god-damn theater. Back then you could smoke on airplanes and in the doctor's office. Now they stick you outside of a bar where they legally serve cirrhosis, and have you freeze your ass off in minus twenty.

Charlie pulled out his pack. "Dropping the boy at Grandma's?"

I bummed a smoke. Charlie didn't bust my balls over trying to quit. He understood as well as anybody that sometimes failing can still be your best.

"Jenny's mom doesn't live in Ashton anymore," I said, borrowing a match from him as well. "Moved to Burlington. About six months ago. Pretty much right after Jenny and I got married."

Charlie screwed up his face. I wasn't sure which part confused him. My mother-in-law Lynne relocating to the scenic shores of Lake Champlain, or the wedding itself? Charlie had been my best man for the ceremony at City Hall. We didn't have the time or money to plan anything extravagant. Reception for six afterward at the Chicken Shack. My wife deserved better.

"Lynne earned her certification to be a traveling nurse. Remember? We talked about this the last time I saw you."

"Was I drunk?"

"When aren't you drunk, Charlie?"

"Good point."

"Besides, it's ten thirty. Kids have bedtimes. Something you don't have to worry about."

Charlie nipped his beer.

A gaggle of college girls burst onto the porch, interrupting our suffering with their enthusiasm. Giggling, then shrieking, then laughing hysterically at something that couldn't possibly be that funny. I'd once bar-backed at a pub over the summer. I decided then that the most annoying sound in the entire world is young, drunk girls having fun.

My instant hatred of these four, who had done nothing besides dare to exist, made me remember what Jenny said back at the house. *When are you ever happy, Jay?*

When did I become such a miserable bastard?

"What's going on with you, man?" Charlie said. "You got that mopey, hangdog expression you used to get whenever your brother came around."

"Maybe he did," I muttered.

"Huh?"

"Never mind."

"Okay, Mr. Big Shot Investigator, why *are* you back in town?"

"Stop calling me that. And can't I just meet a buddy for a beer?"

"An hour's drive? In the snow and cold? This late?"

"Jenny and I got in a fight."

"What did you do this time?"

"What makes you think it's my fault?"

Charlie laughed.

"It's complicated."

"I bet it is."

"Let's just say nine-to-five doesn't live up to the fantasy."

"You fantasized about having a nine-to-five job?" Charlie pointed in the vague direction of the foothills. "Dude, I got a shoebox in my attic. Feel free to borrow some magazines. You need better fantasies."

"No one keeps porn in a shoebox anymore, Charlie."

"It's a metaphor."

"No. It's not. But whatever. That's not what I mean. Before all this went down, I had a goal, y'know? As long as I was chasing after that payoff, I was okay."

"I could've told you nine-to-five sucks. Best you can hope for is landing on workman's comp like my Uncle Jimmy. An insurance office? Gonna need one hell of a paper cut."

"I mean, I thought, if I could get regular work with benefits, get Jenny back, get my son back—if I had a chance to be an everyday dad, be reunited with my family—they would make the rest of it worthwhile."

"You telling me they don't?"

"No. I'm not saying that. Jenny and Aiden are my whole world. I'd be lost without them. It's just . . ."

"What?"

I shook my head. "I don't know, man." I drained my beer. "That fucking job. I hate it. Feel like a monkey in a suit peddling a bicycle. I'm not cut out for corporate."

"What are you cut out for?"

"Beats me. Christ, I feel like I'm sixteen again, throwing punches against the wind. I wasn't like this before. You ever get that way?"

"I ain't the guy to ask. I'm one step from a ditch digger."

"How's that working out?" Last winter, Charlie had gotten himself canned from the phone company and started working for my old boss, Tom Gable, boxing up the remains of old farmers, clearing antiques, peddling merchandise at flea markets along the shore. Lots of freedom. Little room for advancement.

"You know that game, Jay. If Tom didn't pay me under the table and cut out the middleman, I couldn't survive. Once the unemployment runs out, I'll probably have to crawl back to the phone company."

"Seriously?"

"I'd rather shoot myself first."

Charlie banged his pint until Rita returned with two fresh ones, looking pissed she had to set foot outside. "Ah, that's what I love about this place. Service with a smile."

"Doesn't it get to you?"

"What?"

"All of this. The shit we have to do to keep going." I nodded into the black night, toward the seedy Turnpike south of town. "Maybe those bums and dope fiends have the right idea. Shack up in some fleabag, let the government foot the bill."

"Just living is hard enough," Charlie said. "Then you add the rest of it—bills and jobs, having to sign up for overdraft protection? Dude, I don't know how people aren't running out of their houses screaming down the street every morning."

"Pisses me off. The scraps we're left with. While others roll like pigs in shit."

"Any pig-fuckers you have in mind?" Charlie snuffed his smoke. "You're my boy, Jay, and I love you. But do you know that every time I've seen you this past year, you've brought up Adam, Michael, or Gerry Lombardi?"

"Bullshit."

"Fact. Every time. You're getting as bad as Fisher."

"What's Fisher got to do with any of this? Besides, that's not true. I didn't mention the name 'Lombardi' once tonight."

"Yeah? Then who are you talking about? I'm not an idiot, man."

"I took a wrong turn today. Ended up outside an abandoned Lombardi Construction site."

"When? Where?"

"This afternoon. On the way to a client's house. For work. Western plains, in the sticks. That's not the point. Seeing the name, the quarry, the rusted machines and discarded trailer parts—brought back last year. It sucked."

"I'm sure it did, but—"

"Those pictures, Charlie. I can't get them out of my head. What if it *was* old man Lombardi? What if we let him get away with it? Adam and Michael had to know what their father was up to. Remember Adam's head of security, Bowman? That 'roided-up mutherfucker with the Star of David tattooed on his neck? Adam Lombardi sicced that psychopath on me looking for the hard drive my brother stole—"

"Jay—"

"Bowman broke into *my* apartment. Cold cocked me in the dark. Knocked me out. What if my wife and son had been there? You know, I still get headaches—"

"Jay!"

"What?"

Charlie gestured at the college girls who had now stopped their conversation, gawking at me. I realized how loud I'd been talking.

"Listen, man," Charlie said, "for your own good—you need to get past your hatred of that family. Coach Lombardi is dead."

"No shit. Doesn't change the facts. I'm just calling it like I see it."

"No, Jay, you're not. For one, you're making it sound like Adam and Michael Lombardi were born with silver spoons. I never liked Adam, but the guy worked his ass off to build up that construction company of his. And I don't know how someone gets into politics, but the Lombardis aren't the Kennedys. Michael keeps getting reelected for a reason. Gerry Lombardi was a high school math teacher and wrestling coach."

"And a pedophile."

"Maybe. But you have no evidence of that. Nothing admissible, anyway. His sons had successful careers and your brother was acting crazy, breaking into construction sites, terrorizing that family. High as shit. I mean, how would you expect them to respond?"

"Since when did you become such a fan of the Lombardis?"

"I'm not. Come on, man, I was right there with you, chasing after Chris last winter. Nobody's saying the Lombardis are choirboys. But this jealousy and envy—hating them—it's not bringing your brother back." He waited. "And I think it might be pushing your wife and kid away." He stopped, expression pained. "I mean, I don't know, man. I'm drunk."

"No," I said. "You're right."

"Yeah?"

"Yeah." I reached out for his shoulder.

Charlie slapped my hand away. "Need a couch?"

"Might not be the worst idea."

I'd give Jenny the rest of the night off, space best for all parties involved. Everything looks better in the light of a new day.

* * *

It had been a while since I'd gotten good and ripped.

The weekend crowd finally showed toward midnight, place filling up. College girls were replaced by townies and regulars from Charlie's dart league, everyone congregating on the tiki smoking porch, where Charlie and I had remained rooted, at first freezing our asses off until, soon, we felt nothing at all. I didn't think about Jenny or my responsibilities. Beer flowed on endless stream from the tap. People kept shoving shots in front of me. Whiskey, bourbon, scotch. Never a good idea to mix and match. I didn't care. I pounded each back like a challenge.

Soon the lights began to flicker, signaling closing time. Charlie pulled his wallet, slapped down a few twenties, and then polished off the rest of his beer.

I could barely stand. "I think I will take you up on the offer of a couch."

"No problem, amigo. But don't you have to work tomorrow?"

"It's Friday night, Charlie."

We swayed to the sidewalk, a pair of desperados in a border town.

"Go home, Finn," someone shouted from a passing car. "You're drunk."

"See you tomorrow?" a girl called out, though whether to Charlie or me or someone else, I had no idea.

"Shit," I said. "How we getting back to your place?" No way either of us could drive in this condition. We sure as sin couldn't walk. It was almost two a.m., and without the smoking porch enclosure to absorb some of the brunt, I felt every negative degree of Lamentation's subzero assault.

"I'm fine," Charlie said, pulling his keys, which I tried snatching. He was too quick. "Fuck you, Porter. I drink like this every night." He held up the ring, dangling them in front of me. To prove victory, I guess. But he dropped the keys in a snow bank on the sidewalk. We both reached for the keys at the same time, bonking heads, slipping on the ice, falling into a snow mound and wrestling for them on the ground, cracking up, hysterical drunk.

I didn't see the flashing lights until they were on top of us. Then came the familiar voice.

CHAPTER FOUR

"Okay," Sheriff Rob Turley said. "On your feet, you two."

Charlie and I stopped wrestling. We both stared up at fat-ass Rob Turley, hitching his trousers and holster, trying to play the heavy in his wide-brimmed lawman's hat. Which made Charlie and me howl harder.

Turley made me leave my truck at the Dubliner, and chauffeured us out to Charlie's house on the plains. Sitting in the back of the cruiser, I didn't answer any of Turley's attempts at small talk, questions about the wife, the new job and town, the kid, and soon he gave up trying.

Charlie was right about one thing. He was used to drinking this hard. I wasn't. Within minutes of getting dropped off at his place, my best friend was passed out in the bedroom; I spent the next half hour hurling chunks over the railing.

I didn't even remember falling asleep. When I woke to take a piss in the middle of the night, I was facedown on the floral-print couch, string of vomit drool connecting head to hand like some degenerate marionette.

Staggering into the kitchen, I filled a tall glass with tepid tap water at the sink, and sat in the dark rehydrating, staring up at the Lamentation Mountains, waiting for a sun to rise over the peaks.

I didn't open my eyes again until ten a.m., cheek glued to the table. Charlie flipped on the coffeemaker. Neither of us spoke, day-after movements excruciating. Spoons clanking off clay walls made my skull hurt. Back when I was nineteen, twenty, I could tie one on till three in the morning, take an hour nap, and still make it to the farm by five. I was grateful today was Saturday. I'd need half the day to recuperate.

We arranged a ride back to Dubliner to fetch my Chevy and his old Subaru.

"Be nice to your wife," Charlie said as I was getting in. "Jenny's a good woman. You ain't the easiest guy to be around."

On the way back to Plasterville, I stopped at the gas station and filled up. I grabbed a newspaper and another pack of cigarettes, which I stashed for my next emergency. I also bought a dozen roses.

The heater was off when I got home, my wife out. Grocery shopping, I figured, since Saturday had the best bargains at the Price Chopper. I dropped the flowers on the stove and cranked the thermostat. Then I hopped in the shower, mulling over how I should handle the Brian Olisky situation. After everything that family had been through, I didn't feel right ratting him out. Even if it was my job. Returning from Libby Brook so late yesterday, I hadn't bothered stopping off at the office, everyone already gone for the weekend. Which gave me until Monday when I had to turn in my report. The burden weighted my shoulders, and I still felt nauseated from the hard alcohol. I stayed under the hot stream until the room fogged like a sauna and some of the poison washed out of my pores.

Stepping from the water, skin scrubbed new-baby pink, I slipped on sweats and a tee, and put on some coffee. Waiting for the pot to brew, I sat at the table to read the paper. I skimmed an article about the old TC Truck Stop in Ashton, which had been demolished last summer to make way for new ski condominiums.

Looked like they were scrapping that project in favor of a new detention center, advocates citing the need to combat the growing drug epidemic up here. Great. Just what addicts need. More lock-up. Less rehabilitation options. A ballot measure had been proposed in an upcoming special election to circumvent legal hurdles and pave the way. I decided to set the paper aside until I was in a better mood. Anything related to drugs tended to incite my rage, and I needed to remain calm if I hoped to repair my marriage.

After a couple cups of coffee, my hangover started to clear. I ran over the apology in my head, practicing points of contrition. Sounded good to me. Heartfelt and sincere with enough self-deprecation to maybe make Jenny laugh. My wife was one of the few people who appreciated my sense of humor.

That's when I saw the Dear John letter in the empty fruit bowl on the table.

* * *

"What the hell's going on?"

"You read the note?" Jenny said.

"Yeah. I read it. But what the fuck?" I whispered this last part, like Aiden was playing with blocks in the next room. Which of course he wasn't. My wife had taken him, across state lines, almost three hours away, to her mother's place in Burlington. "What is this? You're leaving me?"

"I needed a break. Aiden needed a break. I think *you* need a break."

"Thanks for telling me what I need."

"Don't."

"Don't what?"

"Play the victim."

"When are you coming back?"

"I don't know."

My heart sank. Everything I wanted, right there in front of me, and somehow I'd managed to screw it all up. The panic returned, washing over me in waves. Jenny could sense my anxiety.

"Calm down," she said. "This isn't me asking for a divorce. My mom's been bugging me to come up with Aiden, and with everything going on with you, now seemed like a good time to take her up on the offer."

"You're not leaving?"

"We're married. I don't give up that easy."

I wasn't sure if I was relieved or pissed. I wanted to feel some indignation for having been wronged, except I had no right. Jenny didn't need my permission to visit her mom. That's all the letter said, "I'm taking Aiden to my mother's." I assumed the worst, because, on some level, I knew I deserved it.

"I'm sorry," I said.

My wife waited for the rest.

"I know I haven't been—"

"What?"

"Myself lately, I guess. I mean, since my brother died."

I didn't mention any wrong turns or construction sites. Didn't talk about a wrestling superstar popping too many pills or the painful memories it evoked. These were the excuses I'd used to get myself worked up, feel a sense of self-righteousness. Charlie's bluntness at the Dubliner had put everything in perspective. I was pushing my family away, and all the evidence I needed of that was on the other end of the line.

"I know it's been hard, Jay, losing him the way you did, but you have to find a way to deal. Or it's going to destroy you."

"I have all this stuff inside me, Jenny. Things I want to say to you, good things, but I can't seem to do it. Nothing comes out right."

"I'm not saying you have to call Dr. Shapiro-Weiss, but maybe she could—"

"I already called her," I lied.

"That's good to hear, baby."

"Can I talk to Aiden?"

"Of course. Hold on."

I heard Jenny call our son from the other room, followed by the pitter-patter of busy feet.

"Hi, Daddy."

I knew Aiden was only visiting his grandma in Vermont, but the boxy connection made his voice sound tinny and a million miles away. I got the sudden, aching feeling I'd never see my son again.

"You miss Daddy?"

"Yes."

"How much?"

"Um. Infinity plus forty-six plus seventy-two."

"Wow," I said. "That much? That's a lot."

I loved my son's twisted understanding of mathematics.

"Daddy?"

"Yes?"

"Bye-bye, Daddy. Grandma has cookies."

I heard the phone drop and tap dance off tile. I waited for my wife to come back on the line. But she never did.

I stood in the kitchen listening to a dial tone for ten seconds before I finally hung up. I searched for relief from the conversation. That had been good news, right? I replayed what my wife said. She'd been clear this was temporary, a brief vacation, no splitting up. She called me "baby." But she also got her point across, loud and clear: I needed to get my shit together.

Coffee in hand, I retrieved the Marlboros from my glove compartment, and then headed to my workshop in the garage. I packed the smokes against my wrist and wedged the side door ajar. Until my wife came home, I might as well enjoy the thing I'd missed most about smoking: that first one in the morning.

In a dusty, dark corner I unlocked the top drawer of the gray filing cabinet, and dug around back, extracting the thick, rubber-banded binder. I fanned my collection across the workbench, the curious cutouts and clippings from last year that had been my preoccupation. Or obsession was more like it.

Right after the shooting, the *Herald* ran a series on my brother's death. Not as much about the person as the addiction that defined his life, highlighting how a former star athlete had fallen from grace, an angle the media loves, culminating with the raid on the farmhouse where he died, which the paper parlayed into the push for drug reform. That was the real reason behind these stories. No one gave a shit about a dead junkie.

Chris' passing came to represent what had become of our hometown. Even if I now lived fifty miles west in Plasterville, a very real part of me would always be in Ashton. Drugs had infiltrated much of northern New Hampshire, but Ashton remained ground zero because of the seedy Desmond Turnpike.

I'd cut out every article I could find pertaining to the scandal last December and January. Except no one had the real story. Chris' assertion, that Gerry Lombardi had molested little boys, couldn't be proven, the pictures he'd copied from that hard drive blurry and inconclusive. But what Charlie, Fisher, and I had stumbled onto last winter couldn't be denied either. The computer *had* come from Adam Lombardi's construction site, and there *were* pictures of little boys on it. Even if we couldn't be sure it was Mr. Lombardi in those photos, there had to be a reason Adam and

Michael were so nervous. Of all the bizarre things that happened last winter, perhaps most damning of all was a man named Roger Paul, who had masqueraded as a Concord detective, infiltrating Ashton's hick police force. He ended up snatching my brother, bringing him up the mountain with plans to bury him beneath the ice of Echo Lake. And if I hadn't arrived on the scene, running them off Ragged Pass, he would've gotten away with it. Of course none of this could be proven. My word against theirs. And nothing could be tied to the Lombardis.

The cover story that the car crash and Roger Paul's death was the result of a drug deal gone bad was bullshit. I could see why the local PD wouldn't want that egg on their face. But the rest of the story was whitewashed, too. Not one word about incriminating hard drives. The name Gerry Lombardi appeared nowhere. The only bad guy in any of this: drugs. Not money. Not greed. Not the luckless bastards foraging in squalor on the Turnpike. Drugs.

Once Gerry Lombardi was in the ground, what was the point of digging any further? Even before he kicked it, I'd asked Charlie and Fisher to back off the investigation. The Lombardis were too big a local institution to take down, the photos pure conjecture. I had a wife and child to think about now. I needed to leave this behind.

Still, most nights I ended up in that garage. Long after Jenny and my son were asleep inside our warm home, I'd drink beer in the cold garage alone, rehashing the past and reliving the nightmare. My wife was right. So was Charlie. I needed to move on.

I closed the book.

Sweeping the remains, I cradled the entire sordid mess in my arms, turned one-eighty and dropped it all in the trash bin.

CHAPTER FIVE

WHEN I WALKED into the office Monday morning, I could tell right away something was up. Coworkers I seldom talked to made eye contact, nodding approval. I got two thumbs-up and one handgun salute. Another—I think his name was Marc, or maybe Ron, some bald guy—raised his coffee mug in a toast. A hero's welcome.

They started coming up one by one. Took me a moment to realize why they were congratulating me. Even without filing my report, I had been credited with cracking the Olisky case. NEI investigated potentially fraudulent claims all the time. Finding incontrovertible evidence to refute those claims was rare. Nabbing a confession, almost unheard of. The only problem: I hadn't said a word. The emphatic response shocked me. The reality of the situation was far less glamorous. An overwhelmed, emotionally distraught sixteen-year-old boy had admitted lying. I hadn't done anything but be in the right place at the right time. How had DeSouza even found out?

A little after ten, the boss' door swung open.

"Porter," DeSouza called from the doorway. "Get in here." I'd heard those words before, but never with the warmth and smile that accompanied them now.

"A helluva job, Jay," DeSouza said, closing the door after me, pointing to take a seat. "Helluva job."

I'd hated my boss from the first day I met him. Andy DeSouza embodied every douchebag characteristic I'd grown to despise, the kind of short, slick man who shakes your hand extra hard before finding an excuse to tell you what he paid for his new hot tub.

"I'll admit, Porter, there were times over this past year when I questioned your motivation. Started thinking you may not be cut out for the insurance game. But this Olisky investigation, you really delivered the goods. Came up big when we needed it most."

"Didn't realize it was such a big case."

"Are you kidding me? Do you know much an insurance company loses to fraud every year?"

I shrugged.

DeSouza's face pinched up. "Well, I don't have an exact number. But I can tell you it is a lot. *This* is the sort of case that gets a claims man noticed. I noticed. Trust me, *Concord* noticed. Speaking of which . . ." He left those words dangling there. I wasn't sure what I was supposed to do with them.

It was nice getting praise for a change, but I was still curious how this information had made its way to DeSouza in the first place. "How did you—I mean, how could you deny the claim without my final report?"

"When you didn't return to the office Friday afternoon, I called the Olisky house. Brian admitted he'd been driving. Sounded like you grilled him pretty hard, eh? I'm proud of you."

"Thanks," I said, even though if DeSouza called the Oliskys directly, he'd been checking up on me because he didn't trust me to do my job.

I glanced around at the motivational posters plastering the walls. Hands covering hands, skydivers forming a circle, a single snowflake testifying how special we all are. The worst part was the cloying platitudes stamped underneath, all variations of Believe in Yourself, Work Harder, Take No Shortcuts. Loose translation: keep selling your soul to the company store and don't ask what your company can do for you. I had more in common with the Oliskys of this world than I did the DeSouzas.

I must've made a face, because DeSouza launched into the party line.

"We are in a war, Jay. Every day. Against criminals trying to defraud NEI with their scams. Swoop and Squat. Drive Down. Two-Lane Turn Sideswipe. These crooks are always cooking up new schemes, trying to screw us. We have to stay one step ahead of them. Be willing to go that extra mile. And do you know why we do this?"

I shrugged.

"Because we fight for the little guy."

The way he said it, I half expected him to leap on his desk and rip his shirt open, Big S advertising truth, justice, and quarterly profits.

"We advocate for those who play the game the right way. That is what you did, Jay. You helped keep premium rates lower for the honest Joe, the guy who busts his hump at the factory every day, the mother who pays her bills on time—the folks who don't think rules are just for 'other' people, that exceptions should be made for them. Insurance is a safety net, not a ladder to come up. Scammers like the Oliskys—"

"It wasn't like that," I said. Donna and Brian weren't bad people. A mother and son who didn't have much money tried to pull a fast one. I could understand that. "I don't think the Oliskys were trying to deceive—"

"What do you call lying on an official claim?"

Hard to argue with that one.

"I've been in conversation with HQ down in Concord," DeSouza said, picking up the thread from earlier. "The Big Office needs a call up. Been in the works for a while, and I've been trying to decide who deserves it most. Not an easy decision. I'm sure it comes as no surprise, last year wasn't the greatest for claims."

I didn't bother responding that I hadn't much thought about it.

"Your work on the Olisky case helped make my decision for me." He paused for drama's sake. "I've decided to recommend you."

"No shit?"

"No shit."

DeSouza waited for me to jump through his hoop. When I didn't hop fast enough, he sweetened the pot. "Of course, the Concord position comes with greater responsibility. Which comes with a bump in salary."

"A bump?"

"A big bump." He smiled wide. "So, you ready for the majors?"

I couldn't wait to call Jenny with the good news. This was the break I needed. The break *we* needed. Concord, a promotion, a raise—I could finally deliver on the promise I'd made to my wife when I'd asked her to marry me. For the first time in a long time I could see light at the end of the Turnpike tunnel.

My boss came around the desk.

"It's not a done deal yet, of course," DeSouza cautioned. "But if I were you, I'd start checking out the housing market down south."

DeSouza patted me on the back, leading me to the door. Hand on the knob, he extended a firm paternal handshake.

"Don't waste another minute worrying about the Oliskys," my boss said. "They knew what they were doing was wrong. Which is why the son confessed. You did the right thing. You leaned on him until he cracked. And that effort is about to pay off for you. Big time."

Back at my desk, guilt still gnawed at me, even though I hadn't done anything wrong. I hadn't said a word to DeSouza. Brian Olisky confessed all on his lonesome. What was so wrong with taking the credit? I couldn't do anything to help the Oliskys now.

I hadn't been sitting there five minutes when I heard someone shout above the floor chatter, "Porter, line one."

The only person who ever called me at work was Jenny. I took the call, anxious to share the good news. Only it wasn't my wife.

"Mr. Porter?" A woman blubbered on the other end.

"Yes. This is Jay Porter. Who is this?"

The woman sobbed, sputtering illegible gibberish without vowels.

"Ma'am, calm down. I can't understand what you're saying—"

The woman inhaled slowly, forcing composure. "This is Donna Olisky. We met last week? We talked at the copy place where I work? About the accident?"

"Yes, Mrs. Olisky. I remember you." In fact, I was just basking over having denied your claim a few minutes ago. I glanced up from my desk to make sure no one could hear the conversation. "Why are you calling me?"

"They arrested my son this morning."

Across the room, DeSouza stood in his doorway watching me. When our eyes met, he gave me a double-barrel thumbs-up.

I returned the corny gesture, and told Donna I'd call her back.

"Going for a smoke," I said to no one, grabbing my Pats cap and slipping outside with my cell to the parking lot, where a winter's worth of snow remained piled high on islands.

I wasn't sure why I felt the need to hide a work call while I was at work, but after DeSouza's speech, just talking to Donna Olisky felt like fraternizing with the enemy. Why was she calling me? I didn't have any pull with the police. What kind of trouble could a dork like Brian Olisky have gotten into, anyway? Returning a library book late?

I fired up a Marlboro. Tasted so damn good I wondered how I ever quit in the first place. Donna Olisky picked up on the first ring.

"I'm sorry to bother you, Mr. Porter. I didn't know who else to call—"

"Yeah. Okay." Flurries drifted. I stomped my feet to keep blood flowing. Ground so frozen, every time I touched down I could feel the cold penetrate my sole. "What happened?"

"The police picked up Brian this morning," Donna said, still battling to contain the sniffles.

"What for?"

"For leaving the scene of an accident." She said it so calm and matter-of-fact, like I was the moron for asking. I hadn't considered the possibility.

"I'm not blaming you, Mr. Porter—"

"Call me Jay." I'd met that kid. Cops didn't arrest boys like Brian. "They probably need a statement. You don't get arrested for lying—" I stopped myself, thinking about what I'd said. Lying on an insurance claim was textbook fraud.

"We were having breakfast. They hauled him off like a common criminal."

"Did they actually *arrest* him?"

"Huh?"

"Did the police read him his rights?"

"I don't know!" she snapped. "But they weren't very nice."

"Cops can be like that." I'd been through this drill before with my brother. An actual arrest meant paperwork. Police hated unnecessary paperwork. I started to feel better. "I'm sure they just want to talk to him."

"He has a driver's license," Donna said, still believing I held sway over the situation. "We can't afford the premium. Brian has a chance to go to Europe."

"I know, Mrs. Olisky. He told me. But I don't know what you think I can do. I work for an insurance company. I'm not associated with the police. I don't know any cops. Well, I know this one cop, Rob Turley. But he's an Ashton cop—"

"I want to drop the claim. Officially. I thought maybe if I did that, they'd let him go." More sobbing. I made myself remember this woman's loss. I saw her dead son's picture on the mantel, a shrine erected by a grieving mother. I kept telling myself that it wasn't my problem. Except, of course, now it was.

"Mrs. Olisky," I said. "I wouldn't worry about anything. For one, your son is a minor. There's not much they *can* do."

"I want to drop the claim," she repeated. "Rescind it. Officially. If you send over paperwork, I'll sign it."

"It doesn't work that way—"

"Then can you call the Longmont County Courthouse? Tell them we changed our mind about filing a claim."

"Courthouse? First of all, if the police have Brian, he wouldn't be at the Longmont Courthouse." I tried not to act glib over her unfamiliarity with police procedure. People watch way too much TV.

"They said he's being arraigned this morning."

"Who said that?"

"The police. When I called down the station."

"They said he was being arraigned? Are you sure?"

"Yes! At the Longmont County Courthouse. This morning!"

I knew firsthand that the legal system didn't move so fast. None of this was adding up.

"Please," Donna Olisky said. "Can't you halt the claim? My son can't go to prison."

"No one is going to prison."

"He must be so scared. He's just a boy. I can't leave the store again. I'll get fired. I need this job. Tell them he didn't mean to do it. Tell them I put him up to it. He's a good boy. This is all my fault." The inconsolable sobbing returned.

"Please stop crying. Let me see what I can do."

"Oh, thank you, Mr. Porter, Jay," Donna said through choked-back snuffles. "That's very kind of you."

"I'm not making any promises. Listen. This is my cell. If you need to reach me, use this number. You're going to have to give me a little time, though."

Mrs. Olisky thanked me profusely. Not like I had any choice.

You'd have to be one heartless sonofabitch not to be moved by a mother's crying.

CHAPTER SIX

I RANG LIBBY Brook PD, expecting to be shot down, or laughed at, because the scenario Donna Olisky proposed was ludicrous. Instead I got an extra-helpful receptionist, who confirmed the impossible: not only had Brian Olisky been arrested, he'd been whisked up to Longmont County Courthouse for arraignment this a.m. She didn't know more than that. I called the courthouse. A robot answered, prompting me to push a bunch of buttons, which got me no closer to a live human being. After ten minutes of Michael Bolton musak and frustration, I decided to check this out in person and find out what the hell was going on.

I told DeSouza I had loose ends to tie up before I could turn in my final report. He didn't ask what, which was good, because I wouldn't have had an answer.

Centrally located south of the mountains, the Longmont Courthouse served as one-stop lowlife shopping, servicing most of northern New Hampshire. Every screw-up charged within a fifty-mile radius got hauled here. DUI, drug possession, domestic violence, whatever other hillbilly crimes had been committed over the weekend—this was where the damage got sorted out.

The Courthouse bustled with late-morning business as deputies jettisoned the last batch of scofflaws up the steep steps of Lady Justice; hardened criminals prepared to meet their fate. Except none of these inmates looked terribly hardened to me.

That's one of the benefits of experiencing how the other half lives: you're forced to go beyond stereotypes and prejudice. With a different past, I'd only see the tan jumpsuits and handcuffs, too. Like the rest of the wholesome folk tooling Main Street. Turn head in disgust, hit the auto-lock, drive away a little faster. Most of these convicts, with their bad posture and drippy noses, weren't gangbangers or bank robbers; they were dope-sick addicts who'd attempted some penny-ante bullshit. Junkies will do anything to put off dealing with the reality of their pathetic lives another moment longer.

Watching the parade of drunks, dope fiends, and tweakers, I knew one thing: Brian Olisky didn't belong with these people.

I checked the time. Almost twelve. Bad timing. State agencies take long lunches. Even with the lunch break and my boss' good graces, I knew I had to hurry. And I didn't know where to start.

Last time I'd been here, my brother had been popped for panhandling outside the Price Chopper. Vagrancy. Had to be at least two years ago. I'd come to bail him out. They'd refurbished the place since then, adding another wing of courtrooms. There used to be a help desk right when you walked in. I didn't see any help desk.

I emptied my keys in the bucket and crossed the threshold.

A steady flow of suits, lawyers on both sides of the equation, exited in the other direction, prosecutors and public defenders yammering out last-minute plea bargains on their way to grab an expensive sandwich. Two years suspended after four, credit for time served, yuk-yuk. An hour earlier, they'd been at each other's throats. Now they were laughing, joking, friendly as hell. It's all a show.

Those prisoners lucky enough to get their charges dropped or released on their own recognizance scurried off into the shadows, free to plot their next fuckup, the rest of the chattel refitted with chains and packed in the jailhouse van, whisked back to county, or somewhere far worse.

The clock tower struck noon. The hectic scene of ten minutes ago vanished. Doors locking, gates rolling shut. A bailiff with a large metal key ring dangling from his hip scowled in my direction, took a corner, and was gone, the echo of footsteps swallowed by cavernous halls. I stood in silence.

I didn't know where to find Brian Olisky. I couldn't believe the police would pick up a boy like him. Even if they did, processing took time, arraignments took time. This wasn't any of the state's business until NEI chose to file charges. DeSouza was a jerk, but I couldn't see him clamoring for the arrest of a sixteen-year-old. Even if corporate made the call, no one goes before the judge this fast. Had the woman at Libby Brook PD been mistaken? Had Brian even been here at all?

I poked my head in a couple of deserted courtrooms. Still plenty of good seats left for the two o'clock showing.

Standing in the middle of the hall, I spun three-sixty, scanning surroundings until my eyes settled on a little hole in the wall. At the far end, inside a tiny box not much bigger than a tollbooth, a young woman sat watching me. She didn't hide her amusement over my confusion.

She waved me closer. Nose ring. Pierced lip. Sunburst tattoo curling out collar, orange flame licking slender neckline. Young. Pretty. White Mountain Community College, I figured, probably interning for class credit. Brushing the black hair from her eyes, she ran a tongue over her lip ring.

"Hey," I said.

"Hey yourself."

"I'm looking for someone."

"I bet you are."

"A friend of mine."

She patted the stack of court documents piled high next to her. "When was your friend picked up?"

"This morning."

She giggled. "Then he's still in county. Longmont moves fast. But not that fast."

I wanted to say nothing moved fast in Longmont. On the way in, I'd gotten stuck behind a jalopy flatbed with a "Can't Beet a Farmer" bumper sticker.

I pointed at her paperwork. "You mind checking anyway?"

"Not supposed to give out that information. Except to family." She wrinkled her nose, as if she were one to play by the rules. Before I could respond, she smiled and said, "What's your *brother's* name?"

"Brian Olisky."

She flipped through pages, running a finger down, twirling hair, gnawing her lip. She wasn't exactly subtle. I'd always considered myself a good-looking guy. Mostly because other women had told me so. But I wasn't good-looking enough to warrant this kind of attention, not from a girl who looked like that. Which told me one thing: she must be really bored inside that little box, or she was playing me for some reason. Beat me why.

"I don't think he's going to be listed," she said. "If he was arrested this morning, they'd book him in whatever township, then petition to get on tomorrow's docket, even expedited, and then— oh, wait. That's weird. Here he is. Brian Olisky."

"Great. Can you tell me where I can find him? Or who his public defender is?"

"Everyone's at lunch. If he hasn't seen the judge yet, he'd be on the afternoon docket. Could be with a sheriff in one of the holding cells in the basement? They feed prisoners hamburgers for lunch. But you can't go down there."

"Can you?"

"Can't leave my station."

"But you don't know if he's down there?"

She shook her head. "Could be back in county," she said. "Don't see a PD assigned yet. I can find out and call you." There was that grin again.

I'd thought maybe I was being egotistical, a thirty-something dad mistaking friendly with flirting. I didn't know how girls that age acted. In a couple years I'd be put out to demographic pasture. I already didn't understand new music or techy gadgets. But when she asked for my number, she made sure to lean forward over the counter, pressing her arms against her tits so I could see down her shirt and the black lace bra. A blind man could see she was hitting on me.

I wasn't blind—or a saint—but when I brought up my cell I made sure she saw my wedding ring.

I caught her glance at it, heeding its warning as much as you do a mattress tag before you rip it off. She reached for my hand, soft fingers lingering over calloused knuckles. A year spent working white-collar hadn't erased a lifetime's worth of manual labor's scars. She relieved me of my phone, scrolled through my contacts and added her information, typing in a flurry of thumbs and digits. Anytime I had to add a new name and number, I needed half a week to hunt and peck. She flipped my cell over, passing it back like a loaded gun.

"Better yet," she said, "I get off work at four. There's a bar around the corner, the Chop Shop. Come back and I'll let you buy me a drink."

I winced goodbye. Like I was doing that. I knew damn well

she'd seen the ring; I didn't feel any need to reiterate the obvious. Walking away, I felt self-conscious, face flushed, gut twisting, wondering how pretty girls still held that power over me.

My cell buzzed. I glanced down at my new friend's contact.

Nicki. Spelled with an "i." Of course it was.

* * *

Longmont proper was about forty minutes south of Plasterville, not far from the 302, which put Burlington little more than an hour away. I realized that was half the reason I'd gone up to the courthouse, even if I hadn't acknowledged it consciously at the time. Now I could see Jenny and my son. So much for altruism.

I called DeSouza and said I'd eaten something bad at lunch.

"Gas station sushi will do that to you," DeSouza joked. "No worries, Jay. Go home. Rest up. You deserve it. See you tomorrow."

The tortuous drive along 302's ice-slicked roadways made the trip seem a lot longer than it should have. I didn't bother calling Jenny first because I was worried she'd tell me to turn around. I hadn't been to Lynne's new place in Burlington. Whenever Jenny made the trip, I begged off. I had to look up the address on my cell.

My mother-in-law and I didn't get on too well. No surprise. How many bad comedians cut their teeth with mother-in-law jokes? It's Humor 101. My situation was worse than that. The woman flat out hated me. She made no secret she thought her daughter could do better, a point of view she started voicing back in high school. I remembered Lynne once telling Jenny how Derek Riggs, Ashton High's QB, would make a great boyfriend. I was standing right there in the kitchen when she'd said it.

Lynne attended our marriage ceremony at City Hall last year, and she'd said all the right things, calling me son, welcoming me to the family. Even though her daughter and I had a child together, Lynne couldn't hide her contempt for me. Jenny fleeing in the middle of the night, bashing her "emotionally unavailable" husband, wouldn't improve my standing.

The whole drive up I'd been gnashing my jaw, sucking down cigarettes. By the time I reached the shores of Lake Champlain, I realized those feelings had less to do with my mother-in-law and more to do with the guilt I felt. I hadn't done anything wrong with that Nicki girl, but I'd still enjoyed the attention. Regardless of our current situation, I loved my wife. I hadn't flirted back. Had I? No, that was all on her. Maybe I'd imagined the whole thing and she *was* just being nice. That made more sense. I had to be at least ten years older than she was, and why did I care anyway?

Chomping mints, I tried to clear my mind as I knocked on Lynne's door. Seeing my wife and son would fix everything.

"Oh, hello, Jay," my mother-in-law chirped with phony cheer, standing in the doorway, not bothering to invite me in.

I peered around her. "I was in the neighborhood."

"Burlington is over two hours away."

"Yeah. Took me over two hours to get into the neighborhood... Is my wife here?"

Lynne laughed and stepped aside. "She should be back any minute. Come in. Sit down."

"How about my son?" I saw a corner of the living room had been designated a play area, all toys contained neatly within its borders. Nothing else in the apartment was out of order. Even the magazines on the glass end table were fanned perfectly. My mother-in-law was nothing if not meticulous.

"He went with her," she said.

"Where did they go?"

"To lunch," Lynne said. "She's made friends with another tenant in the complex. Same age. Have a lot in common. You know how outgoing and personable Jenny is. It's not easy for her out there where you live now. Nobody to talk to. She's going a little stir crazy. They went to grab a bite to eat." Lynne walked ahead of me into the living room, peeking back over her shoulder. "I don't think Jenny is a big fan of my cooking."

My mother-in-law was the worst cook I'd ever met. Every meal she made the same: indiscernible variations of low-sodium boiled meats in bland, pale gravies. The woman seemed to have a real aversion to flavor.

The condo spread out in typical condo fashion, condensed quarters cut up for single-person living, a place where old people could enjoy pastel and things not meant to be touched well into their golden years. Best I could tell, there were about fifty units in the complex. I'd bet dollars to donuts, they were all decorated like this one, with ugly paintings of giant watercolored lilies in gilded frames, fake Greek columns and too many mirrors.

I sat down in the chair. Lynne had family photographs propped up on glass end tables. Pictures of Jenny. Pictures of Aiden. Pictures of Jenny and Aiden. I saw one with me in it, out of focus, relegated to the background.

"Jenny says you two have been having trouble? Can I get you coffee? Tea?"

"No. Thanks. And I wouldn't say we've been having trouble. We're happily married." I knew the "happily" was a stretch. Right then "married" felt like pushing it. "The year's been stressful. New job. Moving." I didn't add the part about witnessing my brother's violent death.

"Of course marriage is hard," Lynne said. Then after a slow pause, "Although without the misery of marriage, one can't know the joy of divorce." She laughed.

"No one's getting divorced."

"Relax, I wasn't talking about you, Jay." As if my inference was out of left field. "Just a joke I heard a comedian make the other night. I was talking about me. The best years of my life came after I divorced Jenny's father."

"Jenny doesn't talk about her dad much."

"Why would she? He's worthless. As a husband. As a father. As a man. Couldn't hold down a job for more than a year without screwing it up." Lynne smoothed her hands. "By the way, how is your new job? What are you doing? Selling insurance? Jenny says you aren't happy there."

"Claims investigations," I corrected her. "That's why I wanted to see Jenny, actually. Tell her the good news in person. I solved a big case. Saved the company tons of money. I'm up for a promotion. We'll be relocating to the main office down in Concord." I couldn't resist rubbing her nose in it, even if I was jumping the gun. This woman had sold me short since the day we met.

"That's wonderful," Lynne said, though her dour expression didn't match the cheerful encouragement. "I'm so glad to hear that, Jay."

"I thought you'd be upset."

"Why would I be upset?"

"Concord is pretty far. Won't get to see Jenny and Aiden as much."

"I'm not worried about that. I'll find a way. Besides, I want what's best for my daughter. I don't think someone her age—especially a mother—should be a cocktail waitress, do you?"

The door pushed open, and I heard my son's voice, followed by my wife's.

"Is that Jay's truck outside?" Jenny said from the condo landing.

My son ran in the room. "Daddy!" Aiden shrieked and jumped into my arms. I gave him a big dad hug.

"Hey, little man. You miss me?"

He nodded.

"How much?"

Aiden squinched an eye. "Um. Infinity plus sixty-one plus seventy-four plus ninety-*nine*!"

I pulled back, flabbergasted. "Whoa. That much? That's a lot!"

My son wrapped his arms around my neck super tight. Only a couple days had passed but just feeling his skin against mine made me whole again. I was feeling great. Kicking ass at work. Center of my boy's world. When I saw Jenny's smiling eyes, like she was actually happy to see me, I felt like nothing could bring me down.

Then I saw him.

Clean cut, strong chin, commanding presence. He reminded me of that smug prick Adam Lombardi, the way he stood there in his crisp collar, oozing self-confidence.

"Hi," he said, slipping past my wife. "I'm Stephen. You must be Jay." He held out a hand.

I set my son down, and stared at my wife. I turned back to Lynne, who practically tittered with satisfaction.

"I thought you said Jenny was out with a friend?"

"Yes," Lynne offered without apology. "Stephen lives upstairs." She waited. "He's an investment banker. At Morgan Stanley."

Stephen shrugged his broad shoulders, dismissing the no-doubt hefty six-figure salary. He flashed me a megawatt. "So Jenny tells me you . . . sell insurance?"

"No. I don't sell insurance. I investigate insurance claims."

Stephen and my mother-in-law exchanged a look, eyebrows raised, like I was missing the joke. I hated when people did that.

"Jenny," Lynne said to my wife. "Jay has good news. He just—" My mother-in-law gazed at me in earnest. "I'm sorry. What did you say? Solved a policy?"

"I told you. I don't sell insurance."

"My bad," Lynne said, then back to Jenny: "But he did do something good, I remember that."

Lynne and Stephen laughed.

"What the fuck is going on?" I said.

Lynne gasped, like she'd never heard the word fuck before. No way some guy hadn't dropped a few f-bombs on her before now.

Jenny gave me the death stare. I didn't care. I was the odd man out, the third wheel in this scenario. Me, the husband. This was bullshit.

"I should be going," Stephen said.

"Yeah, why don't you do that, Stephen." I stressed his name, which was a stupid name for guy. Your parents saddle you with that one, you go with Steve. Nobody called him "Stephen McQueen."

The bastard locked on eyes with me. Not long, fleeting. But long enough to issue the challenge. Consider the gauntlet thrown down, fucker.

Then, right there in front of me, the sonofabitch had the nerve to take my wife's hand. "I had a nice time today." He gazed back at me with manufactured civility. "Nice meeting you, Jay." But the nail? He called over Aiden, *my* son, who didn't know better. Crouching down eye level with him, Stephen said, "Next time we'll work on keeping your eye on the ball, slugger." Then he tousled his hair. Put his fucking hand right on my kid's head.

I've never been good at regulating emotions in the heat of the moment. Especially where other men were concerned. Once that lizard switch gets tripped, there's no going back.

Wedging by my wife, I took Stephen by his fancy-boy collar and shoved him against the wall.

"Jay!" Jenny shouted.

I got in his face. "Listen, asshole. You stay the hell away from my family."

Stephen held up his hands. "Hey. Whoa. I think there's been a—"

"Don't play that bullshit with me."

"Aiden, come with Grandma in the kitchen," Lynne said, like she hadn't orchestrated this entire scene. My boy stared up at me, eyes widened in confusion, as my mother-in-law dragged him away from his lunatic father.

I drew back my clenched fist, ready to break Stephen's jaw. Maybe I'd have only punched the wall by the side of his head to scare him. I don't know. Probably the first one. But Jenny grabbed my cocked fist and pulled me off before we had the chance to find out.

"I'm going to go," Stephen mumbled, fumbling for the knob, squeaking outside.

"Yeah, you do that, asshole." I panted, overheating, a bull.

When I turned around and saw the mix of horror and disgust on my wife's face, I knew I'd fucked up.

Jenny didn't need to say it. But she did anyway.

"Jay, you need to leave. Now. I'll call you when I'm ready to talk to you again. Until then, I don't want to hear your voice. I don't want to see your face. Stay away from me."

CHAPTER SEVEN

I SPED ALONG the winding, tortuous route east as light snow began to fall. A dusting coated the roads, sweeping small pirouettes across the empty lanes. I lit a cigarette and punched the wheel, back tires fishtailing with the blow. I accelerated around a hairpin, tempting fate. What the fuck was I doing? *When you're standing on thin ice, you don't jump up and down.*

Even though I knew Stephen, if given half the chance, would try to sleep with my wife—because he was a guy and that's what guys do—my opinion on the subject didn't matter. You can see whatever you want to see—if nobody else sees it, what good does it do you? Invisible trees get chopped down in the forest all day long.

Out the window, Douglas firs and evergreen tips bowed with the wind. The spare change in my cup quaked as the earth shook. I couldn't tell if a storm was brewing or I was driving way faster than I should. My big Chevy block thrummed, rattled. I checked my speedometer, needle pushing fifty around tight curves intended for twenty-five. I saw a call come in on my cell in the center console. I glanced down and ignored it. If Jenny wasn't on the line, I didn't give a shit.

Donna Olisky had badgered me all afternoon, ringing every hour on the hour, forcing me to put the phone on vibrate. I knew keeping her in the dark was lousy, and that I'd have to talk to her sooner or later. But you can't report back on what you don't know.

My botched afternoon in Burlington wasn't Donna's fault, but favors still cost extra—you don't get to look out for someone else's well-being until you've taken care of your own.

Didn't help that my defense was inadmissible. As sure as every winter up here promises misery, I knew Lynne had manipulated that whole charade. A plan had been set in motion months ago: wait for a vulnerable moment to unleash the young, urban professional upstairs, whose pump Lynne had surely been priming since the day she moved in. And I'd played right into the trap. But you can't prove intent, and lunch is still lunch. I couldn't accuse Jenny of anything other than being hungry.

Coming up on the 302 split, I fought temptation to flip a bitch and bull my way back to Lake Champlain. Stand my ground until Jenny heard me out. If given enough time, I could usually stumble across the right words. If the extra rope didn't hang me first. Saner instincts prevailed, and I stayed the course.

Even though my wife had thrown me out of her mother's house, I still had faith I could repair the damage. Jenny was good about accepting apologies. When she calmed down. I needed to stay away for a while, bite my tongue, wait till she returned from enemy soil.

What pissed me off most, I hadn't been able to give Jenny the good news about my promotion. Which had been the whole point of going up to Burlington in the first place. My mother-in-law had bowled my legs from under me, shortchanging my big score, and leaving me no choice but to split, a loser.

My cigarette died out. I lit another. My phone buzzed again. I picked up the cell and saw the name on the screen. But it wasn't Donna, and it wasn't my wife. Sometimes I wondered if the universe delighted in screwing with me. I put it to my ear.

"Hey," said the cool female voice. "It's Nicki."

I didn't respond right way, molars powdering enamel to keep from screaming.

"From the courthouse?"

"Yeah. I remember."

"So, you free to grab that drink now?"

I had to end this now. Nothing good could come of it. I'm a happily married father. I don't screw around.

"Listen," I said, attempting tack. "You seem like a nice girl, Nicki. But I'm married—"

"Yeah. I know, I saw the ring. Sorry about that." She laughed. Well, less a laugh and more a mocking jeer. "It was shitty of me."

"Sorry?"

"Y'know, how I was with you earlier, playing. I thought interning at a courthouse would be fun. Or at least a good experience. Get course credit, walk away with a few stories to tell. But it's *so* boring. All I do is sit in that little box, filing paperwork. All. Day. Long. Can't even check Facebook on my phone. The only way I can pass the time is hitting on old married guys. Lame, I know. But it's entertaining watching how nervous they get."

Old? I'm not old. Since when is thirty-one old?

"Not that you're old," she added.

Talk about a bitch slap. I'd gone from worrying about how to let her down easy to getting batted around like a wounded mouse for the amusement of a house cat. I could practically hear her licking the blood from her claws, satisfied with another kill.

"I want to show you something," she said. When I didn't respond right away, she added, "We can meet in a well-lit, public place if you're worried."

"I'm not worried. I'm busy."

"I have information about your friend, Brian."

"Where is he?" My self-worth had taken enough of a hit for

one day. I wanted back in front of my TV, sweats and a tee, beer in hand. Pop in a DVD and forget this whole rotten day. Mocked by yuppies and college girls. Does it get any worse?

"Place called the North River Institute."

"North River?"

"Listen," Nicki said, "it's too complicated to explain over the phone. So here's what I'm going to do. I am stopping for a drink at the Chop Shop. It's a steakhouse slash cocktail bar a few blocks from the courthouse. Corner of Main and Laramie. If you want my help, I'll be there for the next hour. Or until I find something better to do. If not, nice meeting you, Jay."

* * *

Nicki sat at a small table by the bar, twirling the tiny umbrella between her fingers. Being allowed in the bar meant she had to be at least twenty-one, not that Longmont County cared any more than the rest of New Hampshire when it came to following the letter of the law. But if she was working at the courthouse, I couldn't see her using a fake ID. She might be brazen, but that con was short-lived. She spied me and took another sip of her fizzy pink cocktail. A tall, untouched pint sat across from her. I wondered if I was interrupting something. The rest of the bar was empty.

"You strike me as a beer guy." She slid over the glass. "Crowd will pick up in about fifteen when the courthouse closes for the day. Good luck getting a drink then."

I stared down at the beer, then at her, still deciding whether I wanted to sit with this girl.

"Truce," she said, nudging forward the frothy pint.

"I didn't realize we knew each other well enough to be fighting."

Nicki cocked her head. "Not yet," she cooed, before biting a lip. "Sorry. Force of habit."

A giant picture of a dissected cow hung on the wall behind her, illustrating the various cuts of beef.

"Have a seat. I won't bite, promise."

For the first time I detected the accent. "Where are you from?" I pulled the stool out.

"Took you long enough. The City."

"Concord?"

Nicki laughed. "Is that what you call 'the city' up here? No. I mean, *the* City. New York." She flicked her nose ring. When I didn't react, she peeled her shirtsleeve, revealing the rest of the sunburst flare, a brilliant kaleidoscopic supernova wrapping around her biceps, comet tail shooting up her shoulder.

"People are inked up here, too."

"Yeah," she said. "Except people with tattoos don't say 'inked' or 'tatted.' That's TV talk."

"Okay, Nicki. I get it. You're cool. I'm not. I don't care. You said you wanted to show me something? Show me. I have better things to do than sit around and get insulted by a girl half my age majoring in women's studies at White Mountain Community."

"Actually, I'm twenty-two, and it's criminal justice at Keene State. Just taking a break while I am stuck living with my uncle in Ma and Pa Kettle Country."

"Terrific. But I still don't care."

"Drink your beer," she said through a pursed smirk. She hoisted a handbag to the table, rooting around, extracting a folded sheet of paper.

"What's that?"

"The new address where your pal Brian is staying."

"I wouldn't call him a pal."

"I know. You work for NorthEastern Insurance. I made some phone calls."

I checked the address. North River Institute. "What is this?"

"A diversion program."

"Diversion from what?"

"A life of crime. Rough crowds. Gangs."

I couldn't help but laugh.

"What's so funny?"

"If you met this kid, you'd know. He's a string bean. A tadpole. A nerd."

"Nerd is the new cool."

"Good to know. But the only gang Brian Olisky is in danger of joining is the Doofus Patrol."

"If he was such a square bear, he wouldn't have been brought before Judge Roberts. North River is no joke. It's a juvie. A hardcore rehab. Seen a lot of troubled kids getting sent there lately."

"Brian Olisky is not troubled. He lied on an insurance form."

Nicki pointed down at the rest of the paper I had yet to read. "Says the cops found drugs in the car."

"Bullshit."

"Read."

Below the handwritten address for North River, an official summary of charges spelled it out. "A joint? How long are these diversion programs?"

"Depends. The courts work out sentencing with parents beforehand. A joint decision. But incarceration is open ended and can last for years, if there's enough financing."

Brian's mother never would have signed off on anything like that. She'd been a nervous wreck last time we'd spoke.

"You could've told me all this on the phone," I said to Nicki, folding the police report and address.

"I know. But . . ." She glanced around the room as a couple suits stepped in from the cold.

"But what?"

"I told you. I don't know anyone up here. You seem like a nice guy—"

I held up my ring finger.

"Get over yourself, Jay. I mean, I could use a cool guy to talk to, grab a beer once in a while. Y'know, a friend."

I returned an incredulous stare.

"What? Men and women can't be friends? What are we? In high school?"

I didn't answer. I was thinking about Jenny and how I'd gone ballistic over her having lunch with a guy. Pretty much the same thing I was doing here. Actually less egregious, because every time I looked at Nicki I couldn't help wondering what she looked like naked.

"What is wrong with everyone up here?" Nicki asked. "I'm not looking for a boyfriend. Trust me. I've had my fill."

Draining my pint, I stood and stuffed the sheet in my back pocket.

"Wait. Where are you going?"

"Home, Nicki. I appreciate you getting this information for me." I looked around the barroom, which had now started to fill with a steady stream of prosecutors, clerks, and public defenders. "I'm sure you'll make plenty of friends."

She cocked her head.

"We're real friendly up here."

CHAPTER EIGHT

PARKED UNDER A street lamp, I sat in my idling truck a few blocks from the bar. Strong winds swept down the street with the late-afternoon cold front, whistling outside the glass, kicking up snow. I pulled the piece of paper, rereading the address for the North River Institute, trying to reconcile conflicting reports. A diversion program? Basically a rehab masquerading as detention center. That's how Nicki had pitched it. For Brian Olisky? A band geek who had been arrested, arraigned, and sentenced in less than six hours. There's swift justice. Then there's cruel-and-unusual warp speed. Death Row inmates wait longer than that. What had Brian done to warrant this kind of response? I pictured that skinny, scrawny, pencil neck, imagined how scared he must be inside those prison walls. He wouldn't last a night.

Maybe Nicki had oversold it. Maybe North River was a residential facility designed to intervene before teens went down a dark path. Except Brian Olisky was as far from the dark side as I was from domestic bliss. I had no way of knowing what the Institute was really like without checking it out, firsthand, a mission I had no interest in undertaking. Because this wasn't my problem.

Did I need to call Donna Olisky and explain her son wasn't coming home tonight? Or did she already know? I wasn't sure which scenario bothered me more.

I checked my phone to see how many of her calls I'd missed.

After the disaster with Jenny, I'd seen my phone light up several times. I'd stopped paying attention after a while. When I scrolled the log, I saw the calls from Donna stopped early afternoon. The rest were from Charlie, texts and voice mails urging me to head over the mountain and catch him at the Dubliner if Jenny hadn't returned.

I was relieved I didn't have to break the news to Donna. Someone from the courthouse must've already done that. Why else would she suddenly stop calling? Sucked for her. But my job was done. My stomach knotted up, I toppled a few antacids, choking down the dry chalk, trying to locate Route 302 in the dark.

Steady precipitation returned, thick sleet and wet snow glopping the windshield like spitballs from a juvenile god. My wipers labored through the slush, little motors grinding gears until I could smell the burn. I didn't know this area so well. Whenever I'd had to bail out Chris, I'd come during the daytime. That was ages ago. Tonight I was relying on GPS to guide the way. I still didn't have the hang of the technology, goddamn screen rotating every time I picked up the phone to get a closer look, and the robotic vocal instructions to "turn left here" always came a beat too late. Felt like I was going in circles.

Keeping my eyes peeled for deer, which had a bad habit of jumping out and standing in the middle of the road, I was so focused and preoccupied over Brian Olisky and Jenny and where my life was headed, I didn't spot the cruiser on my tail. Even when the lights flashed and air horn bleated, it didn't register they were talking to me.

I slowed to the side. Blinding high beams shot through the back window of my truck, smacking off the rearview. I cocked the mirror to shield my eyes. Doors opened and slammed shut. I leaned over to fish my registration from the glove compartment.

After the day I'd had, last thing I felt like doing was dealing with Podunk PD for rolling through a stop sign.

I hadn't been pulled over on a routine traffic stop in a while and couldn't find my paperwork, too many crinkled receipts and ATM statements, napkins from the Dunkin' Donuts that I kept for when Aiden's nose ran, which, as a little kid living on the tundra, was invariably. I swatted aside papers in the glove compartment, growing agitated over my lack of organization. A hard knock rapped off the glass.

"Hold on," I said. "Jesus." Without looking up, I reached back with my left hand to unroll the window. Waiting for the requisite "Do you know why I stopped you, sir?" I continued digging around, wading deep in the dish, until I found the registration, crumpled yellow paper like a McDonald's cheeseburger wrapper. I sat back up, expecting a balding reject picked last in gym class. Instead I got highway patrol buzz cut and a pair of crazy eyes better suited for mixed martial arts than law enforcement.

"Put your hands on the wheel where I can see them." The quiet seething in his voice should've been my first clue this wasn't an ordinary stop.

"No problem," I said, flipping the paperwork in the center console. Sudden movement, a stupid move. Sig Sauer unholstered and aimed at my skull, the officer ripped open the door, reached in, and flung me to the ground. I hit the frozen tarmac with the full force of a belly flop on a winter lake, knocking the wind out of me. I pushed myself to my hands and knees, waving a hand to let me catch my breath so I could explain.

I heard more footsteps in the snow, my vision tearing up, blurry. A pair of boots came to rest on each side of me.

No one was interested in explanations.

The pair alternated kicks to my stomach, flanks, and sternum.

The unexpected force made me throw up. One of them grabbed me by the scruff, lifting me off the asphalt like a misbehaving mutt, hoisting me to unsteady feet. He spun me around, pushing me against my truck, face-first. My forehead cracked against the frame. Feet kicked apart, I was patted down. My head rang and I tasted blood in my mouth.

Satisfied I wasn't carrying any weapons, they spun me back around, where a high-powered flashlight shone in my eyes.

"You have a hard time following orders, eh, boy? You been drinking tonight?"

I squinted and tried to focus on the face talking to me. I couldn't tell if it was the same crazy-eyed psycho or his partner. Not that it made any difference.

"He's talking to you, boy. You been drinking?"

"I had a half a beer. About an hour ago." I still couldn't even see who the hell I was talking to. I hated that I couldn't see a face.

"Don't lie to me. Nobody throws up from half a beer."

I didn't mention the roundhouse kicks to my lower intestines. By now I was pretty sure no one gave a shit what I thought.

"Except faggots. That it? You some kind of faggot? Can't hold your liquor?"

"Nah, he ain't a faggot. He was just in the Chop Shop, chatting up that pretty girl."

"Nicki," his partner said, nice and slow. The way he said her name made it clear he knew her.

"He's talking to you, boy."

I didn't hear a question in there, but "Yeah," I said, "my friend. Nicki. I mean, I just met her."

"I think Nicki has enough friends. You got me?"

When they'd first pulled me from the truck and began kicking the shit out of me, I hadn't processed what I'd done. Didn't have much time to think through scenarios while getting my kidneys dislodged. Maybe someone robbed the Price Chopper or Qwik Stop. Mistaken identity. Everyone up here drives a truck. Weirder things had happened. Maybe tonight was just the wrong night to be driving a Chevy on this road. All I knew: they had the guns and the badges, and nothing I said was helping my cause. With that warning, though, I had my reason. Just my luck. A jealous ex who also happens to be a cop.

When I didn't answer right away, I felt the other one close ranks. "He asked you a question."

"Yeah," I said, "I got you. Enough friends."

With the flashlight blazing in my eyes and the searing pain in my abdomen, I couldn't focus, and I stopped trying. I only knew these cops weren't like the cops in Ashton. We were on a desolate road, no houses, no street lamps, just bramble weeds and briar patch. I hadn't seen a car since I'd been stopped. Deep runoff ditches ran the gamut each side, a permanent resting spot for roadkill deer. Let the carcass decompose back to the elements. No one was coming down here looking for the dead.

One of them had my wallet.

"Jay Porter," he read. "75 Genoa. Plasterville."

His partner repeated my name and address, the implication clear: they knew who I was and where to find me. I'd pegged that girl for bad news the moment I met her. Could smell trouble on her from ten feet away.

The cop flipped me back the wallet. Of course I wasn't ready to catch it, and I couldn't see jack shit anyway. The thing bounced off my chest and flopped to the ground. I didn't flinch, for fear of a steel-toe boot and fractured eye socket. I stood statue still until the light switched off.

I waited in the darkness as footsteps retreated. Even then, I didn't move until the squad car K-turned, taking off down the road, in the other direction.

* * *

"What do you think they wanted?" Charlie asked, swiping a chicken wing through the ranch dressing.

After my run-in with the Longmont cops, I'd driven straight over the mountain—or rather around it—to the Dubliner, shaken up and not wanting to be alone. Sometimes walking into a dark, empty house by yourself is more than you can stand.

"No idea." I didn't feel like going into my meeting with Nicki at the Chop Shop, which would prompt more questions about my wife and life.

We sat outside on the tiki porch, Charlie enjoying his ice-cold beer in the ice and cold, licking microwaved BBQ sauce off his fingers, savoring flavors like he was dining on grade A, choice cut. I was shivering balls. My stomach muscles ached, throat raw from retching and breathing fire. My attempts to quit smoking had proved as successful as my efforts to play family man. Now back up to over a pack a day, I exhibited no signs of slowing down.

"So they pull you over. Kick the shit out of you. Then let you go?"

"Pretty much." I regretted mentioning the incident to Charlie, but you can't show up looking like I did without offering some explanation.

"Weird."

I fired another cigarette. I couldn't be certain that cop had dated Nicki. He sure seemed to have a thing for her. Even if it was one-way, *Fatal Attraction* shit, I wasn't calling to find out.

"Maybe you should talk to Turley."

"What for?"

"He's a cop."

"Being a police officer is not like being a member of the fucking moose lodge."

"I know but maybe he can reach out. Y'know, vouch for you."

"Vouch for what? Being okay to drive through their shit-heel town? Trust me. I'm not going back to Longmont anytime soon."

"Why were you out there anyway?"

"Favor. For a friend." I left it there. Charlie didn't press what or for whom.

After a few minutes, he said, "Isn't Longmont where your brother stayed sometimes?

"Yeah. They have a Y over there. Your point?"

"Chris was always getting in trouble. Maybe they knew about you from one of his screw-jobs."

"Possible." I doubted it. That beat-down felt far more personal.

"Isn't that where your brother met that girlfriend of his? What was her name? The one you talked to last year when he went missing? Cat something?"

"Kitty. Katherine. I don't know her last name. I'm not sure they were dating. She was a junkie, too. Chris met her there though, yeah. What are you getting at?"

"I'm not getting at anything. Just trying to have a conversation with my friend who showed up looking like he'd gone twelve rounds with one of the Klitschkos."

"Sorry." I was being a bastard. I still stewed over Jenny and neighbor Stephen, my inability to do a damn thing about it.

"How are things with Jenny?" Charlie asked, picking my thoughts out of the radio waves. "You able to patch things back up?"

"Not exactly."

Charlie waited for the rest. Clipped answers weren't going to cut it. I filled him in on my macho bullshit at Lynne's. How I'd threatened to punch a guy in the head for eating lunch with my wife. Charlie could usually find the silver lining in my storm cloud, fake an attempt that this too shall pass. Not this time.

"Damn," was all he said before turning away to sift through the bird bone graveyard.

"Yeah, I know. I fucked up. You don't have to remind me. Having my mother-in-law whispering in my wife's ear isn't helping." Lynne couldn't come right out and tell Jenny she was better off without me—Jenny, no matter how mad she was at me, would never tolerate her mom openly disparaging the father of her child—but Lynne could still snake the gardens, plant subtle seeds of discontent. Sow enough of them, then she sits back and waits for the things to bloom next time I say something stupid. Which, in my case, was only a matter of time.

"What are you going to do?" Charlie asked.

"What *can* I do? Jenny ordered me to stay away. I can't go all caveman clubbing down doors and dragging her back. I can't let Aiden see me like that again."

Charlie didn't say anything.

"I don't get it. This was all I wanted, man. Jenny and my son. The three of us together. A family. And now that I have it, every move I make just seems to make things worse. Even when I manage to do something right—like breaking this case at work and putting myself in line for a promotion—I still screw it up. I went up there to tell Jenny the good news in person. We can move to Concord, get out of here. Get away from all—" I swept my arm out over the breadth of my hometown "—this." I drained my pint. "Maybe it's not meant to be."

"What?"

"Jenny and me. A contented, regular life. Peace."

Charlie slapped me on the back. "You want to crash at my place again?"

"No. Thanks, man." I'd only had the one beer. "I have work in the morning." I'd burned up whatever favor I'd curried with DeSouza by taking off the whole afternoon. I couldn't do anything else to jeopardize this promotion.

I wasn't looking forward to going back to an empty house, any more than I was waking up at the ass crack of dawn and heading back into that claptrap of an office. In fact, when I gazed into my future, all I saw was dread on the horizon. That little light of mine, Concord, wasn't a perk any longer. I now needed it for the win.

Driving back to Plasterville, a song came over the radio. "Your Love" by The Outfield, this old song from the '80s that had been a running joke between Jenny and me ever since high school. I used to sing it to her when we first started dating, and later on, too, because it always made her laugh. The song was about the singer's girlfriend, Jenny, being out of town, and so he invites a younger girl over to spend the night. I'd tease Jenny, belting out the opening line: "Jenny's on a vacation far away . . ." I have a terrible voice, and Jenny would tell me to stop, the song's message awful, but she'd giggle anyway. Except when I listened to the words tonight, I realized I'd gotten it wrong all these years. The girl's name in the song wasn't Jenny at all; it was Josie. I'd been singing to the wrong girl.

CHAPTER NINE

THE MORNING HAD already gotten off to a rocky start. I hadn't been able to sleep a lick the night before. Those kicks to my stomach had messed up something inside me. Hurt like hell every time I tried to take a piss. Which couldn't be good. I contemplated a trip to the hospital, but dismissed the idea. I hated doctors. I didn't even have a general practitioner, and no way was I visiting the ER in the middle of the night. I'd wait until I literally began pissing blood before I endured that freak show.

Even though she'd cautioned me against calling, I still tried phoning my wife. Didn't matter. Jenny wasn't taking my calls. And my mother-in-law wasn't looking to do any favors.

Wet, cold slop filled the roadways, precipitation stuck between solid and liquid states, which only made a mess of things, weighing down the world. A felled tree and knocked-over telephone pole detoured traffic past the lumberyard, and the moron cashier at the Dunkin' Donuts drive-through added another half hour to my morning commute. I got to work late. Stepping into the office, pant cuffs stained with rock salt, my socks wet and toes squishy, I got a rude reminder that yesterday's victory was an apparition, and any celebration short-lived.

DeSouza stood at the gateway, curling a finger for me to follow him into his office. There was no smile this time. My coworkers, so quick to congratulate and praise me just a day earlier, now shuffled with their heads down, noses in their coffee, careful to look the other way.

When I stepped inside the boss's office, the heavy office door closed behind me with an ominous thud.

"Were you up at the Longmont County Courthouse yesterday afternoon?" The way DeSouza asked meant he already knew the answer.

"Yeah. I told you I had some loose ends to tie up on the Olisky case."

"Was this before or after you phoned in sick with 'food poisoning'?"

I wanted to say "before, because that's how time works, asshole." But I bit my tongue. I was still hoping that one bullshit sick day wasn't going to snuff my chances at Concord.

"I got a phone call this morning, Jay. From the Longmont County Courthouse. Where you were yesterday, asking to review confidential court documents. Harassing a clerk into making unauthorized Xeroxed copies—"

"That's not what happened."

"As a representative of NorthEastern Insurance, you can't barge onto state property, demanding—"

"I didn't demand anything. I went to the courthouse because Donna Olisky—one of our policyholders—called me in a panic, worried about her son."

"I thought I told you to forget about the Olisky case?"

"Sorry, Andy," I said, not sorry at all. "Donna Olisky reached out to me, personally, and asked for my help, after the police had picked up her only child. I thought as a 'representative of NEI' that it might be in our best interest to go that extra mile for a client. *Especially* one we'd just denied a claim on. Y'know, because, above all, we're in a service industry."

When I said the words aloud I almost bought the excuse myself. Advocating for a client *would've* been the right thing to do. But DeSouza didn't even acknowledge my stalwart defense or generosity.

"Why were you digging into Judge Roberts' sentencing history?"

"I wasn't. Who told you that? I don't even know who Judge Roberts is. I don't know what you're talking about, man." I tried to remember if Nicki had given me the name of the judge who'd sentenced Brian to North River. Judge Roberts sounded familiar.

"I am trying hard to make this work, Jay. I like to believe I'm a fair boss. I may get on an employee when I think they can do better. But I pride myself on being fair. When someone does good work, I let them know." He made sure he had my attention. "I let you know you did a good job yesterday, didn't I?"

How magnanimous.

"For this to be a successful partnership, though, it has to work the other way too. A two-way street. Respect. Give and take." He did that annoying thing where he alternated a finger between the two of us as if we were tied together by an invisible, affirming string. "I don't appreciate being lied to."

"I'm not lying to you. I drove up to Longmont because Donna Olisky asked me to check on her son. She was stuck at work. I asked a clerk what happened to Brian. That's it."

"Nicole Parker."

"Huh?"

"The clerk you asked. Her name was Nicole Parker."

Of course he meant Nicki. I could feel the setup. Nicki. The courthouse. Those shit-kicker cops. The way Donna Olisky's phone calls suddenly stopped. Now this. I didn't know the angle just yet. Only that the hook was in, the fix on, and I was taking the fall.

I stared at a huge poster behind his desk, the one with the adorable, mewling kitten dangling from a ball of yarn, clinging for dear life. The caption read, "Hang in There."

"Your friend Nicole—"

"We're not friends. I met the girl yesterday."

"Whatever you two are, Nicole was caught photocopying *sealed* court documents. Classified court documents. Red-handed. That is a serious offense. And when they asked her what she was doing, she said the papers had been requisitioned by Jay Porter of NorthEastern Insurance."

"That's bullshit. I didn't ask that girl to unseal anything."

DeSouza held up a hand. "I'm not interested in excuses." He walked around his desk, sitting on the front edge, leg draped casual, his man-of-the-people pose, tone dropping to dulcet. "I went to bat for you. The court can discipline its employee how they see fit. For my part, I'm willing to let this oversight slide. This time. It's obvious you're going through something right now." His gaze washed over my disheveled appearance, lingering on the bedhead and stubble I'd neglected to shave. Even after I showered and tended to the wounds, my face still betrayed an ass whooping. "You look like you didn't get much sleep last night. Is everything okay on the home front?"

My first instinct was to say "None of your fucking business." But then I recognized a branch being extended to a drowning man. I only had to grab hold and hang on.

"No," I said. "My wife and I are going through a rough patch right now. This last year has been hard on us." I drew out the pregnant pause. "She thought when I started this job, we'd be moving down to Concord. The big city. Y'know? A new start."

DeSouza nodded like he understood.

"She took my son to her mom's in Burlington. Yesterday when I called you, I was already halfway there. I missed them. I wanted to see my family. I took advantage. I'm sorry for lying to you."

Which was the truth, minus the sorry part, even though I resented having to be straight up with a tool like DeSouza. Something must've struck a deeper chord, because his entire demeanor changed.

"Why don't you go home," he said.

"You're firing me?"

"No, Jay. But I want you to take the rest of the week off, get your head straight. Work out whatever you have to with your wife." He came over and reached for my shoulder, giving it a squeeze. "Family is everything."

I scanned the desk behind him for a Mrs. DeSouza but didn't see one. The only pictures he had were of other dudes in huge rubber pants, fly-fishing in streams.

"Concord is still a real possibility," he said. "But we can't have any more mistakes like yesterday, okay? It's imperative if you want this promotion." DeSouza clasped his hands in prayer. "Take a breather, sort out whatever is going on at home. Do what you have to do. Then get your head back in the game. We clear?"

"Yeah, we're clear." I made to leave.

When I got to the door, DeSouza stopped me. "Do me a favor. If Donna Olisky calls you again, have her contact me at the office. I'll take it from there."

I nodded.

"And please no more sniffing around closed cases."

No problem. Whatever was hidden under that lid stank to high heaven, anyway.

* * *

On my way to the grocery store for beer, I phoned Jenny, who still wasn't picking up. I left another message, less apologetic, more pissed. We were going on twenty-four hours of radio silence. I knew I'd done something stupid. Still I expected, as her husband—and the father of our child—I'd get the courtesy of a returned phone call.

Back home, I slipped on some sweats, grabbed a cold one, and kicked back with my fat cat, Beatrice. I flicked through cable movie stations, searching for something to numb my brain. TCM was showing *Gunga Din*, a flick I'd seen so many times I knew the dialogue by heart. The distraction wasn't working.

With all this time off, my wife and son a state away, I knew I wouldn't be able to hold out much longer. Either Jenny would return my calls or I'd have no choice but to drive back to Burlington. Which wouldn't end well for me. That was the thing about my wife: you didn't want to force her hand before she was damn well and ready. She wasn't ready. But I was losing my damned mind.

Nipping my bottled beer, I abandoned the search for temples of gold on the silver screen, and glanced around this new life I'd carved out for myself, wondering how far I'd really come. Bigger television, nicer couch. More square feet, a garage. Renting a little house instead of renting a little apartment. An upgrade, sure, but at what cost? Because without Jenny and Aiden none of this meant squat. What would Concord really solve? I was seeking relief from something I could never escape. Worse, I'd bought into the fallacy of the geographical cure.

Back when my junkie brother was alive, I'd bring him into rehab to clean up. I'd ask the doctors if we could ship Chris out of state, somewhere to remove the daily temptation. The counselors warned me against believing a change of scenery could provide a cure-all. Didn't matter where your connections were or how familiar a street corner was. If you wanted to get high bad enough, you could find drugs anywhere. Wasn't a place on Earth remote enough to keep you away from you.

Outside, the winds smacked iced branches against the windowpane. I stroked Beatrice, fists filling with white fur, feeling the empty ache inside.

I'd made a good dent in the twelve-pack and was contemplating another beer run before the roads got too bad—I hadn't picked up any food since Jenny left—but decided against it. The thought of walking outside to my truck right then, turning over the engine, waiting for it to warm, and starting down that long, snowy road filled me with unspeakable dread. Instead, I turned my attention back to the television and watched a man die in a pit of cobras. I'd dozed off when someone buzzed the bell.

Jenny had a key. Charlie would call before driving all the way out here, which he seldom did anyway. Which literally left no one else. I didn't have a single friend in Plasterville. Then I remembered those two cops.

The buzzer rang again. I set down my beer, shooed Beatrice off my lap, and went to the window. I peeked into the street. I had a clear view. Didn't see a squad car. *Like they're going to announce they're here to cap your ass. Man up, Jay.*

The buzzer.

"Jesus," I shouted. "Hold on. I'm coming."

I jerked open the door, and there she stood, Nicki, holding a sack of takeout Chinese.

"What the hell are you doing here?"

"Nice to see you, too."

"Are you nuts? What if my wife was home?" I looked over my shoulder, whispering. "How do you think this would look?"

Nicki leaned in, whispering back, "I didn't know we'd been hooking up?" She peered past me. "Is she? Home, I mean."

"Not your concern."

"I'll take that as a no." Nicki hoisted the Chinese. "Hungry?"

I couldn't believe the nerve of this girl.

"Can I come in?"

"No."

"Jay, I need to talk to you. I know we got started off on the wrong foot, but—"

"Why are you telling people I asked you to unseal official court documents? You know how much shit I got in at work over that?"

"Sorry. But that's why I'm here. Please. Can I come in?"

I didn't say yes but since she wasn't taking no for an answer I left the door open and walked back in the kitchen.

"I'm sorry," she said again, stepping inside my depressing world.

"Yeah. You mentioned that part." I gestured around the house. "Wonder why I'm home?"

"Because you're done working for the day?"

"I've been here all day."

"I didn't get you fired, did I?"

"No. But damn close. I'm on the heels of a big promotion. Instead I get a mandatory vacation."

"Where is your wife?"

"That is none of your business, Nicki."

She glanced around the place, at the cleared-out, opened drawers, which I hadn't bothered to shut, the drained beer bottles toppled across tabletops, the crumpled cigarette packs, the tea plates I'd been using for ashtrays, all the telltale signs of a lonely man enduring a prolonged stretch of bachelor. The whereabouts of my family *wasn't* any of her business, but no point denying the obvious either.

"My wife and son are in Vermont. Visiting her mother. Okay? Now tell me whatever you came to tell me so I can get back to my movie."

"What are you watching?"

"Something you've never heard of. Go. You have two minutes."

Nicki flipped her handbag on the table, extracting banded photocopies. "After you said your friend Brian was such a straight arrow, I remembered a case involving this other girl, Wendy Shaw. Honor roll, debate club, real square bear. She wrote a scathing blog post about her principal. Judge Roberts also shipped her off to North River. Called it 'cyberbullying.'"

"And I care, why?"

"Hold on. So I got curious."

"Curious? Or needed something to do besides hit on married old men?"

"Don't be so sensitive. I already apologized. I snuck down to records and did some research." Nicki spread the photocopies out on my kitchen table. "It's not the first time."

"What's not the first time?"

"That Roberts has sentenced kids to North River for minor offenses. And not just Wendy and Brian. I pulled his sentencing for the past six months, year. Even further back. You have to see some of those charges. They're ridiculous." Nicki began reading down the reports. "A real pattern is emerging—"

I clasped a hand over hers. "You can stop right there." I stepped back and lifted up my shirt, wincing as I revealed my wounds, the bruised ribs, my flank a slab of tender discolored meat, red, purple, shades of unknown green. The swelling around my eye had gone down. These bruises on my body had spilled blood deep inside me.

"Jesus! I thought your face looked a little fucked up. What happened?"

"Why don't you tell me?"

"Sorry?"

"I have to be out of my mind to even let you through that door. Any exes pissed you gave them the boot? Special friends of yours who work for Longmont PD? Possessive types who don't take no for an answer?"

"I don't know what you're talking about."

"No? Two cops stopped me after I talked to you the other night. On a deserted road. Where they dragged me from my truck. And took turns making sure I got the message to stay the hell away from you."

"I don't know any cops."

"Well, one of them sure knew you."

"He said that?"

"In so many words, yeah."

Nicki wrinkled her nose, shaking her head, pointing a finger at me. "No, no, no."

"No what?"

She was still shaking her head as she fanned the papers. "Even before I started working as a clerk there, Judge Roberts has been shipping kids to North River. Look at this sentencing history. Year by year. Twenty-one. Thirty-three. We're barely two months into the new year, and he's already signed the orders for sixteen more."

"I told you. I don't care. What's that got to do with the two cops I just told you about? Didn't you hear me? They took my license, Nicki, wrote down my address, said they'd be back to finish the job if I even *spoke* to you. You want to explain that?"

"I just did. North River."

I went to the fridge for a beer. I didn't offer her one.

"Have you been following New Hampshire's recent debate about privatizing prisons?" Nicki asked.

"Nope." I popped the top and leaned against the counter.

"Diversion programs are an alternative form of punishment," she continued, undeterred by my lack of interest. "Here's how it works. Parents of the juvenile offender, because they are minors, get together with the judge, and if both parties come to an agreement that this type of intervention makes sense, the judge executes the order, and the juvenile offender is locked up at North River."

"Here's how I know you're full of shit. Brian's mother wasn't at the courthouse. That's why I was there. I'd gone to Longmont to advocate on her son's behalf, so no way in hell would Donna Olisky agree—"

Nicki grabbed a fax from the table, waving it under my nose. I snatched the page from her hand. There was Donna Olisky's signature approving Judge Roberts' recommendation for North River, time-stamped with last Friday's date, a few hours after she'd called me in tears, hysterical.

"How does this North River work?" I asked her. "Exactly."

"You remember that old cockroach commercial? You check in, but you can't check out."

"I think you mean the 'Hotel California.'"

"I hate the Eagles."

"Everyone does, Nicki."

"I like kitsch better. Old commercials, PSAs from the '70s. 'How a Bill Becomes a Law.' Cheesy '80s music—"

"Terrific. I feel like I know you so much better." Nothing kitsch about it when you survived the shit the first time. "What I mean is who funds this thing? If it's not private, the state subsidizes?"

"North River's main source of revenue is from the clients themselves, the parents, and from nonprofit donors. And it's not cheap. These places can run upwards of a thousand bucks a day."

"I've been to the Olisky house. They don't have a thousand dollars, period."

Nicki shrugged. "That's the least disturbing part." She ran her finger down a page till she found the figures she was looking for. "The facility started out with thirty beds. Look at this chart. Over the past three years alone, North River has seen a 300 percent increase in new inmates. Wings and additions are being added almost daily, the grounds in a constant state of construction. Complex is *massive.*"

"Okay," I said. "Once more for the cheap seats—this concerns me how?"

"It concerns your friend."

"I told you. We aren't friends. His mom holds an insurance policy with our company."

"You said he's a good kid. Band geek, right?"

"Yeah."

"Don't you think it's bullshit he's doing hard time for telling a fib and a joint?"

"Sure. But the world's a shitty place. I know at your age, you want to believe if we all join hands and try our best we can make a difference. Plant a tree, buy local produce, change the world. But none of that matters. Go campaign for cleaner ozone, free Tibet, whatever the fuck you college kids think matters. I'm just telling you it doesn't."

"How the hell did you get so cynical?"

"By walking around with my eyes open."

Nicky pointed at the paper trail. "Jay, there are kids, some as young as thirteen, locked up for popping Mom's pills and posting on social media." She flipped through her Xeroxes. "This girl, Wendy Shaw? Who got accused of cyberbullying? Her principal wouldn't let a trans kid go to the prom—"

"Trans kid?"

"Transgender?" She said it like my not picking up her new

American slang painted me a dinosaur. "Wendy rallied support for the student on her blog. Criticized school officials for being homophobic and discriminatory. All she did was *write* about it. Judge Roberts slaps her with that cyberbullying charge. She's been in North River for a year." Nicki plucked another page. "Another boy. Nabbed shoplifting lip gloss for his girlfriend. Almost two years." She practically shoved the papers in my face. "Dining and ditching. Fistfights. Egging a house on Halloween. Pot, pills, E. All sent to North River by Judge Roberts."

I pushed her hand away. "You know why people like to believe in conspiracies, Nicki? Because it means that no matter how shitty life is at this moment, at least it isn't completely random—there's someone who knows what the fuck is going on, a puppet master calling the shots, a wizard behind the curtain—and that however wicked, nefarious, or just plain evil that entity may be, it is still preferable to the alternative. Namely, that we are on our own. Everyone is running this race blind. The train's gone off the rails, ship's rudderless, each crazy bastard as screwed up and clueless as the next." I finished my beer and set it down hard.

"How much have you had to drink?"

"Enough that I don't have patience to play intrepid reporter with some riot girl who just read Sylvia Plath for the first time."

"You don't have to be an asshole."

"No. I don't. But I don't feel like being nice, either. It's been a bad few days, and you've only made it worse—"

"I said I was sorry."

"I know. I appreciate it." I clapped my hands, sincere. "But besides two cops who would have no problem dumping my body in a ditch—"

"Roberts sent them to scare you off—"

"—my boss told me, in no uncertain terms, to drop the Olisky case if I want any hopes of landing this promotion. Which I desperately do. If only to get away from this frozen hellhole. Now, if you don't mind?" I pointed at her so-called evidence. "Take your homework assignment and go home."

Nicki snatched her handbag but didn't pick up the rest of her crap.

I pointed at the paperwork cluttering my messy table. "You forgot something."

"Maybe when you sober up, you can be bothered to think about someone other than yourself. Innocent kids are languishing in prison for nothing."

"When you walk out the door," I said, "that shit goes in the trash."

Nicki shook her head and split without another word.

At least she left the Chinese.

CHAPTER TEN

I DIDN'T THROW away the photocopies Nicki left behind. I abandoned them to the rest of the trash on the table and grabbed a container of pork lo mein, returning to my movie and beer, stewing. Nicki was young, but the girl knew how to push the right buttons. Must be an innate female trait. I was lousy at not thinking about pink elephants.

My default position was almost always no, automatic refusal triggered from days dealing with my brother, who always needed a favor, a ride, a place to crash, money. When someone is forever making demands on your limited resources, you better learn to say no or you'll be run ragged to the poorhouse. But let a few minutes pass, wait for a cooler head to prevail, and some misguided angel would start chirping on my shoulder, the compulsion to do the right thing eventually getting the best of me. A quality both infuriating and redeeming.

Even though I kept telling myself Nicki's discovery didn't concern me, I had a tough time ignoring what I'd heard. Innocent kids doing time over victimless crimes. Maybe calling these kids "innocent" was a stretch; no crime is "victimless." The police weren't plucking random teens off the street without reason. Laws get broken, prices have to be paid. But punishment needs to fit the crime.

Despite technical classification to the contrary, North River sure sounded like a prison. Then what was the play? Overzealous prosecutors? A constipated judge? More than likely, a bunch of well-meaning but out-of-touch adults were overreacting to bad decisions made by today's youth. Which had been the same song and dance for generations.

I gave up and accepted my brain wasn't letting this go. The kick in the pants to do the right thing giving me a pain in the ass. Back at the kitchen table, I scanned the copies Nicki made at the courthouse. Nothing in there she hadn't already told me. Somehow reading the facts for myself made it worse, the horror more real.

There were serious crimes listed, like dealing and assault, but the majority of transgressions were misdemeanors—shoplifting, joyriding, vandalism, and underage drinking, which met with equally harsh penalties. I understood the need for law and order, but sending a fourteen-year-old up the river for snatching a sweater off the clearance rack at the Gap smacked of disproportionate.

The kicker was that in each case, the parents had signed off on the treatment. Box after box notarized. How bad could North River really be if Mom and Dad were on board?

I swept up the Xeroxes and headed to the computer. Under normal circumstances, I'd have Jenny here to help me navigate this kind of digital research. Today, I was hunting and pecking search engines on my own. Not that I had to look far. The North River Institute was the top result.

Most of the press featured glowing testimonials from parents. I had to scroll a few pages before I found a disparaging word, a couple malcontents in a chat room. Then again, it's hard to lodge a complaint when they don't let you out. The real grievances didn't come till several pages later, allegations of physical and sexual abuse buried way beyond the electronic breakers.

The institute pitched itself as an alternative to incarceration, bullet points cramming in as many loaded keywords as possible (Therapeutic, Reparenting, Intensive). In between the testimonials and touted success rates, including an 80 percent "satisfaction with life" for those who completed the program, whatever the hell that meant, the phrase "behavior modification" caught my attention.

I may've been suckered in by party lines if not for personal history. My brother Chris was as far gone an addict as they come. In the end, he didn't care about his life circling the drain, and I didn't have much sympathy for his lame, failed attempts at sobriety. After so long in the wasteland, my brother had quit quitting before he walked through hospital doors. But early on I'd tried to get him cleaned up, and he'd at least gone through the motions. In those days there was a certain kind of facility that scared even me.

One of the counselors gave it to me straight in private. "They will tear you down to build you back up." He explained the strict regiments and controversial techniques critics called brainwashing. "But, frankly," he said, "some of these brains could use a little washing. Reformed addicts who know the game police these houses. They will call you out on the BS and aren't afraid to put a man in his place."

I remembered driving through the gates to check Chris into one of these facilities, taking a look at the jacked-up, ex-con trustees and tatted enforcers, arms crossed and glowering in the doorway, and I turned the truck around.

Maybe I should've let those guys have a run at Chris. Maybe he'd still be alive if I had. I just knew my brother, how he responded to that kind of pressure. Like a sow bug. Slightest bit of pressure and he'd curl in a ball. Besides, I didn't know then what I know now. I'd thought I was protecting him. Dealing with adult addicts isn't the same as teenagers. Right? And North River wasn't a rehab, not in the strict, official sense. As I read through the courthouse copies, I saw more often than not, drugs were involved. The blog girl, a rare exception. There were almost always multiple infractions. An initial charge, for say shoplifting or truancy, would then be augmented with possession, distribution, public intoxication, proximity to a school, some drug-related case that made rehab a feasible and reasonable option.

Donna Olisky hadn't contacted me since last Friday. At first I'd been grateful to be let off the hook. Now that dots weren't connecting, I wasn't so sure. Despite DeSouza's expressly forbidding contact with the Oliskys, I had to know the real reason for the change of heart. Why would a mother go from worried parent to willing participant in the sentencing of her son to somewhere like North River? There had to be a more logical explanation. Unable to reach Donna at home, I checked the clock on the microwave, and tried her at work. A friendly "Welcome to We Copy!" quickly turned sour when I mentioned my name.

"How can I help you, Mr. Porter?"

The return of "Mr. Porter" felt stiff and needlessly formal, but whatever; I forged ahead. "I'm just checking in, Mrs. Olisky."

"About what?"

I wanted to say, What the hell do you think? But instead, I took the high road. "How is Brian? I wasn't able to speak with him at the courthouse." I knew damn well how he was doing, and where he was doing it, but I was attempting tact.

"My son is getting the help he needs." Her cold, dismissive tone annoyed me. Like I was a telemarketer pitching worthless swampland, interrupting dinner. Where was the protective, overbearing mother of a few days ago? Beatrice jumped on my lap, and I stared down at her with a "What the fuck?" expression. My fat white cat pretended to understand. Then she coughed up a hairball. Had this whole world lost its head?

"He's at the North River Institute?" I said, priming the conversation.

"Yes."

"Isn't that strange? I mean, North River doesn't seem like the best fit for your son."

"How would you know what's best for *my* son? This has nothing to do with you."

"You asked me to drive up to the courthouse in Longmont?"

"I never asked. You volunteered."

"Because you were upset."

"Or because you felt guilty denying our claim over a technicality?"

I hadn't denied anything. Her son confessed. To my boss. But I knew pointing that out now would get me nowhere.

"I don't understand, Mrs. Olisky. Last week you were freaking out about Brian feeling lonely for a few hours in a courtroom. Now you're saying he's been locked up inside a juvenile detention center, and you don't have a problem with that?"

"Do you know they found drugs in the car?"

"I heard they found a joint, yes."

"Do you know that's how my other son, Craig, died?"

"Because of pot?"

"Because of drugs! Drugs killed my boy. I will not sit by and watch them destroy the only son I have left."

I thought about their accident. The timeline didn't add up. Even if Brian had been alone in the car at the time of the crash, his mother arrived at the scene before the cops. Why wouldn't she have known about the marijuana sooner?

"I'm sorry, Donna. Mrs. Olisky. I'm confused."

"About what?"

"When did you learn about the pot?"

"It doesn't matter. My son needs help. The courts were kind enough to offer a treatment program for him. I took them up on their offer."

"North River isn't treatment. It's a behavioral modification detention center. And it's not cheap."

"Since *your* company declined our claim, I don't see how *our* finances are any of your concern." Donna Olisky cleared her throat. "I have to get back to work now. Don't call me again."

I flinched when she slammed down the receiver.

What the hell? I stared into the earpiece I held at arm's length.

Why *did* I care? This had nothing to do with me. So what if Brian Olisky had been handed over to North River on a trumped-up, bullshit charge? Why did I care if his mother was buying into the antidrug hysteria up here? Her and the rest of the goddamn state. I could've explained to Donna Olisky how after everything I'd seen pot was a goddamn vacation, pills a picnic. Then again maybe Donna was the smart one. Who was I to offer advice on how to deal with drugs? I'd botched every attempt.

I was ready to leave it there. I had Nicki's photocopies rolled back up and was about to walk out to the garage and ceremoniously drop them into the trashcan like I'd done with my own failed attempts investigating the Lombardis.

Instead, I grabbed my phone.

"Hey. You up for taking a ride?"

*   *   *

"What the hell is this place?" Charlie asked.

We sat in my idling Chevy, shielded by a cluster of pines. Tall, barbed chain-link ran the length of the perimeter, boxing the property. Had to be a few solid acres. The main building, squat, stout, intimidating, sat a football field away across a windswept gully. With high lookout towers and too much room to cover before reaching freedom, the place mirrored a penitentiary.

Like Nicki mentioned, the complex appeared to be in the state of serious influx. I saw the skeletal frame of a new building at the back end of the lot—and not a storage shed either, like a mini high-rise you'd find downtown in a big city. There were other telltale signs of major renovation, too. Sandbags. Cement mixers. Breaking new ground in this weather was impossible, but you could always tack on. Scaffolding wrapped around steel girders, with lifts and ladders, piping for waterline extensions angled sharply and intertwined, a boatswain chair to reach the top floors. Several moving trucks, the long haul kind that transfer entire worlds, split the difference between the fence and D-block. Blue Belle Moving Co. Looked like you could fit the whole prison inside those trucks. Things were enormous.

I hadn't mentioned a destination to Charlie on the ride over, and he hadn't seemed too concerned, not even as we turned down dark, unfamiliar routes and endless farming roads. Charlie was always up for an adventure. We chewed the fat about less pressing matters. The Bruins. The Pats. The Sox. He didn't mention Jenny. I didn't touch on his lack of employment or direction in life. Win win. Now that we were here, I was having a tough time answering his questions why. I wasn't sure I could express my urgency to see North River. Maybe my friend had picked up on that uncertainty—I could feel his uneasiness—I only knew I had an itch to satisfy. Save for the occasional whisper of winter wind, the country night felt eerily calm. One by one lights flicked off. Bedtime for the inmates.

"Are you going to talk to me, man? What is this place?"

"I'm not sure, Charlie. A prison, of sorts."

"Of sorts?"

"A juvie. A prison for teenagers. Long-term drug treatment. I don't know."

"Sorry. I just don't understand why we're here."

Funny, I'd been asking myself that one, too.

I reached under my seat and pulled the folder, in which I'd coalesced Nicki's photocopies, adding a few webpages of my own that I'd printed off the Internet, flipping the entire batch to Charlie. I switched on the cab light so he could read.

"Court records?"

"Remember that kid I was telling you about? Brian Olisky?"

"What about him?"

"That's where they put him."

"The kid who lied about driving?"

I stared at North River. Even the pictures from the website, the ones supplied by the facility itself, boasted a fortress under lock and key. Up close, the place was a mini gulag.

"Not just him," I said. "Other kids, too. Bullshit charges."

"Like?"

"One girl created a fake website," I said. "Making fun of her science teacher, principal, whatever. She's been locked inside North River for a year."

"What's North River?"

I pointed at the complex. "*That* is North River."

Charlie panned around. "What town are we even in?"

"Middlesex."

"Middlesex? Isn't that where your brother's ex-girlfriend lived? What was her name again? Bunny?"

"I told you. Kitty. Short for Katherine—she's not a stripper—and yeah, she lived here. At a halfway house, other side of town. Why do you keep asking about her?"

"You ever talk to her?"

"No. Why would I?"

"Because," Charlie said, "she knew your brother. She knew him during . . . that time. Maybe talking to her would help you."

"Help me what?"

"Y'know, get past his death." He paused. "The guilt you feel."

"I don't feel guilty."

Charlie turned toward the window, embarrassed for me over my bold-faced lie.

Yeah, you're not guilty, Jay. Then why are we sitting on an access road staring at a lockdown ward? It's almost midnight.

"I don't know how to get ahold of Kitty," I said. "It's been over a year since we talked. Since then I've moved, changed numbers. I don't even know her last name. She lives in California, for Christ's sake. What could she really offer me, anyway? Chris is dead."

I'd seen the signs. Private Property. No Trespassing. Turn Back.

Charlie fidgeted. I twitched with edginess too. Which was strange because Charlie was the one person I could always be myself around. As much as I wanted to blame him for the weird vibe, I knew my mood was at fault. I'd been out of sorts all day.

He tried to change the subject, rambling about his dart league, something about a cute Australian girl from the bar. I was mired in my own game of solo Q&A, a psycho's version of solitaire.

Troubled teens? Drug addicts? Rehabs? Juvenile prisons. This isn't for work. I'm on involuntary vacation. My wife's out of town with my son. What am I supposed to do? What's it matter? Even when she's home, you're not there. Oh, shut up. *What are you so pissed off about?* I don't know, man. *You can't save me. You know that, right?* No shit. You don't think I know that?

"Jay?"

"What?"

Charlie stared at me like I was sweet pickling the short bus. "Dude, you're talking to yourself."

"So? People talk to themselves all the time."

"Yeah, but you're answering yourself, too. You okay, man? You haven't looked right since you picked me up. Shit, you ain't been right the last few times I've seen you. You're not telling me something." He held up the photocopies. "At least not the whole something."

I didn't know why I wanted to drive out to North River at this hour, or what I thought I'd find here. They weren't going to let me tour the place during business hours, let alone the middle of night. Nicki had touched a nerve. I ached to do something, find a reason to believe. I couldn't sit in that empty house a moment longer, not without Aiden and Jenny. I kept envisioning her having dinner with Stephen, laughing at his cornball jokes, touching his arm at all the right times, because when she'd walked back into Lynne's condo the other afternoon and I'd seen her smiling eyes it hadn't been over me; it was because of him. All I could do to combat the creeping malaise was smoke cigarettes, drink beer, and stare at water stains on the wall. I couldn't compete with the Stephens of the world as it was. Take away the steady paycheck, and what the hell could I offer? I pictured my empty house, and I could already feel the cold air seeping in, insulation failing, hear the lack of laughter, the absence of other people breathing. So many times during this new life, I craved solitude. Not to be alone. Just to be left alone. I'd walk through the door after a long day of work, and Jenny would have a hundred things she wanted to talk about, mind-drudging domestic details, and Aiden would be jumping around, demanding attention, and I'd wish I had a remote. Press the pause button. Let me grab a beer, put on sweats, take a deep breath, acclimate to suburban dad. I longed for a few minutes, not forever. I felt like the universe had heard my ungrateful bitching and this was the retribution of entitlement. I'd grown to dread the sound of a coffeemaker gurgling at dawn's first light.

"Jay?" Charlie said. "You all right?"

"Never mind. Forget it." I turned off the cab light, flicked the nubbed butt into the sub-zero scrub, and rolled the window back up. "Let's get out of here."

The headlights descended on us from out of nowhere.

CHAPTER ELEVEN

TWO ALL-TERRAIN VEHICLES came at us from opposite directions, jamming my Chevy kitty-corner, high beams catching us in the crossfire.

A beefy security guard, who looked like he'd flopped out of Boston College, pushing three hundred if he was a pound, smacked the butt of a flashlight against the glass until I cracked the window.

"What are you doing here?" he said. "This is private property."

"Me and my buddy took a wrong turn," I said. "No street names. Can't get a signal." I held up my phone, offering its blank screen as evidence of my ignorance. "Do you know the way to the highway?"

"Let's see some ID."

"You're not a cop," Charlie said. "We don't have to show you jack."

The security guard flashed a secret hand signal, some gangland command, and another guard materialized from the shadows, standing outside Charlie's window. Light glinted off a grip of a handgun. I knew then these two would love nothing more than to split my skull open. And neither would be opposed to a two-for-one deal. After getting my ass handed to me the other night, I didn't have the stomach for another beat down. Three days later, I still couldn't piss right.

I slammed the truck in reverse and floored the pedal. The passenger door flung open, hand darting around inside, fumbling for the traction of Charlie's coat.

"Hold on," I screamed.

The guard had a firm grip on Charlie, who two-fisted the Jesus bar, squealing as I punched the transmission in drive. I cranked the steering column, burning donuts in double time until the guy let go.

I jerked, re-righted the front end, speeding to freedom. In the rearview mirror, I saw the big man roll across the frozen dirt. I waited for the echo of gunshots over my shoulder. But they never came.

"Christ, Jay! What the hell?"

"I don't know, man. I don't know what their deal was."

"Not them! You!"

"Me?" Where was the gratitude for saving his ass?

"They were rent-a-cops, dude."

"I don't know what they were. But they looked like they wanted to use us for target practice."

"Target practice? With what? Their flashlights?"

"He had a gun."

"It was a flashlight. A couple of fat guys on golf carts. What did you think they were going to do? Lock us inside with the rest of the junkies?"

"We were on private property. And he had a gun. I saw it."

"Dude. It was a flashlight! Relax."

I checked my rearview to be sure we were clear of any hot pursuit. No one was on our heels. Golf carts? A flashlight? I was certain it was a gun. Was I going crazy?

"Jay, you don't look so good."

"Listen, man, I'm not supposed to be touching this case. DeSouza finds out I'm poking my nose around, I'm out of a job."

"Then what were we doing up here in the first place?"

I could feel him watching me, waiting for a better explanation, but all the ones I had tumbling around inside my brain sounded stupid. I didn't know what we were doing up there. I didn't know what I was doing, period.

I felt my chest tighten. I was having a tough time catching my breath. I steadied on the road and focused on my breathing.

"Shit," Charlie said, rotating his arm and ball joint. "I think Fatty dislocated my shoulder."

My lungs seized up. They stopped accepting oxygen.

"Jay, you okay?"

I tried to nod but it didn't come across right. More like my head swiveled in seven different directions at once.

"Pull over," Charlie said.

"I don't . . . If they're . . . behind us."

Charlie covered his hands over mine, taking control of the wheel. "No one is following us, Porter. Pull over. Let me drive. You look like you swallowed a case of mini-thins. You're going to wrap around an oak tree and kill us both."

I steered to the shoulder.

Charlie and I traded places.

I rested my head against the cool glass, and gazed out into the night. I focused on my breathing, like Dr. Shapiro-Weiss had told me to do. Count. One. Two. Twenty-three. Charlie didn't say anything more as he drove us back to his place.

Like a den mother, he led me to the couch, covering me with a quilt that reeked of mothballs and liniment. Charlie Finn playing caretaker. Hell had truly frozen over.

He thumbed toward his kitchen. "You want a beer or something? Whiskey? You could use a shot to calm down. I think I still have a bottle of Maker's somewhere . . ."

Charlie returned with a pair of glasses. He broke the seal and measured out two fingers, like he was administering cough syrup to a sick kid.

"Okay, Jay." He passed the glass. "Drink up."

I pounded the shot. He poured another. I pounded that too.

"Better?"

I nodded.

"Tell me what's going on. I'm your friend. Let me help."

"That folder I showed you."

"The court documents?"

"Yeah. It relates to the Brian Olisky case. According to the cops, they also found a joint."

"Is that true?"

"I don't know."

Charlie scratched his thinning curls. "How much time did he get?"

I explained the open-ended sentences, North River being a diversion program, parents waiving rights because the children in question were minors.

"So Dad signed off?"

"There's no dad in the picture."

"I thought you said Mom called you because she was worried? Why would she agree to send her son there?"

"She didn't know about the pot. At least that's what she said when I called her tonight. I think they got to her."

"They? Who's they?"

I couldn't answer that. I didn't know. The malicious they? The conspiratorial they? The they really in charge.

Charlie tried to wrap his brain around logistics, my investment, my helter-skelter reasoning.

"Sucks about the kid," Charlie finally said, "but, like, it's not your problem."

"It's more complicated than that."

I tried to explain about Nicki and what she'd uncovered, Judge Roberts' harsh sentencing practices, the recent spike in enrollment at North River. Maybe those cops *had* been sent to deliver a message, stop me from kicking over stones. Maybe they were all in on it. Everyone buying into the antidrug propaganda, quick to point the finger, solve problems with absolutes. Black. White. I was bouncing all over the place, talking points that made sense in my head lost in translation. Words failed me. I couldn't stay on task or follow a single thread to its proper conclusion. I knew how unhinged I sounded. Dredging up the past, fretting about the future. I circled back to Craig Olisky, Brian's dead brother. At some point in my rambling, I began bitching about Adam Lombardi.

"Adam Lombardi?" Charlie said. "What about him? You know he doesn't even live in Ashton anymore, right? Relocated his entire family down to Concord after his father died. In fact, I'm pretty sure he got out of the construction business altogether."

"Bullshit. Where'd you hear that?"

"I don't know. The news? Sold the company. I think he's working full time on his brother's campaign."

That would explain the abandoned site I'd run across last week.

"I hate to say it, Jay. Don't take this the wrong way. You sound like your brother. Everything isn't some conspiracy involving the Lombardis." He dropped his head, muttering, "I swear between you and Fisher . . ."

"Why do you keep saying that? Fisher. What about Fisher? I haven't spoken to Fisher since he got me in at NEI—"

"Gerry Lombardi is dead. His sons live far away. It's over, man. Your brother died because of drugs."

"You don't think I know that?"

"No, I think you do. Up here." Charlie pointed at his head. "But not here." He pointed at his heart. "You want to hold someone responsible. The Lombardis are convenient."

"How can you say that? You were with me last year. You were with me when I chased down Roger Paul in those mountains, with my brother a prisoner in the backseat—"

"Roger who?"

"The guy who grabbed Chris and stuffed him in back of his car! The guy who planned to cut a hole in the ice. The guy I chased down and ran off the road. The guy who died! Who do you think sent him?"

"You mean Chris' drug dealer who'd been trying to collect his money? The one who died in that car accident on Lamentation Mountain?"

"You never believed that, man. That was a bullshit cover story sold to the newspapers. You saw my fucking truck, busted to shit. I was the other vehicle involved in the accident! Come on, Charlie. You know that!"

"All I know is what Turley said. I know what I read in the *Herald*. I know that you ended up with a concussion in the hospital, talking crazy. And truth is, man, you must've hit your head pretty fucking hard. Because you haven't been the same since."

Charlie sat beside me on the couch, put his arm around my shoulder. "Maybe you should talk to that doctor you were seeing. The shrink."

I shook my head. "You sound like my wife."

"Get some sleep, buddy. Everything looks better in the morning."

I nodded, even though I didn't believe that. When nothing is right in your world, the sun coming around again to shine a light on your failure is the last thing you want to see.

* * *

Whether from the whiskey or lingering internal trauma from the beating, I couldn't fully fall asleep, at least not peacefully, enduring an endless, tormented night. Straddling the line between consciousness and slumber, I felt both asleep and awake, very aware of the fact that I was dreaming. I'd read somewhere that your dreams only last a few seconds. Just feels like they go on forever. Not this night. My dreams were never-ending. And it felt like a reckoning, the past coming back to haunt. I saw them all again. High school bullies. Distant relatives. Ex-girlfriends whose hearts I'd broken because I'd only been in love with one woman my whole life. I saw Erik Bowman, Adam Lombardi's head of security, with the Star of David tattooed on his goddamn neck. Bowman, who'd done time in a motorcycle gang with Jenny's ex, Brody, whose scumbag ass my scrawny, drug-addled brother had thoroughly kicked the same day he died, tapping into a secret strength from his wrestling days I didn't know he possessed anymore. I saw the entire town of Ashton, longtime residents who'd come out to pay their final respects to my dead junkie brother, collective expressions on their faces like the expressions I invited wherever I went these days, one that seemed to say, "You poor sick sorry sonofabitch." Which is what happens when you become a scourge, a pariah, a lunatic.

I lay there immobilized, paralyzed like *Johnny Got His Gun*, forced to relieve my mistakes, watching actors dramatize what could've been. No one else could tell me what was real and what wasn't. Because anyone who had been there was now dead. Like my brother. Like the killer sent to silence him. Like my parents who perished in a fatal car crash twenty years earlier under mysterious circumstances. Like a very real part of me. Every secret, every promise broken, every word left unsaid—my memory and my burden to carry alone. I tossed, turned, and ground my jaw until I dreamt I was chewing sawdust, mouth parched, calcium phosphate powder, narrative dissolving into nonsensical, over- heated bubbling celluloid.

* * *

I split with the daybreak, leaving Charlie snoring blissfully un- aware in his bedroom. Stepping outside, I embraced the overcast. I don't think I could've faced a clear blue sky right then.

I filled up my truck, grabbed a paper, a carton of cigarettes, cof- fee, and drove out to see her, waiting on the front steps for her to arrive.

CHAPTER TWELVE

"Jay?" Dr. Shapiro-Weiss said as she walked up the narrow stone pathway to her office. "What are you doing here?"

"I needed to see you."

"Okay. But it doesn't work like that. You can't show up at my office. You have to call and make an appointment. I have other patients scheduled. These are boundaries I need you to respect."

"It's an emergency." I could feel my chest tightening, breaths short and shallow, pulse irregular. I clamped the cigarette in my teeth and grabbed hold of the railing.

I waited for her to tell me to go to the emergency room, at which point I'd get in my truck and drive off. Fuck it. I didn't believe in asking for help in the first place. You dig yourself in a hole, you dig yourself out. Only the weak need help. But shame was the least of my concerns. I was falling down and needed a hand up. If the doctor sent me packing to be someone else's problem, I'd take it as a sign. I wasn't asking twice.

Maybe Dr. Shapiro-Weiss recognized the crossroads too, because she said to come inside and have a seat in the waiting room.

"Let me see if I can juggle some appointments. Might take a few minutes. Don't go anywhere. Breathe."

I nodded and watched her disappear into a back room. The soothing sounds of the rainforest dribbled out the sound system, the calming pitter-patter of water pooling and plopping off lush, tropical leaves, splashing into giant puddles, the delicate sound of thunder crackling in the distance. I closed my eyes and concentrated on the air filling my lungs. Inhale into my mouth, expel through my nose. Rinse, lather, repeat. Concentrate on solid blocks of color. Don't think. Blue. Black. Dark forest green. Gray is good too. I passed out.

I doubt more than five minutes ticked by, but I got a better night's sleep in that short time than I had in the entire six hours at Charlie's.

Dr. Shapiro-Weiss stood over me, calling my name, pulling me back from the brink.

Inside her office, the doctor sat in her cushioned, wicker chair, waiting while I got comfortable on the couch, rearranging throw pillows and trying to figure out where to begin. The diplomas and accomplishments on her wall distracted, overwhelmed me. Degrees, awards, commendations. From all over the country. Prestigious institutions, framed and centered, fancy gold-leaf lettering. What was I doing with my life? To attain this level of success, she had to start studying at an early age. Right out of high school, straight to college, then to university and grad school, post-grad and doctoral work. No time for parties or fucking around, no time for dragging heels, protesting growing up. Not if you want to be somebody in the world. That's how Stephen had become a financial advisor, or whatever the fuck he did. Unless Daddy got him the gig. The only skills I possessed: digging ditches and loading a truck. Grunt labor a trained monkey could do. I didn't belong here.

"Jay?"

"I'm sorry." I started to stand. "This was a mistake. I shouldn't have bothered you."

She gestured for me to sit down.

"Have you been having more panic attacks?"

"I don't know. I think so."

"Why didn't you call me sooner? You must've run out of medication a while ago."

"I don't want to be some pill popper who takes drugs every time he's in a bad mood."

"You have a condition."

"I don't have a condition."

"You have an anxiety disorder. You can call it something else if you'd like. There's no disgrace in receiving treatment when something beyond your control is affecting the quality of life." She waited for that to sink in. "How is your relationship with your wife? Your job? Friendships?"

"I don't have a lot of friends."

"When people with anxiety disorders experience prolonged episodes, it makes thinking rationally difficult, impossible. The skills they've relied on their entire lives short circuit. They behave irrationally. Which can push away those they love. This compounds feelings of isolation. A 'fight or flight' hyperawareness kicks in, and everything becomes dire."

"Dire? You mean like when you're on a mountaintop, and someone is trying to kill you and your brother? You mean dire like that?" The sarcasm didn't come out as cutting as I intended.

"Yes," the doctor said. "Like that. Unfortunately, Jay, because of what you went through, what you saw, what you experienced the last few days of your brother's life, you are still trapped there in many ways. This feeling of being trapped is what causes you to panic. There are medications that can quell the worst of it. Now if you want to try a different type of medication—"

"I don't like taking drugs."

"How much have you been drinking?"

"I'm not an alcoholic."

"I'm guessing more than a few beers every night, though, right? Self-medicating is still medicating. Why were you waiting on my front steps this morning?"

"I didn't know where else to go."

"Has something changed? A new development that brought on these attacks?"

I let it all pour out—the Olisky case, Brian and his dead drug-addict brother, the fight with Jenny, my wife taking urgent action to visit her mother in Burlington in the middle of the night and bringing my son along for the ride, the yuppie neighbor, Stephen, the clerk at the courthouse, Nicki, North River, and Judge Roberts' dubious record. And of course I invoked the sins of the Lombardis, whose crimes I couldn't accept had gone unpunished, even in death.

"No wonder you're having panic attacks," Dr. Shapiro-Weiss said. "Those events you've described are a microcosm of what you experienced last year. It would be like a Desert Storm veteran suddenly finding himself back on a battlefield." Before I could protest how ridiculous a comparison, she held up her hand. "No, you're not in the Army, and I am not undermining what real soldiers go through. What I mean is, both cases can trigger the PTSD."

"You think I have post-traumatic stress disorder?" I wanted to laugh. Only I couldn't.

"Jay, I want you to stop qualifying your anguish. What you experience is unique to *you*. You don't need to gauge your feelings and pit them against how much someone else suffers. Personal pain is just that: personal. And, yes, what you went through with your brother last year, and even before that—losing your parents, having to assume the role of caretaker at such a young age—all these events are traumas." She set down her pad and pen and leaned in. "None of this makes you weak. I know that is what you think. But it is not true. I've had ex-NFL players sitting in that chair, six foot five, three hundred and fifty pounds, sobbing because they watched their dad hit their mommy when they were small boys and couldn't do anything about it. I've had police officers who thrust themselves in to do-or-die situations every day, putting their very lives on the line, because once upon a time they couldn't save a sister or a friend and this is their penance. These are strong people. Trapped in a hell of their own making because of events beyond their control."

"Big difference when you're a kid and can't fix a problem. I'm thirty-one years old."

"Which is why I used the soldier analogy. Trauma is trauma. Effects can be cumulative. You've reached a tipping point. Whatever happened at work and in your personal life has dredged up memories and emotions you've kept buried for a long time. You ignored them, and now feel like you should be able to fix everything if you can only do a better job, control outside circumstance more." The doctor positioned her hands, miming stranglehold. "But you can't. This isn't about willpower. This isn't about toughness or resolve. This isn't about skill sets. This war raging inside you is about reconciliation. Learning to accept the past, make peace with your loss. Your brother's habit was *his* problem. From everything you've told me, you did everything you could to save him. This is the hard part for someone like you to understand. And by 'someone like you,' I mean someone who *is* strong, someone who is resilient, someone who is used to fighting the fight on his own. Recognizing that you can't do it alone is not a sign of weakness." Dr. Shapiro-Weiss paused for emphasis. "It is a sign of strength."

* * *

The doctor sent me off with a new script for lorazepam, an anti-anxiety pill, which I filled at the pharmacy on the way home, feeling self-conscious and judged when the pharmacist asked for an ID because it's "a controlled substance." Walking back to my truck, even before I stuck one under my tongue, I felt better. I remembered Chris once telling me how the only time he felt like himself anymore was right after he'd copped, when he could pat the dope in his pocket. Didn't even need to fix. The real relief came knowing he had the drugs. I'd never understood what he meant before.

I tried to appreciate what Dr. Shapiro-Weiss had said, about how there was a difference between a doctor prescribing medication for a patient and a junkie shooting dope to get high—about how the strong sometimes need help; every tragedy wasn't my fault. I wanted to believe these things but had a tough time. I stopped at the grocery store for another twelve-pack, just in case.

When I unlocked the front door to the house, I could tell Jenny wasn't back. Didn't matter that I didn't see her car in the driveway or that all the lights were off, the rooms silent. I could feel the emptiness, the loneliness. It cut like a hot knife through the gut of a dead deer.

I stripped off my clothes and hit the shower, cranking the heat, steaming the bathroom. I turned the water as scalding as I could stand, as if I could flay the ugly parts away. Two hands planted on the tile, I let it rain over me for a long time.

When I stepped out, I was ready to curl up in bed and pass the fuck out. Then I heard Jenny's voice.

"Jay, you here?"

I slung the towel around my waist and rushed into the kitchen, sopping wet, slopping footprints in the thick carpet and across the hardwood floor. I was so glad she was home. Everything that had been wrong in my world would be set right. In seconds I'd see my son, my family would be back together, and I could set about reassembling the janky parts that had spilled inside me. All I needed was that opportunity.

Except it wasn't Jenny.

"Sorry," Nicki said, pointing at the door. "It was unlocked. I saw your truck..."

"Do you ever think of calling first?"

"I didn't think you'd pick up if you saw my number."

"So instead you just walk into my house?"

She stifled a giggle.

"What's so funny?"

"Looks like someone's been hitting the gym."

I realized I was standing there half naked.

"Wait here," I said, gripping the towel in place. I made for the bedroom to slip on my jeans.

"You have any coffee?" Nicki shouted.

"In the cupboard," I shouted back. "Knock yourself out."

I couldn't find a clean shirt. With Jenny gone, my laundry was piling up. Every tee shirt in the hamper smelled like rotting cheese. Nicki shouted something again, but I couldn't hear. I headed back into the kitchen, shirtless, slicking back wet hair with my fingers.

"What did you say?"

"I wasn't flirting. I just meant you're in pretty good shape for an old man."

"I'm thirty. Which isn't old. And I've worked outdoors all my life. You don't need a gym to stay in shape if you're not a lazy fuck. But never mind about my body." My cheeks burned. "What are you even doing here? Shouldn't you be at work?"

Nicki spun around, leaning against the counter, arching her back and letting her shirt rise enough so that I could see her belly button, stomach tight as a snare drum. "Nope. Fired."

"Sorry to hear that."

"Don't you want to know why?"

"Got caught looking in to Judge Roberts' sentencing again?"

"Making 'unauthorized' photocopies." She even did the fake air quote thing I hate.

"Some people never learn."

"Yeah," she said, flatly. "I don't think they knew what I was photocopying. You have to log in at the courthouse with your employee ID number every time you make a Xerox."

"Fascinating."

"Funny thing was, I wasn't even looking into Roberts. Just some peripheral stuff. Places they ship kids out of state. I hit my limit of acceptable photocopies, apparently. Everyone's a bean counter. Do you know how many kids get sent out of state? To private prisons? Kentucky. Arizona—"

"I don't care, Nicki."

"You don't care?"

"Nope."

Nicki pointed at the blank space on the kitchen table. "Where are those photocopies I left with you?"

"Threw them out."

"Really?"

"Really," I said. And when she wouldn't relinquish the expression of disbelief, I added, "Doesn't matter."

"The lives of hundreds of kids don't matter?"

"Don't make it sound like they're all innocent little cherubs. You don't get arrested unless you break the law. You don't get sent before the judge unless you did something wrong."

"Wow."

"What?"

"Cynical is one thing. I didn't take you for such a heartless bastard. The other day, you seemed so concerned about your friend."

"I told you. He's not a friend. My company insured his mother. Business."

"A nerd locked up in North River for a joint?"

"And lying on an insurance claim, yeah. Attempting to defraud a company out of thousands of dollars. Kind of a big deal. And you don't know how long he'll be in there. He could be out in a week."

"Bullshit. You read that report I left."

"Maybe I did. So what?"

"Then you would know that the average stay at North River is three years. Three years for shoplifting hair products. Trying to buy beer underage. A joint. And that's the *average*. Meaning there's kids in there a lot longer."

"And shorter. Because that's how averages work." I wasn't so hot at math, but I'd retained that much from high school.

"Come on, Jay. There are lives being ruined, irreparable harm being done."

"Not. My. Problem." I opened my arms, revealing my joyless, messy, rented house. "I have bigger problems to worry about."

"Your wife still hasn't come back?"

"That's none of your fucking business."

Nicki stepped toward me. "Why do you hate me? What have I done to you?"

"I don't even know you enough to hate you! But since you asked. You've done nothing but fuck up my life since the day I met you. You keep bugging me with this . . . bullshit! I don't know what you think I can do. I'm a junior claims investigator at a two-bit insurance company. I don't have any access to court records or a pipeline to the police. And by the way, next time mention you're dating a cop."

"I told you. I'm not dating a cop. I've never dated a cop. I don't know any cops! Do I look like I'd date a cop?"

"Well, one of them sure seemed to know you."

"Think about it. You and I were digging around—"

"I wasn't digging shit."

"Fine. I was digging. But you don't know Longmont. It's an old-boy network. Judge Roberts has those pigs on payroll. He was sending a message."

"About what? You're the eager beaver, the nosy one. I'm just a guy trying to do his job."

She went to touch my arm. I pulled away.

"You're scared," she said.

I jabbed a finger at her face. "You are nuts. You are one of those crazy, psycho girls. If I had a pet rabbit, I'd lock it up. Come home and find it boiling in a pot on the stove one day."

"Huh?"

Of course she was too young to get the cultural reference. I grabbed her hand. "See, honey, it would never work out with us."

We both turned around at the same time when we realized we weren't alone.

I hadn't even heard the door open.

CHAPTER THIRTEEN

MY WIFE SEEMED more perplexed than anything, although her confusion didn't last long. She stuck her keys in her purse and acted like a normal person. I introduced Nicki as "a friend from work," even though Jenny knew everyone I worked with, having just suffered through NEI's Christmas party a couple months ago. I was standing, dripping shirtless, holding hands with a girl young enough to be my student if I were a college professor. Except I wasn't any professor.

Nicki mumbled a polite hello, and then gathered her handbag and excused herself, quick as possible. Took her twelve seconds to get out the door, although her exit felt more like a never-ending, drawn-out scene from a Lifetime movie.

When we were alone, Jenny said, "We have to talk."

"I know how bad that looked, but it's not what you think."

"Okay," she said.

"I'm serious. I just met that girl. She works—worked—at the Longmont Courthouse. See, there was this kid. Well, first there was this woman. Who had a policy with us? Olisky. Donna Olisky. She said she was driving, but it was really her son. Remember? I was telling you about him? The accident? Brian. The kid with the brother who died, the wrestler? Anyway, I was checking up on that, and that girl, Nicki, she uncovered some strange shit about this one judge who's been sentencing kids to a sketchy juvie. Place called North River. Minor offenses. I mean, they're minors but the crimes are no big deal. Shoplifting. Some drugs, too. She wanted my help. That's it. I swear."

"I said I believe you."

I stared at my wife, unable to get a read on whether she was being sarcastic or trying to draw me out into the open where she had more room to maneuver—and I had less places to hide—like a boxer taking advantage of speed and reach. I cast a sideways, suspicious glance.

"Jay, what do you want me to say? I believe you."

Somehow that response bugged me even more. "Wait a second. You walk in here, see me half dressed with a pretty, young girl. I tell you nothing is going on, and that's that?"

"Are you lying to me?" my wife asked.

"No!"

"Okay, then."

I felt this indignant surge to fight and protest my innocence. But I'd already been acquitted. Why was she letting me off the hook? There had to be an angle. Then I remembered that douchebag up in Burlington. Stephen. Tits and tat. Quid pro quo. A sneaky trick, pretending to be cool in order to make me look like a bigger asshole.

"This is about the other day," I said. What better way to prove a point? "I lose my temper because you had a lunch date with a guy. But you walk in, see me half dressed with some girl, and you're going to act like the grown-up? I get it." I wasn't sure how any of this added up to my being the victim, but like I learned with the Patriots' last season: when you have no defense, your best bet is to keep your offense on the field as long as possible.

"I don't worry about you screwing around, Jay. That's never been your problem. Sometimes I think it'd be easier if that *was* your problem. Running around and getting some on the side would be a pleasant distraction at this point."

Then it hit me. She was alone. She carried no bags. My son wasn't here. My wife wasn't coming home. "Where's Aiden?"

"With my mother. In Burlington."

"Why?"

"Because," Jenny said, in that pretend-patient tone a person adopts when she's grown sick of explaining rudimentary basics— five is less than eight, a lamb is a baby sheep, fire hot, hungry eat— "we need to talk."

"About?" I asked the question. I didn't want to hear the answer.

"About how I can't go on like this. About how this relationship isn't working. It's toxic."

"Toxic," I repeated. "Which women's magazine did you read that in?"

"What we're doing here is not good for me. Or you. Or our son."

"Now we're not 'good' for our son?"

"Not the way we are going right now, no, we're not. Aiden might only be three years old, but he can still tell something is wrong. Do you want to expose him to us always fighting? Or going days without talking to one another? How do you think that affects his growing up?"

"I'm a good dad," I said.

"Yes," Jenny agreed, "you are. A good dad."

Subtext implied. A good dad. But a lousy husband.

I dropped in the chair. Next to the cigarettes and tea plate ashtray overflowing with butts. I knew the house stank like the tiki porch in the summertime. Didn't matter that I'd propped a fan in the window, blowing out the smoke. Acrid remnants remained. My wife glanced down at my pack but didn't say a word. We had more pressing matters confronting us. The ink had barely dried on the wedding certificate, and here we were, negotiating terms of surrender.

"And what do you propose we do?" I said.

"I don't know. That's why I'm here. To talk. Figure it out." Jenny sat at the table. Facing one another at opposite ends like we were signing a peace treaty, discussing where borders would be drawn, what land traded hands. In a flash I got a horrible premonition, as if someday, perhaps very soon, we'd be sitting down like this again, only next time with lawyers, making it official, hammering out details about who got nothing. Because the only thing of value was our son, and he belonged to her. Kids stay with the mom.

"Y'know, before your mother steamrolled me—"

"She didn't steamroll you—"

"Sorry," I said. "I meant to say before your mother blindsided me, I'd driven to her house to tell you good news. I cracked a big case and am up for a promotion." I smidged my fingers together. "I mean, I'm this close to getting sent down to Concord, the big office. Which will come with a raise. We'll be able to afford a down payment on a house—"

"I called your office, Jay."

"So?"

"So Andy DeSouza told me he gave you the week off."

"I told you. That's not my fault. That girl, Nicki, she got this crazy idea, and she sucked me into it."

"Into what, exactly?"

I took a deep breath before explaining about Judge Roberts, North River, and unjust sentences. I left out the parts about police brutality. If Jenny had seen the bruises on my ribs, she hadn't asked about them. The house was pretty dark. I spoke slow, made sure to ramble less and make myself sound as sane as possible. Good ol' level-headed Jay. Except that "good ol' level-headed Jay" hadn't shown his face around here in a while. Even as I was talking, reasonable had been replaced with a stranger, whose train accelerated too fast around corners, coming dangerously close to crashing over the cliff. I could see the revulsion reflected in my wife's expression as I resolved to ride this to the end of the line. So of course I poured on the gas.

"Nicki isn't wrong," I said. "There *is* something there. I mean, some of these kids, Jenny—we're talking twelve, fourteen. Sentenced to hard time for a pair of Percocet? Two years in a juvenile detention center? I took Chris to one of these places once. They are the real deal. Behavioral modification. Like hazing. They have one goal: break you down to build you back up in *their* image. You know how stark raving everyone up here gets when the subject of drugs comes up. I mean, I know I'm not unbiased, but, damn, you should see this North River—"

My wife shook her head, and when I tried to talk louder, she shook harder.

"This," she said, "*this* is what I am talking about."

"What? I'm doing my job. I thought that's what you wanted. Me to give a shit about something?"

"I want you to move on! With us! With me, your wife. With your son! Your family! Not with some college girl gone wild."

"So you *are* pissed about Nicki!"

"No wife wants to come home and find her husband standing without his shirt on in the middle of the kitchen with a hot young girl. No, Jay. Big fucking surprise. Yes, it would piss off any wife. From here to Nebraska. Okay? But that's *not* the problem. You say you're not sleeping with her—"

"I'm not sleeping with her—"

"And I said I believe you! But you're not here, either."

I feigned surprised, panning around. "I'm not here? So where am I? One of Saturn's moons? Because this sure looks like my fucking kitchen."

Jenny hopped up. I did too.

We stood toe to toe. Another knockdown, drag-out. How many of these we'd had over the years, I'd lost track. I readied for the attack, like any wild animal, most dangerous when cornered, wounded, pitted for survival. But I was also tired. Too despondent, too disheartened to will outrage and win this time.

Now my wife saw my ribs. "What happened?"

"I fell."

"How much are you drinking?"

"I wasn't drunk. There's, like, ice everywhere. I'm fine. You bitch about communication. You complain I'm shut off. But you haven't returned a fucking phone call in three days."

"I needed space."

"Yeah? And I need my son. Who you took. Across state lines. And then you don't have the courtesy to pick up a telephone? I'm still your husband. More importantly, I'm still Aiden's father."

"I know. You're right. I should've called sooner. And I shouldn't have kept Aiden from you. I didn't know how else to navigate the situation. I didn't want to hear your voice."

"Well, ain't that fucking wonderful. So while I can't see my son because you can't stand the sound of me I've got your mother whispering in your ear."

"I know you hate her but—"

"Bullshit. She hates *me*. Always has."

"That's not true. Believe what you want to believe. But even if it *were* true—and it's not—have a little faith. I wouldn't be so easily swayed, okay? I'm not this delicate flower, too naïve to make up her own mind. People talk shit. They always do. What is going on with you and me is between you and me."

"And what is going on?" I looked around the depressing setting, afternoon skies dampening walls, throwing a dark blanket over furniture and floor. I hated the way the northern wilds
could do that. Draw all light, suck it up like soda through a straw.
"Because here you are, without my son, after not returning calls,
with none of your things. Obviously you're not planning on staying. So what's the deal, Jenny? You're moving out? That it? Want
a divorce?"

Jenny didn't respond right away. Then again, I didn't give her
much a chance, jumping right back in.

"Just fucking great."

"I didn't say anything about a divorce."

"Hey," I said, "I mean, who could blame you? You gutted it out,
tried marriage for almost, like, a *whole fucking year*. Makes you
fucking Mother Teresa, right? Goddamn martyr, stay married to
a monster like me for twelve months. Actually . . ." I pretended
to do the math in my head. "Not quite a year. More like nine
months. But, still, I mean, close." I clapped my hands in a juvenile
display. "Wow, just wow. Should fucking pin the medal to your
chest. Fucking heroic."

"We've been doing this dance a lot longer than a few months.
We've been at it since high school. And the problem now is the
same as it was then."

"Which is?"

"Your brother."

"What the hell has he got to do with any of this?" I stopped
and pretended to think. "You mean my dead brother, Chris? The
junkie who's been gone for over a year? And truth be told, a lot
longer than that. The same guy I barely saw the last five years of
his life? The drug addict I avoided like the fucking plague? That
brother?"

I meant the barb to be a stinging indictment of how ridiculous my wife was being.

Instead all she said was, "Yes."

"I'm seeing Dr. Shapiro-Weiss again," I blurted.

"That's good to hear."

"She says I have a PTSD thing going on. Because of Chris. So, y'know, I'm dealing with stuff."

"That's good," my wife said.

"I don't want to lose you, Jenny."

"I know."

I waited for reassurance, my heart flipping inside its cage, desperate for release, blood pressure surging; I could hear the swells rising in my ears, riptide threatening to drag me from shore for good, surrender me to the undertow. I thought admitting I needed help—telling her that I was getting that help—would be some magic elixir. But I was too late. We'd run out of time. I felt my chest clutch up. The pills the doctor had given me were in the other room. Right on the dresser. Relief ten feet away. But I didn't want to risk moving from that spot. I had this sudden, all-consuming fear that if I took a step away from her right then, let her out of my sight for even a second, she'd be gone forever.

"Tell me what you need me to do," I said. "How do I get you and Aiden to come home?"

"I don't know."

"Why did you even come back here?"

"To talk," she said. "And I needed clothes for Aiden. Some of my things."

"So you're moving out?"

"No. Not moving out. Just taking space. Time."

"Until what? What the hell are you waiting for?"

"I'm not sure. I guess I'll know it when I see it."

* * *

Afterwards I retrieved my script and sat at the kitchen table while my wife gathered those things she'd come back for, clothes, makeup, whatever a single mom needs to survive. I didn't watch her pack. I kept my back turned and lit up right there in the house. Didn't bother with a window or the fan. Who gave a shit? I listened to the soft patter of feet, the opening and closing of dresser drawers. We lived on a quiet street, everyone at work or cloistered behind suburban walls. Nothing stirred outside. I could hear every squeak inside our fractured home, and these echoes of extraction stabbed parts of me unknown.

I poured a cup of coffee from the pot Nicki had made, swirled in milk and sugar, sat back down without sensation, a burn victim long after the fire, all nerve endings cauterized, deadened, the pain now seared as a permanent part.

Jenny dragged her haul into the kitchen. My wife leaned over and kissed me on the head, the way you take leave from a mildly annoying cousin you tolerate once a year on the holidays, responsibility served, parting a relief.

I asked when I could see my son. Jenny said since I had the week off, come up tomorrow if I wanted. Just call first. Then my wife walked out the door, and I was alone.

I'm not sure how long I sat at that table, but long enough for the coffee to go cold. Fuck coffee. If I was going to drink something cold, might as well be a beer. I cracked the day's first, and headed out to the garage. I reached into the trash bin and dug out the giant scrapbook I'd thrown away, last year's secret obsession to exonerate my brother that hadn't been a secret to anyone.

Last year when Chris had gone missing, I'd needed a picture of him to show around the now-demolished truck stop. The one photograph I had, this old, faded yearbook snapshot, had been taken back before he was a skeleton, when he had a regular haircut and looked human. When I saw my aunt and uncle at the wedding, the social event of the season attended by seven people, including the goddamn justice of the peace, money so tight, I'd asked them to bring any old pictures they had of my brother and me, our parents. My history.

I hadn't taken more than a cursory glance at the gold-embossed wedding gift. I ripped the pages from the three-hole punch and transferred Chris and my folks to the back of the binder. Tossed the album. I didn't need the constant reminder sitting on a shelf.

Beer in hand, I lit another cigarette and dropped the binder on my workbench, peeling back the cover, skipping the articles I'd compiled on Adam, Michael, and Gerry Lombardi, heading straight to the photos of my family in the back. They were all dead now.

My brother had been ten years older than me, so when he was a teenager, I was a kid. And when Chris was a kid, I wasn't born. We're talking '70s, '80s. Taking photographs then wasn't like it is today, the way Jenny documented Aiden's life digitally on her iPhone, uploading them to the desktop, memories that would never fade or decompose, stored in permanent electronic folders. These photos I had of Chris, Mom, and Dad were Polaroids, snapped on cheap Nokia crap, yellowed, disintegrating with the passage of time.

I ran a finger over the cellophane protector. Little red house. Dirt lawn. Chris in denim outfits, sporting an assortment of butt-chop haircuts. Mom, so young, with too much makeup under her eyes. Dad, shaggy and less serious. There were pics of him goofing around, wearing funny hats, a far cry from the stern and responsible man I'd known as a father.

The three of them at Christmas. The three of them on vacation by the beach. Picnics in the park. They were a family. They all seemed happy. Until I showed up. Once I appeared on the scene, the tone shifted to somber. Then a terrible thought: maybe it all turned to shit when I was born? So long after their first, maybe I was the accident that disrupted the harmony? All I remembered was Chris and our father screaming at each other, my mother silent, off in the distance. I knew my father to be a good man, the kind of man I aspired to be. He was good to me. But there was undoubtedly a distance. My father reacted and battled my brother. My mother seemed broken. Even as a kid, I knew she drank too much. As a child, I attributed these stresses to my brother's acting out. I'd wonder what if Chris wasn't here? What if it was just my parents and me? Maybe then things would've been better. Maybe then we'd be happy. And when they died, even if I didn't blame Chris the way the rest of the town did, I'd think if he hadn't been born, maybe my parents would be alive today. I viewed Chris as the aberration, the mistake. But what it if it was the other way around? What if I was the one who shouldn't be here?

CHAPTER FOURTEEN

I'D SUCKED DOWN half a pack of cigarettes and drained another case of beer running through the photographic seasons like a perverted version of *The Wonder Years*, watching satisfaction erode with each vacant expression.

I opened the garage door and stood at the edge. Still hadn't put on a shirt, hair damp. Nothing dries in the cold. Probably catch pneumonia. The skies over the mountains threatened storm. I inhaled a deep, icy breath, which hurt my lungs. But the air here was clean, pure; I knew it filled me with something good.

Turning to go back inside, I spotted the car. Several houses down, just sitting there. The last house on the block. Sedan. Brown, black, maybe dark blue. Engine running, taillights glowing. In the day's dying light, I couldn't see too well, but I could make out the two shadowy figures inside. I checked up and down the street. I hadn't met all my neighbors. Had no interest. But this car did not belong here.

My heart started speeding again. How much did I have to drink? Or were the cigarettes making me jumpy? The pills the doctor prescribed weren't cutting down on the anxiety. I knew whoever was inside that the car had been sent to do me harm. Haul me away, take me in, make me disappear. Even without seeing anyone's eyes, I could feel intentions of malice. Veins throbbed up my wrists, thrumming inside my biceps, my breathing harsh, hostile, agitated.

When the landline rang, I practically jumped out of my kicks, like I'd grabbed hold of an electric fence.

I closed the garage door and headed inside, snagging a dirty tee off the arm of a chair. The ringing droned, annoying and obnoxious. I should've known who was calling before I even put receiver to ear.

"Jay," Andy DeSouza said. "Why aren't you picking up your cell?"

I carried the landline, cradle and all, to the window and cracked the shutters. The car down the block began coughing exhaust as it pulled away slowly, taunting me.

"I had to call HR to get this number."

"Yeah," I answered, waiting for the car to move faster. "What's up?" Get the hell out of here and leave me alone.

"Were you out at the North River Institute last night?"

The car drove off up the snow-packed street, creeping around the corner, two taillights blazing red around the bend, a pair of demon eyes casting judgment.

"Your truck was spotted on a road up there."

I let the blinds fall. "What? You're having me followed, Andy?"

"So you admit it. You *were* out there?"

"What do you care what I do in my free time? Which I now have an abundance of, thanks to you. Oh, and I appreciate you telling my wife I'd been suspended."

"I think I was pretty clear not to look into—"

"What's your damage, man? I'm sitting in my house, doing squat, because *you* told me not to come to work. Then you rat me out to my wife? Now you're calling to bust my balls because someone saw my truck on a road? What the fuck?"

"This isn't the kind of attitude that's going to get you to Concord—"

"You know, Andy, you've been dangling that bullshit prize since I got here. You're like one of those rigged fucking games at Chuck E. Cheese I take my kid to in Pittsfield. Slip a buck, try and snare a plush bunny with a metal claw. But you know what? You can never win the bunny. You can never hook any of the good stuff. It's fixed. A con game."

"I can't tell you how disappointed I am, Jay. Y'know, Concord—"

"Andy?" I stopped him. "Do me a favor. Take Concord and stick it up your fucking ass." I slammed the receiver.

The phone immediately rang back.

"I said fuck off!"

"Whoa, Jay. It's me. Everything okay, man?"

"What do you want, Charlie?" I peeked back through the curtains. Light snow fell through porch light, fresh powder in the street unblemished by tire tracks. I took a deep breath, feeling for my smokes. "I just lost my job."

"You got fired?"

"Or I quit."

"Shit. What's Jenny going to say?"

I unscrewed my script, toppled a pair of pills, took a swill of warm, flat beer, and lit another cigarette. "Doesn't matter," I said through the slow burn. "She packed up her shit earlier. She's gone."

He didn't say anything.

I stared down at my feet when I realized I'd been walking in circles. Literally in circles. Like one of McMurphy's rejects lobbying to see the World Series in the nut ward.

I forced myself to take a chair. "Why are you calling?"

"To apologize," he said. "I'm not sure I helped last night. I'm not sure I've been helping at all. I mean, last night, you didn't need that."

"No, Charlie? You condescending prick. And what do I need?"

"A friend."

That disarmed me. Charlie Finn was my friend. About the only one I had these days. I didn't need to be reminded he cared. When you fall on black days, bad news is easier to digest; kindness can be cruel.

"Anyway," he continued, after the brief, uneasy silence. "Fisher wants to see you."

"Fisher?" I knew he and Charlie still spoke but why would the guy want to see me now? "For what?"

"Are you okay to drive?" Charlie asked.

"I've had a few beers. Why?"

"Fisher wants to talk to you."

"So why didn't he call me?"

"He asked me to call you. We're meeting at the Olympic Diner. Tonight."

What the hell was so pressing? Fisher and I hadn't spoken since he set me up with the job at NorthEastern last winter . . . Right. My failure reflected badly on him. Nice try. I wasn't getting read the riot act by Fisher.

"It's important," Charlie said.

"Tell Fisher I don't want to hear it." He must've learned I told Andy DeSouza to fuck himself—what other reason for the urgency? Except I'd told my boss to fuck off less than two minutes ago. How fast can bad news really travel?

"Fisher's coming from the other direction," Charlie mumbled, as if to himself. "You shouldn't be driving if you're drunk."

"I'm buzzed. I'm not drunk. But if you think, after the day I've had, I'm taking lip from that greasy little fuck—"

"He wants to help," Charlie said.

"I don't want my job back."

"Jay, it's not about your job. I mean, not directly. You need to see something. You have to trust me. It'll be worth your while. Promise. Won't make sense over the phone. I still don't want you driving, though. We're getting that storm tonight—"

"What storm?"

"How out of it are you, man? Turned on the news lately? Listened to the radio?"

"Nope." I'd been cloistered inside a goddamn bubble.

"Supposed to be, like, the worst blizzard since '78?" He exhaled. "Not gonna hit until well after midnight. We have plenty of time."

"Time for what?"

"Let me call Fisher. Maybe I can convince him to make a pit stop and pick you up first. But it's the other direction." I could hear Charlie's hamster wheel spinning as he tried to plot a way to collect me from Plasterville. "Or we can both go out there—"

"Don't worry," I said. "I'll head to Ashton." I didn't feel like sitting around an empty house anyway, peeking out blinds like a basketcase.

"You shouldn't drive—"

"Relax. I have a friend I can call for a ride. See you at the Olympic in an hour."

* * *

How many reckless high school nights ended up at the Olympic? After every party, kegger, or concert, we always managed to find our way to the twenty-four hour dinette on the Desmond Turnpike, its long, tin carriage gleaming hopefully in the parking lot. The reservoir ragers and drunken hook-ups of wild-eyed seventeen-year-olds with their whole lives ahead of them had given way to two dudes in their thirties, whose lives hadn't gone exactly as planned.

Seeing Charlie in the bright light tripped me out. In the washed-out grays of the bar or his bunker, flaws were more easily concealed. Back in the day, my best friend had been lean and handsome, a real lady-killer. Now he was paunchy, a few ham sandwiches short of blowing up like Brando. I could see what Charlie would look like in another five, ten. And the picture wasn't pretty. The reason was simple: alcohol. Charlie liked to drink, and even beer can take its toll. I tried to add up how much beer I'd downed over these last few days. Counting by twelve and rounding down, I still ended up with a frightening number.

"Why are you looking at me like that?" Charlie asked.

The pretty Greek waitress reached around me and refilled his coffee mug.

"Sit down," he said. "You're making me nervous."

Charlie didn't realize the girl was with me, until Nicki slipped in the booth opposite him. He didn't say hi, content to gawk like a weirdo. She popped back up.

"I need to use the restroom," she said to me.

I pointed down the long row of red vinyl stools propped along the counter, past the strudel and Danish hiding under scratched plastic hoods.

When I sat down, Charlie whiplashed, catching Nicki's ass as she walked away. He spun around, thumbing over his shoulder.

"Are you hitting that?"

"Am I hitting that?" I repeated. "No, Charlie, I'm not 'hitting that.' I'm fucking married."

"I thought you said Jenny left."

"My wife needs time to think. I needed a ride because you kept bugging me. Nicki is a friend. That's it." Truth was, I could drive fine; the heightened, agitated state had left me stone-cold sober.

"And if my wife did leave me, I think it'd take longer than half a day to rebound."

"Sorry, man." Charlie fiddled with his spoon. "I thought, y'know—"

"What?"

"If you and Jenny are having problems, maybe . . ." He arched his brows, bobbing. "*Y'know?*"

"No, I don't know. I don't do that."

"What? Have sex?"

"Screw around." It was true, and one of the better parts of my character, one of the few I had left to feel good about. I didn't cheat. Never had. I had no intention of starting now.

"What about Gina? In high school?"

"Any girl I've been with over the years, Jenny and I were on a break." There had been a lot of breaks. Before he could chime in, I added, "And other girls were never the cause. Jenny and I are . . . complicated."

Nicki returned and slid beside me. I realized she'd excused herself so Charlie and I could have a few moments alone. Maybe she wasn't as unperceptive as I thought.

I also realized I hadn't gotten around to introducing her. "Nicki interns at the Longmont Courthouse." I'd already filled Nicki in on Charlie's backstory. "She's the one who found out what happened to that kid, Brian."

"Cool," Charlie said, still staring without a hint of self-awareness.

He smoothed a hand over what was left of his thinning hair, sucked in his gut, trying to dial up the suave and smooth Charlie from days gone past. The gesture didn't translate. Vince Vaughn in *Swingers* is a lot different than Vince Vaughn in, well, anything else.

"Where is Fisher?" I asked.

Charlie ignored me until I snapped my fingers and caught his attention.

"What?"

"What's going on? Why's Fisher so hot to see me? I haven't even talked to the guy since he got me that fucking job—"

"I told you it's not about the job."

"Then what's it about? Start talking, man, or we—" I motioned between Nicki and me like we were a tag team "—are walking out that door."

"That place we were last night," Charlie said, accepting he couldn't hold me off any longer.

"North River. What about it?"

He had been busting my balls so hard over being there I was surprised he recognized the name.

"When I told Fisher about it—"

"Told Fisher about what?"

"North River."

"When did you tell Fisher about North River? How often do you guys talk?"

"I don't know. Every day?"

"Every day? Are you in a long-distance relationship now?" I looked at Nicki, who broke into a grin, entertained by the witty banter. "What the fuck?"

"Let's wait until Fisher gets here," Charlie said. "You know I'm not good explaining stuff. I start talking it's not gonna sound right."

"I don't give a shit."

"It's all connected, man."

"What's all connected?"

"North River. Judge Roberts." He waited. "Last year."

"What are you talking about?"

Nicki perked up at the mention of Roberts' name, meeting Charlie's eye, the two of them nodding in agreement. I felt stuck in an old *Twilight Zone* episode where everyone's gone crazy but me. One thing I'd learned about this life: the moment you believe you are the only sane man in an insane world you can rest assured you are truly fucked.

When the front bell dinged, I knew if I turned around I'd see Fisher. I saw Fisher all right.

The last time I'd seen the guy was at my brother's wake, when I'd asked Charlie and him to drop this whole Lombardi business, forget the hard drive we'd found, the pictures. There wasn't enough evidence, and given my recent brushes with death, I wasn't jeopardizing the well-being of my wife and son.

Fisher had always been a goofy-looking little fucker. The greasy ringlets and Dumbo ears, the wisp of porn mustache. But still a regular guy. The man who walked toward us now sported long Jesus hair, a scruffy beard, and John Lennon glasses. He wore a tweed jacket with goddamn patches at the elbows. A full-fledged, card-carrying, New Hampshire hippy. He toted a leather satchel, too, like some professor at a liberal arts college, or maybe, y'know, a poet.

I panned across to Charlie, who seemed unfazed by our friend's new appearance, which meant he'd seen him recently, further adding to the sensation that everybody was in on the joke but me.

Fisher stopped at the table and dropped the bag, which landed with a thump.

We all turned.

"We got him," he said.

CHAPTER FIFTEEN

"YOU SURE SCREWED the pooch, eh, Porter?" Fisher said, sliding into the spot next to Charlie. Despite the radical fringe wardrobe, he was the same smart-ass Fisher. "Involuntary leave? Ouch."

I didn't bother correcting him that my temporary break had turned permanent vacation.

For as uncouth and crass as Fisher could be, at least when he saw Nicki he had the decency to act like a civilized human being and not some knuckle-dragging troglodyte looking to club his next conquest.

"Hello," he said, reaching over the table for a respectful handshake. "Fisher."

I was relieved they didn't already know each other, given the conspiratorial vibe enveloping the table.

"Just Fisher?" she responded, teasing. "No first name?"

"Nah, when you're this big, the one is enough. I'm like Sting."

Nicki returned a dumbfounded stare.

"He's a singer—"

"I'm messing with you. I know who The Police are." Then she turned to me. "And I've seen *Fatal Attraction*." Her voice went up a shrill octave. "*I'm not gonna be ignored, Dan.*"

"Okay, Fisher," I said. "What's this all about? Charlie dragged me out here. There's a storm blowing in. I had to call Nicki for a ride—"

"That case you're looking into," Fisher said.

"I'm not looking into any case. In fact, I'm not even working at NEI anymore."

"Neither am I."

I looked to Charlie, who shrugged.

"Since when?"

"I don't know. Last summer?"

"No one told me."

Fisher snorted. "Why would anyone tell you, Porter?"

Good question. We weren't close, almost never spoke. We worked in different locations, hours away. Our paths seldom crossed, our mutual friend Charlie is all we had in common. Still, Charlie might've mentioned it. Maybe he had. Given my recent move and marriage, Charlie and I hadn't been spending as much time together, this past week notwithstanding. And it seemed whenever we did meet up copious amounts of alcohol were usually involved.

Fisher nodded at me. "Fired?"

"I assume so. I told Andy DeSouza to get fucked."

"When?"

"This afternoon."

"Did he actually say you were fired?"

"I hung up before he had the chance."

"And you didn't quit?"

"Not exactly."

Fisher brushed me off. "Like you're the only one to tell Andy DeSouza to get bent. Porter, if they canned everyone who did that there wouldn't be anyone left to work up there. Trust me, DeSouza's a babysitter. A minor league manager. Concord knows what you did. Hell, I heard about it. I still have friends there."

Nicki acted impressed, like Fisher's props improved my status in her eyes. Why did I care what this college girl thought of me?

"I didn't *do* anything," I explained to everyone at the table. "Brian Olisky blurted out he'd been behind the wheel."

"Yeah, and you saved NEI like ten gee."

Funny how that number kept going up. "Doesn't matter. Whatever good grace I banked, I've pissed away. I shouldn't have been up at North River in the first place. DeSouza forbade me from looking further into the Olisky case."

"Andy DeSouza is a pussy. I'm telling you. You want Concord, it's still a possibility."

"How do you even know about any of this? I thought you left NEI. Why do you care?"

Both Fisher and Charlie had the same shit-eating grins on their faces. I hadn't been imagining it. Something was up. "Okay, spit it out. What's going on?"

"So remember last year," Fisher said, "at your brother's funeral, how you told me to drop investigating Lombardi?"

"Yeah." How could I forget?

"I didn't."

Fisher dug around in his satchel and retrieved a rubber-banded binder. Like my own collection of clippings and chicken-scratch. Only his was bigger. Fisher had clearly been doing his homework. He dropped the stack with authority on the countertop, parting papers earmarked with color-coded Post-its.

"I was talking to Charlie this afternoon," Fisher began, focus waning as he multi-tasked. "He told me how you two had been chased off by security guards at North River. Something rang a bell. Knew I'd seen that name before."

"Hold on," I said.

He stopped riffling and peered up at me through his round, hippy lenses.

I pointed at his pile of papers. "What is all that?"

"Research. Since leaving NEI, I've devoted a great deal of time to this."

"This being investigating the Lombardis?"

"Yeah."

"When I'd asked you not to?" I turned to Charlie, who refused to meet my eye. He'd known all about Fisher's continuing to dig around and hadn't said a word.

"So I didn't listen to you, Porter. Shoot me."

I made to stand up, an empty threat, since Nicki had driven me. Boxing me in, she wasn't budging.

"Hold on," Charlie said. "Hear him out."

I reluctantly sat back down.

Fisher found his damning evidence, slipping the page, a cheesy entertainer in Atlantic City plucking the perfect card. He tapped the magic word.

There it was, clear and bold: UpStart.

"What's UpStart?" Nicki asked.

"You never told her about Lombardi's charity project?" Fisher said.

"No," I answered without looking at her. "Why would I? We're not dating."

"Last year," Fisher explained to Nicki, "we—Charlie, Jay, and I—had a run-in with a family up here. The Lombardis. Very influential." Fisher glanced my way. "Some crazy stuff happened—I'll let Jay fill you in on the rest since it involved his brother—but UpStart's their baby. The organization is presently financing a campaign, funneling a great deal of money your way."

"Whose way?" I said.

Fisher motioned at Nicki. "She works at the Longmont County Courthouse, right?"

Nicki nodded, omitting the minor detail that she, too, had recently been canned. "What kind of charity?" she asked.

"UpStart's a nonprofit for at-risk youth up here," I said. "This guy Gerry Lombardi ran it. Before my brother died, Chris accused Gerry of some pervy shit with kids. Said he had pictures."

"Did he?" Nicki asked. "Have pictures, I mean."

"My brother was pretty far gone by then, but yeah. Blurry ones on a stolen computer. Couldn't prove jack."

"Sure looked like Gerry," Charlie muttered.

"Doesn't matter," I said. "Gerry's dead."

"Right," Fisher said. "And now UpStart belongs to his sons, Adam and Michael."

"You know Adam doesn't even live up here anymore?" I said, parroting what Charlie had told me. "Relocated his whole family south. Sold the business."

"No shit," Fisher said. "I live in Concord. Who do you think told Finn that?" He pointed at a sheepish Charlie, before deciding he'd have better luck with Nicki. "In terms of detention centers, North River's a gray area, right? Stuck between private and public? The state pumps in some money, matching family obligations, the rest comes via donations, local nonprofits, etcetera."

She nodded.

"How do you know about any of this?" I asked him.

"I told you," Fisher repeated. "I've been investigating. It's in my files."

Charlie flapped his arms, trying to flag down a waitress.

"Your files," I said. "So what? You turned pro?"

"No," said Fisher. "I am taking a few journalism courses over at Tech, though."

"What's that got to do with anything?"

"Nothing. But you asked what I was up to."

"I don't give a rat's ass about some community college class you're enrolled in. I mean why do you care about North River? You're not at NorthEastern Insurance anymore." I stopped. "And even if you were, this doesn't concern NEI anyway."

"UpStart," Fisher said.

"What about them?"

"They bankroll diversion programs. And one of the big ones is North River."

"Big deal. It's nonprofit. No one's making money. That's what nonprofit means."

"That's not true," Nicki said.

"Huh?"

"Nonprofit. The term doesn't mean what most people think it does."

"I know you can't turn a profit or you start paying taxes." I might not have had a business degree but I knew that much.

"Right," said Nicki. "And one of the ways a place like North River doesn't turn a profit is by paying their officers and staff exorbitant salaries."

Fisher reached into his bag of goodies and plucked another page, sharing it with the class. Nicki staggered over the six-figure salaries, whistling low.

"Just gotta stay out of the black," Fisher said. "Any money you make, you funnel back in to the product. Trick is to always be losing."

"Like *Brewster's Millions*," Charlie said, proud of himself for having contributed to the conversation.

"Plenty of other ways to keep cash off the books," Fisher said.

"What are you talking about?"

"Old-fashioned kickbacks."

"Bribes? To who?"

"Judge Roberts, for one," Fisher said.

"Wait. You're telling me you have proof UpStart is paying off Roberts? For what? To send kids to a facility that they *pay* into? How is that a sustainable business model?"

"Yes. And no," Fisher said.

"Yes and no what?"

"No. I don't have proof connecting UpStart to Roberts. Not directly. Adam and Michael Lombardi are too smart to leave behind blatant paper trails. If there's bank records or wire transfers connecting payoffs to judges, you better believe that money has been funneled six ways to Sunday. They'll launder that shit until every dime sparkles and not a cent can be traced back. But I can tell you *why* UpStart would be so interested in increasing enrollment—"

"They want to drum up public support for a new private juvenile facility," Nicki said.

"Glad someone is following along."

I stared at her.

"It's been the talk of the courthouse since I signed on. The drug epidemic out of control and all that. Some very vocal proponents want to privatize. Think about the revenue stream. You're always assured customers."

Charlie wrinkled his brow like he understood what was going on. Even if he had been listening to Fisher behind the scenes I knew he was as lost as I was. The waitress stopped at our table and Charlie ordered a basket of wings. His coping mechanism for confusion: eat through the uncertainty.

"The way these places work," Nicki said, outlining North River's enrollment figures on a spreadsheet, "diversion programs are, like, alternative sentencing, right? Kind of state-funded. Kind of privately financed. Families kick in, but they still get a huge chunk from investors. According to your friend Fisher, UpStart is one of those investors."

"We're not friends."

Fisher appeared hurt.

"And so what?"

"Don't you think it's weird?" she asked.

"What? That UpStart, one of New Hampshire's biggest organizations dealing with at-risk youth, would support a residential facility that houses at-risk youth?"

All eyes fell on me. But Charlie was the one who spoke up. "Jay, you've been hoping for proof that Lombardi's guilty."

"Yeah. On molestation charges. Not creative bookkeeping. I'm not interested in revisionist history. Besides the old man is dead. And *you*, Charlie, told me I was nuts any time I brought it up." I could already see Jenny's eyes rolling if I pressed the need to pursue this further.

"It's not just North River," Fisher said, taking another crack. He laid out names and numbers on Excel sheets, northern New Hampshire divided up by county and jurisdiction. Courthouses and judges on one side, sentences meted out on the other.

Nicki grabbed the page and spun it in her direction, pointing at a line item halfway down. "These are the figures from the district, how many kids Longmont—and in particular Judge Roberts— has sent away to the North River Institute. Look at this, Jay." She kept her finger on the line. "Can you see the increase in the last six months alone? The uptick over the past year is *insane*. Read those charges. Public intoxication? Truancy? Loitering? Possession raps tacked on to slap-on-the-wrist tickets, and those kids end up behind bars. They are padding numbers, big time."

I saw that Roberts' conviction rates had skyrocketed of late, a majority sentenced to North River, and over nothing much at all—but one and one wasn't amounting to jack shit. Not without some endgame prize.

"You're telling me the Lombardi brothers are financing this whole project, trying to sell out seats at North River. Okay. Why? What's their play?"

Fisher cast a knowing glance. This was the news he'd been waiting to spring, the real reason he'd summoned me on a dark and stormy night.

He pulled out a folded newspaper, the late edition I hadn't gotten around to reading. He pushed it across the table to me.

Law to Privatize New Hampshire's Prison System Expected to Pass.

I skimmed the article. The proposed facility would cover more than just New Hampshire; the rest of New England's most dangerous weed-smoking scourge would be housed as well. I got to the meaty section: the who, the what . . . the where.

UpStart headed a group of investors preparing to build the state's largest private prison. And the proposed site for the massive juvenile detention center? The newly available TC Truck Stop on the edge of my hometown.

CHAPTER SIXTEEN

"This is just like Big Daddy," Charlie said.

He was behind the wheel of his old Subaru hatchback beater, half maroon, half-rusted piece of shit with long gashes and cigarette holes in the upholstery. The car belonged to his mom before she died. When Charlie lost the phone company gig, he lost the company van too, dragging this monstrosity off the automotive graveyard and back into action.

The latest forecast didn't have the blizzard wreaking havoc until much later. We had plenty of time to get out in front of the storm. I argued that as long as we were here, might as well check out the families in town. Nicki and Fisher went to call on a couple kids on the other side of the mountain, while Charlie and I paid a visit to the parents of Wendy Shaw, the sixteen-year-old girl who'd been locked up over a year for defending a gay classmate. One of the things I'd gleaned from my year as an investigator: people have a much easier time hanging up a phone than they do slamming a door. Plus I knew if we called it a night, Nicki would be the one taking me home to Plasterville. Empty house. Late at night. The heels of rejection on the precipice of a disaster, I didn't want to deal with temptation. Fat guys on diets don't walk past the cake shop.

"Remember, from *The Simpsons?*"

"I don't know what the hell you are talking about, Charlie."

"The fake spin-off featuring Chief Wiggum as a private investigator in Louisiana?"

I tried to read route numbers as we snaked through the twists of the mountain. Fat flakes started to fall, lullabying through headlights. The engine was hot enough to melt them on impact, but the soft, fluffy down had begun to slick the roadways. Still several hours till midnight, I wondered if the forecast had gotten it wrong.

"*The Simpsons*," Charlie said. "It's a cartoon. Been on television over twenty years—"

"I'm aware of *The Simpsons*, yes. What the hell does that have to do with any of this?" I'd grown up in these mountains. You'd think I'd be able to find my way around in the dark by now. The Ashton foothills were nothing but a labyrinth of secret alcoves and hiding spots.

"It's an episode. On *The Simpsons*. 'Chief Wiggum, PI.' But a pretend show. It's not real."

"None of it's real. It's a fucking cartoon."

"That's not what I mean," Charlie said, growing exasperated. "You remember Chief Wiggum? Y'know, the fat, dumb Springfield cop?" He chuckled to himself. "Kinda like Turley."

"Make your point, man."

"It's a spin-off, dude. Troy McClure hosts. Principal Skinner is 'Skinny Boy.' Wiggum's kid—what's his name? Wrote the Valentine's Day card to Lisa—I choo-choo-choose you? Ralph!" Charlie chuckled over the funny memory. "Every week's episode features the same villain, this New Orleans kingpin, Big Daddy. Get it?"

"No."

"Lombardi is Big Daddy."

"You're an idiot, Charlie."

The inside of his car smelled like a rat had died in a bag of

McDonald's french fries. At least we could smoke. I lit a cigarette with an old Zippo I found in the ashtray.

"It's a good analogy," Charlie said, softly. "Why are you so pissy?"

"I don't know, man. How about because you've been busting my balls a whole year? Anytime I'd mention the Lombardis, you'd give me hell, while the *entire time* you knew Fisher was playing Hardy Boys on the sly, investigating shit I'd asked you to drop."

"I wouldn't call it investigating. More like—"

"What?"

"A hobby."

"A hobby I asked you both to drop."

"Like you dropped it?"

"You didn't have to make me sound nuts any time I brought it up."

"I didn't want you driving yourself crazy. Last winter tore you up, man. I saw how rough that was on you. Sure, I knew Fisher was still poking around, but not the extent of it. Obsessing over this wasn't helping you any. I didn't want you blowing a good thing. You had the family. A good job."

"Not anymore."

"I figured if Fisher ever stumbled on something worthwhile, I'd bring it to you then. Until that time well, y'know."

"No. I don't."

"Before North River popped up on the map, I honestly didn't think he'd find anything." Charlie dug out a cigarette. "I'm never getting those things."

"What things?"

"A Jenny. An Aiden. A family." He squinted to find a path in the darkness. "I see the way people look at me. At the Dubliner. Around town. You."

"Forget about it, man."

"I'm never leaving this place. I'm getting fat, losing my hair. I drink too much. Shit, I know I peaked in high school. It's cool. But I'm not meeting a nice girl at the bar and settling down. I'll die alone."

"We all will, Charlie."

"I was trying to protect you."

I scrolled down the names and addresses I'd cribbed from Fisher's notebook, double-checking best I could through my eyes watering from the smoke. The problem with finding houses in these parts, people moved up here to stay lost.

"Pretty sure the Shaw place is over that ridge," I said.

"I'm sorry I didn't tell you sooner." He patted his person, searching for a lighter.

I knew his heart was in the right place. I pulled out the old Zippo I'd pocketed, passing it along. I pointed out the windshield. "Take that left."

We cleared a cluster of witch-hobble and moosewood, curving around a boulder, steering toward the glowing patch of porch light. Didn't matter that these homes were in the middle of nowhere or that folks cherished their privacy: no one ever switched off their porch light.

"So we cool?" Charlie said.

"Yeah, we're cool."

I was hoping the Shaws were going to be receptive. I could use a little light shined. One thing I could not wrap my head around was why these parents had signed off. Nicki said incarceration at North River was a mutual decision. Courts *and* Mom and Dad. Why would parents do that to their own kids? I'd wanted to reach out to Donna Olisky again, circumvent this entire process. Except last time we'd spoken, Donna hadn't been feeling all that friendly, and I doubted she'd had a change of heart. After all, in her mind, I'd cost her family five large. Plus, I wasn't sure who'd alerted DeSouza that I'd been hanging around Longmont. Could've been Donna as easily as security guards reporting license plate numbers. Unless someone else was watching me. There was a reason that car sat parked down the block.

I knew taking on this fight again wasn't going to improve my life, not professionally, not personally. My ribs and kidneys still felt tender from last week's beating. But what could I do? I owed a debt. My dead brother deserved vengeance. I was finally close to getting that for him, so much so that I was having a tough time focusing on anything else.

That's the problem with tunnel vision: you can't appreciate peripheral danger. Until it's too late.

* * *

The Shaw homestead would've been just another unremarkable shelter in the foothills of Lamentation Mountain, secluded from the road, shrouded in secrecy, swallowed by tall winter evergreens. Except that unlike many of the old farmhouses you find out here, which were hundreds of years old and in need of major renovation, planks peeling off the frame, shingles checkering the rooftop, this home had benefited from a serious makeover.

As our headlights fanned up the driveway and the exterior, I could see the extent of repairs and expansion. A second story had recently been added, walls still unpainted plywood. An entire new home had been built atop the existing one, transforming a meager ranch into a split-level, doubling its market value. There was a new veranda, a new roof. Sandbags, paint cans, and a ladder lay on the side of the house buried beneath blue tarp.

"There goes the neighborhood," Charlie said.

"Why don't you wait here?"

Soon as I set foot in the snow, a barrel-chested man in bibbed overalls, with a bushy beard and ham hands, pushed open the front door. A frail boy, twelve or so, stood behind him in the doorway.

"You lost?" the man said.

"Sorry to bother you. Are you Ken Shaw?"

"I'm Shaw. What do you want?"

"I was hoping to speak with you about your daughter, Wendy."

Ken Shaw spat, hitching up his giddy. He stared past my shoulder, at Charlie's clunker belching fumes in the driveway. "Who are you?"

I'd pulled a business card from my wallet, deciding whether to pass it along. Given the trouble I'd suffered at the office lately, mentioning the job wasn't the smartest move, but I'd also learned that if you say anything with self-confidence and authority, people follow your lead. I figured insurance sounded less threatening than independent investigator. Especially to these libertarian mountain men up here with their inherent distrust of, well, everything.

I tried to hand him the card, but Shaw stepped from the porch, backing me down the stairs. Damn thing flew out of my hand, carried off on the wings of the night.

All trace of pleasantry gone, a sneer formed on his lips, apple cheeks blazing beneath farmer scruffiness. "What did you say about my daughter?"

"I didn't mean any disrespect, Mr. Shaw." You'd think I'd asked if his baby girl entertained sailors on the wharf. I showed my hands in surrender. I come in peace, I mean no harm. "Wendy's in the North River Institute, right?" I didn't know what response I'd been hoping for—by that point I could see Shaw wanted to throttle me, hard expression twisting harder with each passing moment—might as well get to it. My time here was almost up.

Charlie waited in the shadows. A quick engine rev cut through the howling squall, my friend's way of letting me know he had my back when I was ready to run away. Ken Shaw paid no heed, content eyeballing me with the significant height and weight advantage he enjoyed. I didn't know why the farmer pegged me for such a threat—I'd said little more than hello—but he treated my presence like a wolf sniffing around his hens.

The snow started coming down steadier, slanting with the mountain jet stream, howling through the valley. Shaw's eyes whittled mean, trap stuck between sneer and scowl.

He barked an order over his shoulder to the young boy, who retreated inside.

"I'm sorry, Mr. Shaw," I shouted into the wind. "I think we got started off on the wrong foot. I am here to help your daughter."

Ken Shaw turned around and walked up the steps to his front door. Reaching inside, he brought out a shotgun. The big man cocked his big gun.

That was all the incentive I needed.

I jumped in the car and Charlie peeled out the driveway. Looking back I could still see the madman on the porch, standing guard over the henhouse with his shotgun. On the new second floor landing, the young boy stared out a window. Our eyes remained on one another until the entire home receded into darkness.

The storm had rolled in sooner than expected, and by the time we made Charlie's place, the damage piled high, snow falling hard and heavy, at least three inches in less than an hour. Soon Ashton would ground its plows. Without tire chains and four-wheel drive, I wasn't making it back to Plasterville tonight. I had nothing to go back to anyway. I called Nicki to see how they'd made out.

"Any luck?"

"Nope."

"What are you doing now?"

"Driving around, waiting for you to call."

The sound of highway whisked by in the background. Fisher was behind the wheel.

"What now, genius?" I heard him say, voice muffled by speeding engines and racing winds.

"You guys better get off the road," I told her.

She repeated my message.

"Tell him no shit."

She put the phone to his ear, because I could hear him better.

"You at Charlie's?" he said.

"Yeah. Just got here."

"We'll see you in a few. I can't see shit in this blizzard."

Nicki got back on the line. "Guess we'll see you at Creepy Charlie's soon."

I glanced over at Charlie, who sat bloated and balding in a chair with a beer, staring at a wall without pictures, lost in deep thought.

"Yeah, sorry about that." I didn't want to throw Charlie under the bus, not with my friend sitting there. Nicki got it.

"No worries," she said. "Happens all the time." She laughed. "Maybe that's why I like you so much."

"Why's that?"

"You don't seem to notice."

"I'm not blind, Nicki. Just married. There's a difference."

Then it hit me. Jenny had told me I could see my son tomorrow. Which would soon be today, buried beneath a nor'easter with no exit off the mountain. My head was too far up my ass to hear about the blizzard—I possessed a strange, unfortunate ability to compartmentalize—but Jenny would've known about the storm. I felt a gully in my gut a mile wide when I realized my wife didn't want me anywhere near my child.

CHAPTER SEVENTEEN

NO ONE SPOKE much at Charlie's. Following fifteen coffees at the Olympic, racing to get ahead of the storm, we'd been so geared up. For what? A big crash. We had no business kicking over stones. Where was the crime, anyway? A judge who favored punishment over rehabilitation? Businessmen who liked to make money? Prime real estate used to build stuff on? If there were impropriety—if incriminating evidence existed anywhere in that hodgepodge collection of loose-leaf—none of us were qualified to lead the charge.

Fisher attempted to broach the subject at one point, outlining a plan of action, and I told him to shut the fuck up. I said it hotter than I intended. I was in a mood. Mixing whiskey and beer is never a good idea. Not that it stopped me. I knew I was losing her, could feel the pangs in my heart, ties being cut without a word, the rest of the night a blur. I kept drinking. Conversation dried up after that.

Next morning, the plows were back out, roads cleared. Nicki drove me back to my place. Final accumulation tallies fell well below doomsday predictions. A foot, tops. In other words, a typical Wednesday.

Nicki was ten years younger than the rest of us but she owned a much nicer ride. Funny, most girls I knew her age were slobs when it came to their cars. The floors of Nicki's Jetta were freshly vacuumed, cupholders wiped clean, interior sterile and unlived in, like Grandma's place with the plastic still on the furniture. Of course that meant I couldn't smoke. Nerves on edge, the ride took forever. I rested my head against the cold glass and pretended to sleep to avoid the threat of talking.

Dropping my keys on the counter, I sifted through the day's mail I'd brought in with me from the foyer. Credit card bills. Gas bills. Water bills. A flyer begging for donations with pictures of kids looking a helluva lot happier than me. I flipped the pile to the table with the rest of the crap that would now be my problem.

I switched on the TV. Just for the background noise and color. I stood at the window. No cars idled down the block. I wondered if that car from yesterday had been there to watch me at all. Could've been a husband and wife letting the engine warm before an exciting date night on the town, dinner and a movie, in bed by ten. At least the snow was pretty. For as much as I bitched about the weather up here, I couldn't imagine living in a place like Florida or California, where the sun shines all the time. I needed these quiet moments. This was the part of winter I enjoyed. The fresh snowfall, everything pristine, untainted. Give it a few hours and all this prettiness would be gone, trampled on by dirty boots, tires spitting mud, rendering white powder brown and ugly. For now, though, the world remained perfect.

My cell buzzed. Any thought my wife might have the decency to check in passed when I didn't recognize the number.

"Mr. Porter?" The voice apprehensive, small.

"Yeah, this is Jay Porter. Who's this?"

I heard a hand cupping the receiver. "This is Seth Shaw. I found your business card on our porch."

That weird little kid from last night. He sounded so timid, I felt bad even asking his name. I'd seen his old man, who I assumed beat the shit out of him.

"How can I help you, Seth?" I realized, for some reason, I was whispering too.

"It's about my sister, Wendy." The boxy connection made me picture the boy crouched in a closet. "We got a lot of money after she went away."

I walked into the kitchen and grabbed my cigarettes. "Who got money?" I couldn't find a lighter so I used the stove.

"My dad and me. To fix the house. A lot of money."

I'd seen the house. Additions like that didn't come cheap.

"How old are you, Seth?"

"Fifteen." And then before I could respond, he added, "I'm small for my age. There's a problem with my spine. I'm a regular person. I'm not stupid."

"Didn't say you were. Do you talk to your sister?"

"Not in person. Used to get letters all the time saying how awful it was inside there. Haven't gotten any letters in a while. Wendy has been in North River for a long time. You know she's not my real sister, right?"

"I don't know anything about your family, Seth, other than Wendy got in trouble for making a website."

"Her mom married my dad. Like when I was three. I've known her my whole life. My stepmom died when I was seven. My dad never liked Wendy. But she's my best friend. My sister didn't do anything wrong. She wasn't bullying anyone. She was trying to protect someone from being bullied."

I wished I could reach over the line and hug this kid; he sounded so wounded. I wanted to help his sister, too—that's why I'd gone out there in the first place. But if I suspected kickbacks and fraud, the knowledge didn't suddenly grant me superpowers to fix the mess. I lacked any smoking gun. Seth was a lot smarter than I gave him credit for.

"Mr. Porter, they pay to keep my sister locked up."

"Who pays?"

"I'm not sure. But I saw the man who brought the check to the house. I'd skipped school that day and was downstairs in the basement. My father drives trucks. He's out of work. He didn't know I was home. A man came to our door. I climbed on the couch and could see them on the porch through the cellar slots. I saw the man give Dad a bag. Heard him say, 'Good luck with the repairs.'"

"When was this?"

"Like eight months ago? Contractors started showing up right after that. I asked my dad how we could afford all the repairs. We'd barely been able to keep the bank away since my stepmom died. My father said he'd applied for a government program that helps people like us who don't have a lot of money get their houses fixed. You didn't see our house before, Mr. Porter. It was falling apart."

"Do you know when he applied for the program?"

"My dad said before he met Linda. That was my stepmom's name."

"So, over ten years ago?"

"Yeah."

"But you see didn't a penny until they locked Wendy up? You don't know the name of the man who brought the money? Maybe you found his business card lying in the snow, too?"

"He didn't drop a card. He was driving a construction truck."

"Didn't say 'Lombardi' on the side, by any chance?"

"No. Began with a 'T.' Red letters."

"Did you see anything else?"

"No. Just the logo on the side of the truck as he was pulling out."

"Okay, Seth," I said, "Thanks for calling. I'll do what I can—"

"Oh, and the driver had a tattoo. On his neck."

"A tattoo? On his neck? Thought you said you didn't see anything else?"

"It was a pretty big tattoo."

"You remember what kind of tattoo?"

"One of those Jewish stars."

*   *   *

Charlie wasn't picking up, and the number I had for Fisher was out of service. Which showed how often I talked to the guy. I called Nicki. Got her voice mail. I was anxious to share the news. Even if I wasn't sure what the news meant.

I remembered that first day driving around looking for the Olisky house, taking a wrong turn and stumbling across the abandoned construction site with old Lombardi equipment rusting in ditches. That's where I'd seen the name before. On the guard shack on the way out. Tomassi. Red lettering and logo. At the time, I'd assumed vendor, on-site management, security of some sort. A quick Google search yielded Tomassi as the largest construction outfit in Massachusetts, one of New England's oldest. Big fish gobbled up smaller fish all the time. This had to be the construction truck Seth saw. The more distressing factor was the Star of David neck tattoo, which could only belong to one man: Erik Bowman, Adam Lombardi's old head of security, with whom I'd had a run-in last year when he broke into my place searching for the hard drive my brother had stolen. Made sense a guy like Bowman would land another job in the same field. Except Bowman was no ordinary security guard. He was a former motorcycle gangbanger who beat, intimidated, and murdered, a thug with no conscience. In addition to knocking me out cold, I was pretty sure he'd killed my brother's junkie pal, Pete. Not that

I could prove it. Now he was delivering hush money to keep a girl locked up in North River? Which made sense if he were still working for Adam. But he wasn't.

My cell vibrated. I took the call without a glance, expecting Nicki or Charlie, still buzzing over the implications of Bowman's involvement.

"Are you okay?" my wife asked. "You sound out of breath."

I didn't bother with the truth, that my lungs were working overtime funding a two-pack-a-day habit. "Running to catch the phone," I lied.

"You picked up on the first ring."

"Must be a delay on your end." I knew how stupid that sounded.

"Yeah," she said, either not buying my excuse or not caring. "I didn't know if you were still planning on coming up to see Aiden today?"

When she mentioned my son, I remembered her offer coming on the eve of a nor'easter. "Thanks for the invite, by the way. Great time to plan a trip. Last night was supposed to be the storm of the decade."

"I forgot you were getting slammed down there. I heard it was a false alarm though, no?"

"You forgot?"

"Yeah, Jay. I forgot. Same as you did, apparently."

"They close the mountain roads out of Ashton, you know that."

"Except you don't live in Ashton anymore."

"I was there last night."

"How am I supposed to know that?"

"Or maybe you didn't want me coming up to see Aiden in the first place."

"I'm over two hours away. The storm wasn't going to hit us up here."

"So, what? Now Burlington's your hometown?"

"Think whatever you'd like," my wife said. "Are you coming to see your son today or not? I need to know so I can plan my day—"

"It's wonderful you're trying to fit my relationship with our child into 'your day.'"

"You said you wanted to see Aiden. I'm trying to set that up. You were complaining yesterday that I was keeping him from you."

"You are! By being three hours away in fucking Burlington."

"Okay, Jay, I'm hanging up now. Call me when you are ready to see Aiden."

"When I'm ready?"

"Yes. When you are ready to see your son, call me."

"I'm *ready* now. But I can't control the fucking sky. If my son was home, like he should be, I could see him now!"

"Are you sure about that?"

"What's that supposed to mean?"

"Even if we were there, you'd be getting drunk in the garage with your scrapbook, brooding over your dead brother, which is how you spend all your free time. Ignoring me. Ignoring Aiden. Chasing ghosts."

"That's a rotten thing to say."

"Sorry," Jenny said, "you're right. Call me later. After the storm's cleared. We'll set something up."

"It's already passed. The worst of it is out to sea."

Jenny groaned. I could hear the frustration. I didn't blame her. I was sick of dealing with me.

My wife took a deep breath. "Let's start again. Would you like to see your son today?"

"Yes."

"What time is good for you?"

"What time is good for you?"

"What time is it now?"

"Like ten thirty. I think."

"I have a few errands to run," Jenny said. "Why don't you plan on getting here later in the afternoon. You can take Aiden to dinner. Spend a few hours together."

We hung up without saying goodbye.

CHAPTER EIGHTEEN

I COULD TAKE Aiden to dinner. Me. Alone. We weren't a family anymore. I'd pick up my son at the door and return him two hours later. I was grateful for the one-on-one time with my boy but couldn't ignore the implications. The prearranged visit felt like a court order granted to a fuck-up father. How did we end up here?

At the computer, I surfed the net for news on the Senate bill, the one designed to loosen regulations regarding privatization. I scoured the *Monitor* and *Herald* archives as well as New Hampshire's official state page—even listened to a podcast—all relevant info hiding in plain sight.

When Lombardi Construction leveled the TC Truck Stop and Maple Motor Inn last year, the plan was to build a new resort, the town looking to cash in on the ski craze up here. Or maybe I had been too quick to assume, inferring without due diligence. Words like "diversion program" and "juvenile prison" hadn't been on my radar, and now that they were, I saw them everywhere I looked. A necessary weapon in the fight against youth crime and teenage drug addiction, the need for privatization spelled out clear as the northern lights.

But why would Lombardi sell the rights to build the damn thing? Tomassi was linked to the construction of the new detention facility, tentatively dubbed the uninspiring Coos County

Center. You had to figure they'd come up with something sexier before the grand opening. The amount of money bandied about was staggering, and hard to comprehend. Eighty-million-dollar budgets, another twelve slotted for requisitions, six more for advertising, few hundred thousand here, couple mil there. According to the experts, the bill's passing was a formality, with the potential revenue projected to be in the billions. Ski resort. Juvenile prison. What did it matter? That much money only begets more of it.

Dinner in Burlington left me with a few hours to kill, and I wasn't going to spend them stewing in that house, scrounging around electronically, zooming in and out of satellite images, taking virtual walks in the dark. I set out to visit the old truck stop. I didn't know what I expected to find. Contact info for Bowman would be nice. Fat chance they stored that information in a trailer. I had no intention of hopping a fence like a lunatic, rooting around a private construction site to find out. But I needed something tactile, tangible to make this feel real again.

Ringing Charlie from the road, my call went straight to voice mail. I left a long-winded, rambling message about the Shaw boy and Bowman, my theory about Tomassi being another Lombardi subsidiary, or at least a link in the chain, friends with financial benefits, whatever, because no way Adam sells off a piece of the pie that big without securing a slice for himself, even if I wasn't sure how any of that constituted a law being broken. Lombardi had been awarded the contract to build the ski resort. Why would it matter if they also built the prison? Unless fostering the need, proposing the bill, winning the contract, and then also anointing yourself king of it all smacked of such overkill, even a bunch of greedy fucks like the Lombardis had to cut some bait. Something sure as hell was up. No way this planet contained two Bowmans.

Coming around the mountain, I sped up the Desmond Turnpike, all its degenerate glory on full display.

College papers and advocacy rags often ran features on the Turnpike. The place had become an infamous institution, like Route 66, only less scenic and with more blow jobs and overdoses. No one pulled off the shoulder and snapped pictures of speed freaks going duckpin bowling. This was a stretch of road where you kept your eyes locked straight ahead, got to where you were going, which was anywhere but here. People didn't remain on the Turnpike. Not by choice, anyway. After Chris died, I saw this world in a different light.

I'd read an op-ed a while back, a rant from a landlord, bitching about freeloaders. His prospective tenant, some woman who "couldn't speak a lick of English," wanted to rent one of his shit rooms, and she'd had the nerve to apply using Section 8 housing vouchers. The landlord had done the math. Adding up the Section 8, the free medical care and SSI, the extra kids popped out to beef up payout, food stamps, incidentals, he had determined that everyone on this Turnpike was earning over one hundred thousand dollars a year, parasites sucking off the tit of hard-working Americans.

I watched these welfare hobos, disheveled men and wispy women, hats in hand, shuffling along the side of the road, fistfuls of change to redeem at Taco Bell, because if they could make food any cheaper Lord knows they would, and wondered where they stashed the rest of that hundred grand. They could sure use some of it about now.

The old truck stop grounds clipped the northern edge of town. A chain-link fence, ten feet high, wrapped around the expansive property, protecting valuable construction equipment from scavengers. All the familiar landmarks had been obliterated. The restaurant, filling station, motel, showers, gone; in their place, the new machinations that would house New England's most dangerous teenage threats. Where the old Peachtree restaurant used to stand, steel beams now outlined what would become a laundry room or kitchen, solitary confinement where they'd stick the worst offenders. Where the police had dragged Pete Naginis' bloated body from the wastewater run-off, a giant billboard staked claim to brighter futures. White slate, red font. I tried to picture what the complex would look like when they finished building it. Right now, the scope was sprawling but shapeless.

No one walked snow-covered grounds. Which wasn't a surprise. I didn't imagine I'd find Bowman waiting for me. Construction up here halted during the winter months, and this project was on hiatus anyway. As blowing snow swirled at my feet, I let my eyes rove over the site, the loaders and drills and concrete, and I realized what I'd been searching for.

During the last few years of my brother's life, this demolished truck stop was Chris' base of operations. It was where he'd trade drugs, sell his body, pawn whatever he had left of value, anything for a fix. My old apartment was midtown, meaning Chris had to pass by my place to get here. Most nights he didn't stop in to say hi. The few times he did, he knew better than to ask for money, especially at the end. We could go months without seeing one another. So he'd end up here, doing what he had to. Thinking of my brother sucking off a trucker for twenty bucks killed me. I wasn't rich, but I always had twenty bucks. Who doesn't? Like Dr. Shapiro-Weiss and countless other substance abuse professionals had told me, I knew giving money to a junkie was enabling a habit. I also knew twenty dollars spared a little humiliation, might've let him know that his baby brother still gave a shit about him. At least for one night. And now that he was gone, I'd give anything to have him know that.

Charlie's rust bucket pulled behind my truck. He and Fisher climbed out, Fisher looking riled up, pissed off. Charlie walked toward me, but Fisher remained rooted, skulking in the background.

"Where's your coat, Jay?" Charlie kept his distance, like I were a rabid raccoon in his kitchen.

I stabbed a finger through the fence, in the general direction of steel and rivet. I wanted to say something meaningful. The words didn't come.

"Yeah," Charlie said. "It's a construction site. I can see that. What was up with your message? You sounded—are you okay, man?"

Fisher glowered at me, arms crossed, trying to act tough.

"What's his problem?" I asked.

Charlie seemed surprised by the question.

"Fuck you, Porter," Fisher snapped. "If it was up to me, you could freeze your ass off out here!"

I threw up my hands.

"Last night?" Charlie said.

"What about it? Sorry it didn't pan out." I said that last part to Fisher. Then to Charlie, "But Seth Shaw? The sick kid we saw at the house—"

"C'mon, Charlie!" Fisher shouted. "I told you coming out here was a waste of time."

I moved past Charlie, who protested with a feeble arm as Fisher charged forward.

"What is your problem, man?"

"I came up to Ashton to help *you*," Fisher said. "Drove all the way up from Concord to try and help *you*."

"And I appreciate it. You need me to throw you a parade? What the fuck?"

Charlie wedged between us, Fisher grabbing for my coat, trying to shove me. He looked ready to take a swing. Total joke. Little shit was half my size. I never liked him anyway.

All I could do was turn to Charlie. "What is he talking about?"

"My house? After we got back to wait out the storm?"

"What about it?"

Fisher reached around Charlie, who pushed his friend back. Fisher held up his hands like he didn't want any trouble. Then he thrust both fists at me, middle fingers extended, jamming them right under my nose.

Charlie shoved him away. "Go wait in the car."

"Eat shit, Porter," Fisher said turning his back to me.

Charlie walked me off toward the site.

"What is going on?"

"You really don't remember, do you?"

"Remember what?"

"Fuck. Last night, you were pounding whiskey and beer. You polished off the Maker's. I tried to get you to ease up, but you were on a pisser. Fisher and Nicki were . . . getting cozy . . . in a corner."

"Bullshit. Nicki wouldn't go for Fisher." The thought of a girl like her making it with a cretin like him was laughable.

"Yeah. That's pretty much what you said when you called Fisher a 'big-eared ugly mutherfucker.'"

"I said that?"

"And a lot more. You were vicious."

Charlie went on to detail my abuse, word for word, which I vaguely recalled the more he talked about it. I got fleeting images of Fisher hitting on Nicki and me getting jealous, if that's even the right word. I'd started out busting balls, mildly funny ribbing growing increasingly meaner with each swallow of whiskey. By the end, according to Charlie, I had Fisher near tears. No wonder no one talked to me in the morning.

"Shit," I muttered, moving past Charlie, who told me not to bother right now, let Fisher cool off.

"Hey, man," I called out to Fisher. "I'm sorry. I was drunk."

"Fuck you!"

"Jesus, I said I'm sorry." I walked toward him, feeling the need to explain. I hated acting like a dick. "It's been a bad couple weeks, man. Jenny and I are having trouble. Work's been a nightmare. This shit with Chris—"

"Shit with Chris? Your brother is dead, asshole."

"I am aware of that."

"You're not aware of anything, besides your own little world. You're a selfish prick. Always have been. Self-centered and mean. You think you shit chocolate, like you're better than everyone else. Which is probably why your wife left you."

"You know what, Fisher? I take it back. You are a big-eared ugly mutherfucker."

The little bastard sprang at me, an ornery honey badger attacking from its burrow, claws out, aiming to draw blood. Charlie threw himself between us, Fisher gouging air. He caught me with one of his ragged nails. I smeared blood off my cheek.

"You're nuts!"

"I'm nuts?" Fisher said, pretending to laugh. "That's a good one, Porter. I'm not the jackass running around in the freezing cold without a coat, making up stories about boogeymen."

"Okay, Fisher. Twelve hours ago, we had a conspiracy. Now we have nothing."

"I never used the word conspiracy. That's your paranoid horseshit. I told you UpStart's push for a private prison is connected to North River. That's all. I was doing you a favor. Charlie played me your crazy voice mail. Put it on speaker so we could both laugh at you."

I knew Fisher was doing his best to pay back the insults from last night, cut me where the blade would do the most damage. But Charlie would never betray me like that. I tried to stay on track, take the high road.

"Listen to me. Tomassi is paying—"

"Lombardi sold his company to Tomassi," Fisher said. "I explained that to you last night."

"I'm telling you. Bowman paid off—"

"Bowman, Bowman, Bowman," Fisher repeated the name like I'd said I'd seen a chupacabra or jackalope. "Tomassi is one of the oldest construction outfits in New England. They gobble up smaller companies all the time."

"Then why is Bowman delivering hush money?" I appealed to Charlie, who I could see wanted no part of this. "Tell him about that juiced fuck who broke into my apartment and knocked me out cold last year. The tattoo on his neck. How he works for Lombardi. Tell him about the motorcycle gang—"

"Motorcycle gang," Fisher scoffed.

Charlie didn't say anything.

"You were all gung ho last night."

"Yeah?" Fisher said. "Well now I'm not."

"Listen, man, forget last night. I'm telling you—"

"No, I'm telling *you*. I don't want to hear it. I thought we were friends. But friends don't do each other like that."

"Friends don't do each other like that," I singsonged. "What is this? High school?"

"Might as well be," Fisher said. "You were an asshole then, too." He tugged Charlie's sleeve. "Come on, man, let's go."

Charlie looked torn, stuck between two friends.

"Fine," Fisher said, "I'll walk."

"No, hold on." Charlie turned to me. "Sorry, Jay. Call me later."

He looked at my truck, ramped halfway up a snow bank. "Go home. Okay? Get some sleep. You're scaring me, man. You're not right."

I watched my friend walk away, leaving me in the cold.

The swirling winds of the valley kicked up ice, flinging tiny daggers back in my face, stinging my skin raw, fury enveloping me.

I waited until they drove off.

Then I ran straight ahead and leapt, scaling the chain-link fence.

CHAPTER NINETEEN

I WASN'T INSIDE the construction zone five minutes before I saw the sheriff's car pull up.

Back at the station, Rob Turley brought me to an interrogation room. He draped a coat over my shoulder, setting down a mug of hot coffee, brewed fresh from the break room dispenser. I'd been out there in nothing but a tee shirt, my teeth chattering with bone-rattling shivers.

Turley and I had never been close back in high school, but we spent a lot of time together last winter looking for my brother. Still didn't like him much. He seemed a lot older now, more grown up, carrying the responsibility of being lawman for a town of three thousand. The other night when Turley picked up Charlie and me wrestling outside the Dubliner, I had been wasted. Given the hour—after midnight, northern skies blunted, the moment blurred in a drunken haze—I'd tried to forget about how embarrassed I'd been having Rob Turley, of all people, find me in that state. Now, under fluorescent precinct lights, I couldn't hide. I watched his terse expression morph into genuine concern, and I wanted to punch the patronizing fuck.

Turley nudged the coffee forward, like I was a meek, battered housewife who needed to be coaxed into giving a statement.

He hadn't cuffed me or read me my rights. I wasn't under arrest. Still, I resented the power play.

After a prolonged silence, I locked eyes with him, flexing my shoulders with a "what the hell?" shrug. He didn't need to bring me down here. I hadn't broken any laws. How did he even know I was there? Did Fisher rat me out?

"You tripped the alarm," Turley said, as if hearing my thoughts. He pointed through the wall. "Security system runs straight to the police station switchboard. Tomassi's got about a million dollars' worth of equipment at the site. Can't let some enterprising criminal back up a U-Haul and cart off a Bobcat, y'know?"

"I'm not a thief."

"No one said you were."

"I wasn't trying to steal anything."

"What were you doing there, Jay?"

The question, straightforward and obvious, was one any cop would ask. I didn't have an answer. I couldn't explain how the voice inside my brain screamed, "Go!" How I'd had to obey. My plan to break into a trailer and rifle through employee records, bat-shit crazy.

"Am I under arrest?"

"You were trespassing."

"That's not what I asked."

"No, you're not under arrest."

I stood up.

Turley motioned for me to sit. My threat, like the one I'd leveled at the Olympic last night, purely for show. The Ashton Police Department was a long haul from truck stop grounds.

"How are you doing?" Turley asked.

"How am I doing?"

"Yes. How have you been?"

"What do you mean? Like personally? What do you care?" Like we were two old pals meeting for coffee.

Turley's roly-poly face pinched up.

"You got something to say, man, say it." My actions may have rung irrational, hopping a fence into a restricted area a dumb move, but I wasn't playing heartfelt feels with Rob Fucking Turley.

"People talk."

"I need to get to my truck," I said. "Can you, or one of your deputies, officers, subordinates, whatever the fuck you call them, give me a ride to get it?"

"Yes," Turley said. "Someone will give you a ride to get your truck. When you answer my questions."

"Answer your questions? So you're holding me hostage?"

"No one is being held." He pointed at the door, calling my bluff. "You are free to leave anytime. I'm sure you know the way to the truck stop. Long walk. Need to use the phone for a taxi? No problem. Might be able to get a cab to show up in about four hours. Want to try Finn? Have at it. But you want *my* help getting your truck, yes, you need to answer some questions."

"I'm only here because *you* drove me here."

"Yeah. I did. After you were caught trespassing. On private property. Stop playing the victim."

"I hopped a fence. Big deal. I didn't touch anything. You stop playing ball-busting heavy. I know what you are."

"And I know what you are, Jay."

"Yeah? And what am I?"

"A Porter." He let that sink in. "I seem to recall your brother breaking into a construction site last year, and me having to deal with the same bullshit. I've sat in this same seat and had your brother run that same smart-ass mouth. I sit here, I take it. I fake a smile because I am a nice guy. I've known you our whole lives. You think I'm a clown, don't respect this office or job. No problem. I understand sometimes people are sick and make mistakes because they don't know better. But I have better things to do than bail another one of the Porter boys out of another mess."

I stood to leave. I didn't care if I had to walk five miles in the ice and cold. This mouthbreather didn't know me. I made for the door. Turley stood to block my path. On reflex, I jabbed a quick right. Not a real punch. More a shove for him to move out of my way. Didn't hit square, more a glancing blow off his fat chin. In some tricky cop move they must teach at the academy, Turley let my motion carry me past, catching my arm. Planting an elbow in my back as he threw me into the table. He pressed me in place, twisting my shoulder behind my back. Huffing and out of breath, he pulled the handcuffs from his belt but didn't slap them on.

"Have you lost your mind? Assaulting a police officer? What is wrong with you?"

"Let me go!"

"You know how long I can lock you up for that?"

"Do it then! But let my arm go. You're hurting me!" Turley had my arm so wrenched, felt like the thing was about to snap off, tendons stretching past breaking points.

He snapped the cuffs back on his belt and let go of my arm.

"Sit," he said.

I rotated my arm, wincing.

"I'm trying to help you," Turley said.

"I don't want your help."

"You are acting crazy."

"I'm sick of people saying that."

"I'm gonna tell you something, Jay—and I know you ain't gonna want to hear this right now—but I dealt with your brother a lot over the years. I got stuck plenty listening to his rambling junkie non-sense. But I could still communicate with him. Could still carry on a conversation, get an answer at least, however wacky. You—you're—"

"What?"

"Everyone around here knows you ain't been the same since Chris died."

"Nice to know I'm still the talk of the town."

"Okay, we're all nuts. You're the only one who sees what's really going on. Let's go with that. So tell me, Jay. What's happening?"

"Don't play me like I'm some paranoid schizo you have to placate."

"No one is placating anyone," Turley said, calm as my therapist used to be when she'd ask me to explain about the contract killer sent to bury my brother in the ice. "Just want to hear it. In your own words."

I tried to explain. I started in the middle, and then traced back to the beginning, before I flashed forward, flashed back—I think I even flashed sideways at one point. I threw out everything I had. The thoughts coalesced in my head, but by the time the words escaped my mouth, logic had jumbled, timeframes eroded, and nothing made sense.

The entire time I talked about Judge Roberts, Brian Olisky, Andy DeSouza, Fisher's girlfriend from high school, Gina, who I'd hooked up with—while Jenny and I were on a break—Turley nodded with compassion, sipping his own coffee, reserving commentary. He let me spew about the Lombardis, Gerry, his sons, Adam and Michael, Tomassi, the teenagers locked up in North River; the police who kicked my asshole up into my guts; Wendy, Seth, and Ken Shaw, reparation in exchange for incarceration; Nicki and the guilt I felt over nothing I'd done; Jenny and some soft-handed douchebag named Stephen; and lastly, my son, Aiden, who would surely grow up to hate his father because, after all this time, I still couldn't get it right. I talked about drinking more than I should; about an ex-biker named Erik Bowman, a boogeyman who should exist only in meth-fueled nightmares but who had somehow crossed netherworlds into my waking, walking consciousness.

And the entire time, fifteen, twenty minutes of nonstop blathering, alternating between gesticulating wildly with rapid speech patterns and flailing arms, and then slamming brakes to catch my breath—calm, cool, collected—intense deceleration making me sound even more unstable, Turley's expression never changed. I talked. He sat and listened.

Until, coffee gone, guts purged, we sat in silence. Of course he had no response to any of that. Hearing myself say these things aloud, jumbled, erratic, incoherent, I knew how preposterous I came across, how dangerous I sounded.

I'd learned a great deal from dealing with my junkie brother over the years. But no lesson greater than this: when authorities deem you a danger to yourself or others, they can—and will—lock you up. I needed to spin some serious damage control if I wanted to avoid a seventy-two-hour, court-mandated IEA in the local nut ward.

"Wow, Turley," I said, manufacturing a smile. "Thank you."

"Thank . . . me?"

"I didn't realize how much I had bottled up. I think I just needed to get it out. You know I have a therapist now."

"A therapist?"

"Yeah. Dr. Shapiro-Weiss. Over in Longmont. She prescribed me some anti-anxiety medication. I have the pills at home."

"Jay, I'm not sure you should be getting behind the wheel—"

"You can call her. It's . . . these outbursts are panic attacks."

"Panic attacks?"

"That's what happened, I think. Why I jumped the fence. Because of my brother. The pressure. All that shit I just said."

"That was a . . . panic attack?"

"Yeah. Crazy, huh? Sorry about, y'know, pushing you."

"You took a swing at me, Jay."

"Panic attack," I said.

Turley studied me a moment, before pushing himself up. "Wait here."

He came back ten minutes later, and said he'd give me a ride back to my truck.

I didn't know if he'd called my psychiatrist and she'd backed my play or what. I assumed so, because he wasn't recommending I be committed. And I couldn't think of any reason on God's green earth why he should let me walk out of that station after I'd just tried to slug a cop.

CHAPTER TWENTY

BY THE TIME I got back to my truck, there was no way I'd make Burlington by dinnertime. I had no choice but to call Jenny and reschedule.

At first she was very accommodating.

"No, I understand, Jay," she said. "These things happen."

I hadn't even offered an explanation.

"Is he there? Can I talk to him?"

"Of course. Hold on." I heard her say, "It's your Daddy." And then rustling on the other end as my son dropped whatever toy he'd been playing with to talk to me. Feels good as a dad when you win out over a piece of plastic.

"Hi, Daddy," Aiden said.

"I'm sorry, buddy. I wanted to come up and see you today. But I had to . . . work. We'll do it tomorrow, okay? Just me and you. Something real special. Like pizza."

"Daddy?"

"Yeah?"

"I'm eating pizza now."

"You are? Is it super tasty or regular tasty?" The two markers by which my son judged all cuisine.

"*Super* tasty."

"Pepperoni?"

"No," my son said. "Seeven doesn't eat peppewoni. He's a wedgatarian."

I heard the phone ripped from my son's hand.

"Okay," Jenny said. "Let me know when you want to come up. We'll talk soon."

"Where are you?"

"We're having a late lunch."

"Who's we?"

"Don't, Jay." My wife's voice hushed to a stern whisper.

"Who are you with?"

"I told you, he's just a friend. I'm allowed to have friends."

"Yeah, Jenny. We all need friends."

* * *

I was filling up the tank at the Qwik Stop when she returned my call.

"Where have you been?" I asked.

"Um, sleeping," Nicki said. "We were up half the night. When I dropped you off, I was a zombie. Surprised I didn't crash into a tree."

I jammed the nozzle in the hole. "Well, you're awake now."

"Yeah. Thanks to you. What's up?"

"I was thinking. We should check out some other names on that list. Find some kids who graduated the program. Other parents. The names we got from Fisher at the diner." I explained about Seth Shaw's call and Erik Bowman dropping off the bag of cash.

"What do you think it means?"

"My guess? The parents who don't initially sign off on North River receive an extra incentive. It's an investment."

"By whom?"

"Lombardi. The more kids get locked up in North River, the

greater the demand for a private facility. That's what you said, right? Roberts is a patsy. We need to tie these bribes back to Lombardi." I told her about my morning poking around the Internet, how the juvie would house all of New England's least desirable. "A prison like that would rake in a fortune." I left out the crazier parts about my afternoon—the Tomassi construction site, Fisher's wrath, my assault of a cop. "And private is nothing but profit."

"So, you want some company while you go knocking door to door?"

"Something like that."

Nicki met me at my place. We spent the next several hours driving around northern New Hampshire in my truck, visiting houses on both sides of the mountain. Most, like the Shaws, were in the middle of major renovations. Hardly anyone was home to answer questions. The few times they were, nobody itched to talk. One couple told us to fuck off; another that it was none of our business, they didn't appreciate being told how to parent, and then they told us to fuck off.

Clouds hung heavy as night started to fall, evening as bruised as an eggplant in the bargain bin.

"What next?" Nicki asked, as we pulled out of yet another rural driveway. "This isn't getting us anywhere. Want to check out North River? Maybe someone would be willing to talk to us. Let us tour the facility. We could say we're interested in sending our child there."

"I doubt it. You don't look quite old enough to have a teenager."

"Good point," Nicki said. "You could say you're my dad." She smirked.

"Very funny. But we wouldn't get far. I was up there the other night. They aren't looking to roll out any red carpets."

"Okay," Nicki said, brushing the black hair out of her eyes, making sure to catch mine. "I'm up for anything."

I pointed at the glove compartment. "Pull the map out of there."

Nicki held up her phone. "Ever hear of GPS?"

"Not where we're going."

"Which is?"

"Look for Saint Thomas Place, Libby Brook."

Took me a while to find the two silos and broken-down plow in the brooding countryside night. I parked next to the sparkling SUV with restored steering column and new coat of paint shimmering in the porch light. Nicki followed me up the steps to the front door. The house was a different color. Canary yellow. A happy, inviting hue.

Donna Olisky didn't greet me as warmly this time. Like her son had the other day, she tried to shut the door in my face, but I pushed back. I think Nicki was shocked that I barged inside like I did. But, fuck it, I knew there was no one else home.

"Get out of my house!" Donna screamed.

"Or what?" I said.

Donna made for her landline. I cut her off, yanking the cradle and ripping the cord out of the wall. I didn't mean to pull it so hard.

Donna Olisky gasped. So did Nicki. I knew I was coming on too strong, but I was tired of getting dicked around.

"Sorry." I pulled my wallet. I'd withdrawn cash at the gas station, planning on buying Nicki dinner first. I didn't want to explain the credit card charges to my wife. I placed forty bucks on the table. "That should fix that. Now, I want some answers, Mrs. Olisky."

"About what?"

Out the corner of my eye, I saw the shrine to her dead son. I turned my shoulder to block the view. I needed to stay focused on the task at hand.

"I see your SUV got fixed."

"What concern is that of yours? Your company declined my policy—a policy that I paid thousands into over the years, so that when I needed it, I could make a claim. But *you* rejected that claim, Mr. Porter."

"Yeah. Insurance sucks. They like to take your money. Don't like to pay it out. But I don't make the laws."

"No. You just break them, busting into homes uninvited."

"How did you get the money to fix the SUV?" I pointed outside. "The house has a new paint job, too." I glanced around the interior. Holes spackled over, new wallpaper. The grandfather clock's pendulum swung with renewed vigor.

"Not that it is any of your business, but I applied for government assistance with home repairs. The state has programs to help people like me."

"Like you?"

"Single parent homeowners, yes. You can look it up. There are a variety of state-assistance options and programs available. I was approved."

"When?"

"Why do you care?"

"Because your son was sent to North River. And then you get money. I find the timing strange."

Donna took leave and went to a drawer, where she extracted a piece of paper, returning to shove it in my face. The official seal of New Hampshire, stamped and signed. Formal approval of the HUD request and a receipt for a ten-thousand-dollar check.

"Satisfied?" she asked.

I studied the amount. "When did you apply for this program?"

"When my husband left last year. What's it to you?"

"And the money shows up after Brian goes to North River?

After you agree to Judge Roberts' recommendation that he be sent there?"

"Brian was caught with drugs—"

"Pot."

"Drugs!" Donna started sobbing, pointing at the shrine. "I watched one boy die because of drugs. I wasn't standing by and losing another!"

"So someone called and said if you signed off on North River you'd get the money?"

"Get out of my house!"

Nicki tugged at my sleeve. "Jay, I think we should go."

Donna Olisky kept sobbing, shoulders heaving, pouring on the histrionics.

"Answer me! Did someone tell you this request would get approved if you agreed to North River? Yes. Or no."

"My son needs help!"

"Answer me! Was that the deal?"

"Yes! Someone from the State called and said to go along with the recommendation for a diversion program. I didn't do anything wrong! I love my son! He needs help! I am not losing another boy!" Donna Olisky dropped into a chair, cradling her head in her hands, weeping.

Maybe she hadn't been acting. I reached out to soothe her. Nicki caught my hand before I could do any more damage, pulling me away, toward the door, which was the right move, even if it meant leaving behind a mother brokenhearted and bawling and me feeling like a bully.

Back on the road, I checked my rearview, waiting for the cops Donna Olisky surely called once she found a working phone. There had to be another in the house, or enough spotty cell reception to report a home invasion, if someone wanted to get creative. No lights ever appeared. A mother too grief-stricken? Or too guilt-ridden? Relieved, I still felt like an asshole, and, worse, I didn't care. If you're going to be the bad guy, might as well embrace it. Go big or go home.

I didn't ask Nicki inside when we got back to my house. She just followed me in. That was the reason I'd taken her along tonight. She knew it. We both did.

I went through the pretense of asking if she wanted a beer, and cracked the last pair.

Being at my house wasn't the smoothest move or smartest bet. Nicki's place made more sense. But her car was here, and if they were coming for me, they were coming for me. What could I do about it?

"You want to talk about what happened back there?" Nicki asked.

"Not really. More of what we already knew. Someone—I'm wagering Lombardi—is greasing the skids, bribing parents to sign off on these diversion programs, cooking books, running up the numbers. Maybe they push an assistance claim through. Fast-track HUD. Drop off an envelope stuffed with cash when that isn't enough. Sure as fuck have Judge Roberts in their pocket. Most of these parents are so hyped up over the drug hysteria up here, they don't need much convincing. Roberts gets his piece. The Lombardi brothers get their way. That new prison gets built, and the rich get richer."

"I mean . . ."

I put my beer down and stepped into her. She stopped talking when I pulled her to my hips and kissed her, lips soft like warm vanilla sugar. She fumbled to set her beer on the table, but the bottom clipped the edge, toppling over, suds spilling onto the floor. She reached up for my face, kissing me back violently. Twirling around, our faces still mashed together, she tried to steer us toward the bedroom, but I redirected us to the couch in the living room. We fell down together, me on top, her tongue in my mouth, breath growing hotter, groins grinding as she lifted her ass off the cushion, friction pressed hard against my jeans. I didn't bother with unbuttoning, just jammed my hand down the front of her pants, sliding over the smooth, tight belly. Over the silky panties, already damp with anticipation, I wrapped a finger around the elastic, slipping slick inside her, probing as she ground her hips and moaned, bucking. Nicki let go of my face and unbuttoned her own jeans, tugging them down, allowing me better access, ass rising, pushing my fingers deeper.

She felt for my belt, unfastening the buckle, slipping a cool hand over my hard cock.

"Fuck me, Jay," she hushed in my ear. "I want you inside me."

"Stop."

"What?"

"I said stop." I pushed off her and stood up, trying to stuff myself away.

Nicki lay on the couch, jeans tugged halfway down her thighs, panties peeled off her ass, legs parted, willing and aching, staring up at me. Her expression caught between shell-shocked and wounded, she didn't bother to cover herself up.

"What the hell?"

"I'm sorry," I said. "I can't."

Nicki's eyes locked on my dick, which wasn't going along with the change of plans.

"I'm pretty sure you can."

I left her half naked, and walked into the kitchen.

I guzzled my beer, keeping my back turned.

A few moments later, I felt Nicki glide up behind me, slipping arms around my waist, cooing in my ear. "What's going on?"

I tried to pull away.

"We both want this, Jay," she said, rubbing her hands over my abs, back down my pants. "We're not doing anything wrong."

I jerked her hand away, holding up the back of my hand and the wedding band.

"Yeah. You're married. I know that." Nicki panned around my empty home. "Where is she, huh? She moved out a week ago."

"She didn't move out. We're taking time apart. That doesn't mean I can have sex with other women."

"No, just make out with and fingerbang them? Get a handy?"

"Stop. Please."

"That's why you called me today. You didn't need me to run errands with you. You wanted to fuck me. I want to fuck you. What's the problem?"

"You're the one who got this shit started. Because you cared so much about what was happening with Roberts and his bullshit sentences—"

"I still *do* care." Nicki stepped around to face me. She hadn't bothered to button her jeans all the way and I could see the top of the pink panties, low cut to reveal bare pelvic bone. "Doesn't mean we can't be together."

She reached out to touch my face. I caught her by the wrists.

"You have to go," I said.

She didn't listen, letting me bind her as she moved in to kiss me again. It felt so good to be wanted like that, and Christ knows I didn't have much to feel good about lately.

I turned away, and could feel the heat of her stare intensify, desire and passion giving way to stronger emotions like anger and hate, until she surrendered.

"Fine. Have it your way, Jay."

I let her wrists go. She buttoned up, grabbed her coat, bag, and keys. Didn't say anything else as she walked out the door, taking with her the last ally I had in my make-believe war.

I tried to get some work done, take my mind off sex. Which meant beer and chain-smoking cigarettes, poking around the Internet, scanning the State's webpage again, its HUD program and assorted social services. But it's pretty hard to concentrate with blue balls. My eyes glassed over the mind-numbing details—contact info for Manchester, application forms, vouchers, home equity conversion. I logged off. This is what I had turned down getting laid for.

Don't be crazy, little brother. You've never been the kind of guy to sleep around. That was never your game. Oh, shut the fuck up.

Out of beer and smokes, I grabbed my truck keys and was halfway out the door when the landline behind me rang. No one ever called with good news. No one ever called with answers. Every single phone call I'd received over the past week had been crammed with lousy news, bad results, and the promise of worse returns.

I jammed my keys in my pocket. I didn't recognize the caller on the ID. Who cared? Telemarketers be damned, I picked up anyway.

"Do not go outside," relayed a man's voice, cool, reserved.

"Who is this?"

"Go to your front window. Look down the block. See that car?"

Phone in hand, I walked to the window. I'd turned off my lights on the way out. I didn't turn them back on. I peeked through the shutters. A car idled down the street. Same car as the other day. I could see the shadows of two people sitting inside but little else. I let the blinds fall, and returned to my front door, shutting it softly and slipping the deadbolt.

"Who is this?" I repeated.

"Erik Fingaard. We met last year."

"I don't know anyone named Fingaard."

"I think you know me better by the tattoo I have on my neck."

Bowman.

CHAPTER TWENTY-ONE

I DRAGGED A kitchen chair to the window, watching the car at the end of the road.

"What do you want?" I said.

"To help you."

"That so?" The last time I'd seen Erik Bowman, Fingaard, whatever his real name was, he'd been flexing muscle as Adam Lombardi's right-hand enforcer, swiping a CD that contained incriminating photos from my truck. This a few weeks after sucker punching me in the dark, roughing up junkies at the Maple Motor Inn, and in all likelihood killing Pete Naginis. In other words, about the last guy I'd expect help from. Or be willing to take at his word.

"I get it," he said. "You're leery. I would be too. But you're going to want to hear what I have to say. It's about Lombardi."

"Which one?"

"Both of them."

I watched the car down the block. "I'm listening."

"This isn't something we can do over the phone. We have to meet. In person."

"Yeah, I'm doing that, Erik. Tell you what. Head over to the McDonald's on Addison. Grab a Big Mac and fries. Order a shake too. Wait for me. Even if it takes twelve, eighteen hours, I swear I'm coming."

"We can pick somewhere public, if you want. I have nothing to hide. But I ain't coming up to your house."

"Good. 'Cause I'm not letting you in."

"I'd be more worried about the men in that car. You don't have any choice right now other than to trust me."

"I'd think I have a lot of other choices. The first being to tell you to fuck off."

The car down the block didn't move. I could feel its attention fixate on me.

"Whatever choices you think you have, you won't have them long."

"And why's that?"

"You remember that other night up in Longmont? That was a warm-up. You don't want those two cops getting another crack at you."

I thought about the timing of the phone call, how I'd had one foot out the door. "How did you know I was walking out of my house?"

"I'm parked in the cul-de-sac behind your place. Past the vacant lot. I can see your house."

I walked across my kitchen, into the half bathroom, peeking through the window. Too many branches on dead winter trees. "Flash your headlights or something. I can't see you."

"Can't do that, Jay. Then they'd see me. And I don't want them finding me any more than you do you. I don't work for them anymore."

"Them?"

"Adam and Michael."

"Falling out?"

"Something like that. Listen, we're wasting time. I'm telling you, you're not safe. I'm not sitting here much longer. You're going to have to make the call, and you're going to have to make it fast. So what's it going to be?"

Like going to Atlantic City and laying it all on black. Or walking out on a good-paying job you hate. Never the smartest bet, but "fuck it" always feels freeing. And I didn't see anyone else offering answers.

"What do you want me to do?"

"Flip on your kitchen and living room lights."

I turned on both.

"Good. Go switch on the TV, and then kill the lights in the living room. Like you're settling in for a long, quiet night in front of the tube with easy access to beer and the bathroom. It'll buy you a few minutes."

How long had he been watching me? I did what he said. "Now what?"

"Grab everything you have on Lombardi—"

"How do you know—"

"Grab everything you have on Lombardi, including anything your buddy Fisher and the girl gave you. Especially the girl. Don't make any judgment calls, Jay. If it pertains to Adam or Michael, bring it. Got it?"

"Yeah, I got it."

"Good. Then sneak out the side door of your garage. Stealth. Don't let them see you. They see you, we're both dead. You'll see my car once you get on the other side."

"Why are you doing this?"

"Those two hung me out to dry. I'm not taking the fall. I'm going to help you nail the sons-a-bitches."

He clicked off.

Peering out the kitchen window, I didn't see Nicki's Jetta, just the empty spot where it had been. She must've gotten away free, unless there had been a second car. What would they want with her? What did they want with me? What were they waiting for? I called to warn her. She didn't answer. No surprise. I didn't even know where she lived. I left a quick message telling her to be careful.

I stood in the glow of my television. Was I really about to trust the same guy who'd broken into my apartment last year and knocked me out cold, the same thug who murdered my brother's friend? I stared at the car lurking down the block.

The devil you know is always better than the devil you don't.

Moments like this I wished I had a gun. After last year, I'd thought about getting a permit for one. But I wasn't going to be that moron whose son accidentally blows his brains out.

I slinked back into the kitchen and gathered everything I had on the Lombardis, sweeping all the intel into a paper bag, a sacked lunch for the late shift. When I was sure no window compromised my position, I slipped a knife from the cutting block. Then I crept outside through the side door of the garage.

Our house rested at the bottom of a shallow dale, submerging the lower half from street view. Peering over the hill, I could still see the car, engine swirling fumes into the fog that drifted in. On this side of the house, you couldn't see much through the woods. Once I got far enough across the cul-de-sac, whoever was in that car would have a clean shot. If they were looking to take it. The set up, a real possibility.

I inched along the outside of my house and took a deep breath. It was now or never.

I took off through scrub brush, kicking at the pricks and dead, tangled weeds aiming to ensnare me, hold me captive until whoever wanted me most could claim his prize. Spiny branches from winter-starved oaks stabbed me; prickers snagged my coat, hooks holding up the carrion. The more I thrashed, the more entangled I became, which only made me thrash more. I had to rip roots from the soil to break free from their grasp, hauling a couple small trees with me into the clearing on the other side, where a car and the devil I knew waited.

* * *

"Smart move," Bowman said when I ducked inside blowing on my fingers, scraped and bleeding from the thorns. He didn't say anything more as he started driving, checking his rearview. I kept one hand on the paper bag containing the research and the other tucked inside my coat.

Beneath passing streetlights, I could see Bowman wore his hair longer than he had last year, and there was the start of a beard, but I'd recognize him anywhere. No mistaking that tattoo on his neck. Giant yellow star. Thing was huge. Was he really offering to help? How big of an idiot was I to trust him? Like poking a dead dog with a stick, I was desperate to believe.

"Where you taking me?" I asked.

"Somewhere we can talk."

I contemplated where that somewhere might be. Secluded, out of earshot, a permanent resting spot where bodies aren't found until the thaw of spring?

"Don't worry," Bowman said. "You can stab me with that knife you keep patting in your pocket if you don't like where this goes."

"If you don't shoot me first."

"Yeah," he said. "Guess there's always that chance."

We drove east, veering off the main road, venturing farther into the unchartered wilderness. Dead blackberry plants brambled quiet country ponds. All the natural cover you'd need. Cut a hole.

Drop in the fish food. Call it a day. Nothing I could do but sit and wait.

Soon a soft glow illumined in the distance. As the light grew brighter, I saw the familiar logo.

"I don't know about you," Bowman said, "but I could use some coffee and donuts."

CHAPTER TWENTY-TWO

THE TWENTY-FOUR-HOUR Dunkin' Donuts was part of a Mobil gas station on the side of the Merrick Parkway, extra small with only a few booths and tables. Butted against the base of the Lamentation range, the mountain rose up, overhang of bedrock so steep even snow couldn't stick.

I stood outside the car a moment, looking through the donut shop glass, weighing luck against providence.

Bowman held open the front door.

"Come on, Jay. What do you think I'm gonna do? Cap your ass and dump your body in the cruller batter? Let's go. I'm freezing my nuts off."

Besides the acne-riddled cashier, who also wouldn't be getting laid anytime soon, the only other person inside the donut shop was a hobo who'd wandered in from the forest. Wrapped in a padded puffer, duct-tape-stuffed at the seams, he sat at a table and sniffed his fingers, a gooey white substance I prayed was egg.

Bowman ordered two coffees.

I reached for my wallet.

"On me," he said, unwrapping a thick roll of rubber-banded cash from his jeans. "How you like your coffee?"

"Light and sweet."

"A real man's man. And a half dozen donuts," he said to the clerk. "I'm fucking starving. Mix 'em up. Anything but Boston Cream. I hate Boston."

At the table Bowman clamped down on a jelly. He pointed at the donuts in the bag. "Eat up, Jay. They're good for you. Fried sugar and bread. Everything a growing boy needs."

Bowman kept his back to the wall so he could keep an eye on the door. I'd never seen him this up close before. Deep crags and crow's feet rivered his face, the burden of a hard-lived life etched and unforgiving. Forty-eight or fifty-eight, neither would've surprised me.

I snared a glazed and gobbled up half in one bite. I was running on fumes.

"Okay, let's see it," Bowman said, licking jam off his thumb.

"What?"

"You got in a car with me, drove the darkest dirt roads, and *now* you want to play it safe? You're clutching that paper bag like a purse." He held out his hand. "Come on, man, let's have it."

"First, tell me what's in it for you. No offense, but I have a tough time buying you'd want to help me do anything."

Bowman leaned back. "You're right. I don't give a shit about you. But I do care about breaking free of Adam and Michael. More like the enemy of my enemy. I know for a fact you've been poking around."

"Poking around?"

"Xeroxing courthouse documents. Visiting former guests of North River. Hanging around construction sites. Asking too many questions. You're making the Brothers nervous. This Roberts thing is no joke."

"Judge Roberts?"

"Whatever your little girlfriend—"

"She's not my girlfriend."

"I give a shit. She made a photocopy up in Longmont. They want it back."

"They send you to break into her apartment too?"

"If I wanted to fuck you over, I'd pick a better spot than a donut shop."

I passed the bag, which comprised everything I had—my own clippings, charts and graphs from Fisher, Nicki's contribution to the cause. I couldn't imagine what he was looking for. Even the supposed classified court documents were part of a public archive.

Bowman stacked it all on the table, licking a thumb, perusing page by page.

"You and the Brothers Lombardi aren't seeing eye to eye these days?"

"You could say that."

"What else could you say?"

"A guy like me is dead weight—and the first thing that gets cut when criminals go legit."

"How so?"

"I did a seven-year stretch at NH Correctional. Back when I was a kid your age. Breaking and entering horseshit. Prison ain't nowhere you want to spend a night, let alone seven years. But I tell you this. I met more mensch in NHC than I ever did in the construction racket. It's a business filled with liars and crooks, every last one of them. And Lombardi is the worst."

"I'm guessing you'd know."

"Not a lot of employment opportunities for ex-cons." He pointed at the Star of David tattoo on his neck. "Bit of a hiring deterrent." Bowman kept leafing through the stack, carrying on a conversation in between slurps of black coffee. "You have no idea what you stumbled on last winter."

"Yeah, Gerry Lombardi was a creep."

"I don't know anything about that."

"And here I thought we were becoming friends."

"I don't know what that old man did or didn't do. But their father's perversion wasn't what had Adam and Michael so rattled. That hard drive your brother got his hands on contained something far worse."

"Like what?"

"I don't know, Jay. I'm not exactly an inner-circle guy. I handled more of the grunt work."

"You mean breaking and entering, assault . . . murder?"

Even at the accusation, Bowman remained unfazed. "I've done a lot of things I'm not proud of. But I didn't kill your brother's friend."

"Is this like a criminal's code or some shit? Beating and battery is okay, but you draw the line at murder?"

He stopped reading to catch my eye. "I never said I haven't killed a man. Just not that man."

I gauged the distance to the door, adding how many steps I could manage before I reached the edge of the forest versus the likelihood a bullet would split my scapula first.

Disinterested in my crisis of faith, he continued. "Whatever was on that hard drive is tied to this UpStart business, I can tell you that. You only copied the pics. We got back the hard drive. Which is the only reason you're still here. Even when Gerry was alive, doing whatever he was doing, Adam and Michael were planning this center. It's why Adam spoke out about the drug epidemic so often, why Michael lobbied so hard to get legislation passed for a private facility. The Coos Center is priority number one. It's why they blew up the truck stop and motel. It's why they paid off judges like Roberts to ship kids to North River. Necessity feeds the mother. They want this prison."

"You can prove that?"

"If I could prove that, Jay, why the fuck would I need you?"

"Why *do* you need me?" I pointed at the trail of papers. "Those are public records my friend Nicki copied, newspaper articles I snipped out. Available to anyone with a buck and pair of scissors."

"Your girlfriend got her hands on something special. Someone from the courthouse called Michael. The Brothers have been freaking out ever since. I need to get out of here."

"Here?"

"New Hampshire. New England. Maybe the country."

"Had to fuck up pretty bad to need to run that far."

"That part doesn't concern you," Bowman said, "But, yeah, I wouldn't mind landing somewhere those two can't find me. And a parting payback shot would be nice." He closed the folder. "You don't have it."

"What?"

"What you need."

"I thought you worked for Tomassi Construction now. Delivering payoffs."

"I'm a jack of a lot of trades. Listen, kid, none of this would make any sense to you. It's a need-to-know basis. I'm telling you what you need to know. Don't worry about me or my life, what I did or where I'm going, okay? You're on the right track. Judge Roberts, HUD programs pushed through, the new juvie center. But the spike you need to nail those pricks to the wall isn't here. Now think back. Your little girlfriend—"

"I told she's not—"

"—got into some records. Out-of-state extradition. Population overflow—"

"That's everything I have."

He slammed his fist on the table. The hobo jump-farted in his sleep. The dropout cashier recoiled, terrified.

"If they want her that bad," I said, "why haven't they sent someone to toss her place?"

"They have. The girl hasn't been home in days."

Where the hell had she been sleeping?

Bowman stood to leave.

"Hold on," I said. "Where you going?"

"Away from here."

"How am I supposed to get home?"

"Not my problem." He slid on his jacket. "Call your girlfriend. You're going to want to do that anyway."

"Well, thanks for the date." I would've pushed harder for a ride back, since I was now stranded, except for two things: one, I had no interest in running into those Longmont cops, and two, I didn't want to spend another minute in this guy's company. He had that wild, unhinged look of a man with nothing left to lose, someone who wouldn't mind going out in a blaze, a lethal combination I didn't want to spark.

Bowman nodded at the documents. "Don't go back to your place. Have your girl pick you up here. She has a photocopy. I know that for a fact. Every copy made at the courthouse needs an ID. Either she made it or someone using her name did. What you're looking for involves the kids shipped out of state. Kentucky. Arizona. You find that information and you slip it in an envelope, ship it down to the *Monitor*, care of Jim Case."

"Who's Jim Case?"

"He's a reporter. Been poking around this Roberts stuff too. Making the Brothers very nervous. He's next on the list, if you know what I mean. Get him those papers. Then you and your little girlfriend take a trip out of town."

"I'm married."

"Leave your wife and son in Burlington. They are a lot safer up there."

"I don't even know what I'm looking for."

"Figure it out. And then get out of Dodge. You're in the crosshairs, kid. You and the girl."

When Bowman got to the door, he turned over his shoulder. "Sorry for punching you in the back of the head last year. When you hit a man you really should look him in the eye. Good luck."

CHAPTER TWENTY-THREE

I KEPT TRYING to reach Nicki, who still wasn't answering. I left increasingly dire messages, attempting to explain the danger in thirty seconds, avoiding asking where she'd been sleeping because I didn't want to sound like a possessive ex-boyfriend. If Bowman was right, she couldn't go back home now, wherever "home" was. The thought of her sleeping with someone else burned me up, although I knew I had no right. What did I really know about the girl? Besides that she was from New York City and had been studying at Keene before taking a semester off and getting stuck with a relative up here. An uncle, I thought she said.

There are few things in this life as depressing as contemplating life's mysteries inside a Dunkin' Donuts on the side of a highway in the dead of winter.

The gas station next door sold cigarettes. I made sure to be extra friendly to the clerk, over-explaining how my car had broken down and I was waiting on a friend. I couldn't afford to get tossed for vagrancy. I'd watched the hobo get the boot a while ago. I didn't know which jurisdiction I was in or what police force might get the call, but I didn't want to find out.

If those two Longmont cops couldn't find me at my place, how long before they checked Charlie's? I dreaded calling him. Mostly because I was worried he wouldn't pick up the telephone. I could take getting ignored by Nicki or even my wife, but the day Charlie

Finn stopped taking my calls I'd know I'd burned my last bridge, abandoned forever on the Island of Misfit Toys. I didn't have any choice. I couldn't sit on a gas station curb smoking cigarettes all night. I hadn't seen a single car pull in. Not that anyone picked up hitchhikers these days. Plus, where would I go?

Charlie wasn't thrilled to hear from me. I could hear the Dubliner in the background. He didn't sound too drunk. When I explained where I was and who'd brought me there, he agreed to come get me. I ordered another coffee and donut so I'd have an excuse to wait inside where it was warm. The whole time I kept hoping Nicki would call back, but she never did.

I tried to remember the day she got fired. Interstate extradition? Maybe. Kentucky, Arizona? Sounded right. By that point, she'd already crawled under my skin, bugging me. I wasn't the greatest listener under normal circumstances.

What if Bowman was setting me up? If they couldn't find Nicki, maybe I could. Maybe that's what they wanted, for me to bring her out in the open. Except I'd been running around town with the girl for the last few days, in plain sight. She'd just been in my house. If those cops were looking for her, why hadn't they grabbed her when she left? She'd been parked right out front. Or maybe they'd arrived a minute too late, the timing too convenient. Or maybe those weren't the same cops. I was pretty sure the car was the same one as the other day, but a lot of cars look alike, Crown Vic the preferred prowl vehicle for undercover. Which meant I was taking my cue from a criminal and murderer. And still Bowman had given me more to work with than anyone else.

Sometime around midnight, Charlie pulled up, alone. I hadn't anticipated Fisher tagging along for the ride but I wouldn't have been shocked to see him. Either way, I was glad I didn't have to deal with his bullshit.

This time of night granted wide berth on the parkway. The thoroughfare, like the Turnpike, traversed mountain granite, but located on the other side of the range, the road invited less traffic.

Charlie immediately brought up the elephant.

"And why do you believe Bowman?"

"His real name is Erik Fingaard."

"Whatever you're calling the guy," Charlie said, "he's the same asshole who knocked you unconscious and dumped Pete Naginis' body behind the truck stop."

"He admitted punching me out," I said, "and a lot of other fucked-up shit, too. But he denied killing Pete."

"Did he pinky swear?"

Charlie's skepticism was understandable. You don't get a second chance to make a first impression. Especially when that impression is one someone wants to stomp into your skull. I couldn't explain why my gut told me to trust Bowman.

Charlie reached for a smoke. "So, where to? You said you don't want to go home. I guess you can crash at my place." He sounded exhausted.

"Sorry about last night." I passed my pack. "Sorry about, y'know, everything."

"I love you, Jay. You're the closest thing to family I got." He took a deep breath. "Just tell me the plan, man. You say Bowman's on the level? Sure. Why not? Can't hurt mailing a package to the press."

"Won't matter if I can't get Nicki to return my call."

"Don't shit where you eat, bro."

"I didn't fuck her."

"None of my business. But I could see where that was headed soon as you walked in the Olympic. The way she looked at you. The more you denied it."

"I love my wife."

"You wouldn't be the first guy to love his wife and get some on the side."

"I told you I didn't sleep with her. We fooled around for, like, thirty seconds, a minute tops."

"I'm sure Jenny will love to hear that explanation."

*　*　*

After Charlie went to sleep, I logged onto the web. The Department of Health and Human Services (DHHS) handled most substance abuse cases in New Hampshire, overseeing juvenile subdivisions like CHINS (Children in Need of Services) and DJJS (Division of Juvenile Justice Services). Both had the power to remove a child from the home, especially when drugs became an issue. The worst of the worst were generally sent to the Sununu Youth Services Center in Manchester. That's not where Brian Olisky and Wendy Shaw had been sent. North River had flexibility, operating as a diversion program. Did that mean they could send kids packing across state lines? Is that where Brian and Wendy now slept? Anything's possible if parents sign off. I couldn't find reports of New Hampshire shipping inmates out of state. But I learned Vermont did it all the time. In fact, our neighbor to the west paid out over sixty million to a company called Justice for America, Inc., which oversaw privately owned, for-profit prisons. Most of these facilities were located in Kentucky and Arizona. How did that work? My eyes were going cross trying to figure it out.

I delved into the *Monitor* archives, searching out bylines from the reporter Bowman mentioned, Jim Case. No scalding exposés on the Brothers, but I could see he was playing for the other side, a vocal opponent of the push for privatization, a liberal crusader urging rehabilitation over throwing away the key. Everyone had a horse in this race. Maybe Case just needed a cause to rally around, a pulpit from which to preach. At least this part of Bowman's story checked out. Which made me remember something else Bowman cautioned: the reporter was next on the list.

A Google search revealed an address and phone number for Jim Case. Just like that. You can find anything on the Internet these days, a detail that did nothing to assuage my paranoia. I cross-checked to make sure I had the right guy, the name common enough. Didn't take long. Jim Case had a public Facebook page, Twitter account, LinkedIn profile listing full name, hometown, age, which I matched against other articles and recognitions, all his contact information out there for the whole world to see. Email. Phone number. Mailing address. Nothing was private anymore. I reached for the phone, then thought better. What could I explain to a stranger at two a.m. over the telephone?

I crashed on the old floral print couch. Taunted by hissing radiators and groaning wood, the lingering scent of lavender and liniment, sleep came uneasy. I hadn't enjoyed a full REM cycle since Jenny moved out. Mix in the alcohol and anxiety, the dehydration, I mirrored the walking dead. Half alive, half something not human anymore. Bedtime offered no solace. Whatever questions plagued me during the daytime shadowed me into slumber.

Lucid dreams transported me back to the final act of last January's tragedy. I'd just run a man off the road. He lay dead in the ravine. My brother and me stashed in an empty farmhouse in the foothills, the cops coming for us both. My brother talking crazy, making up stories about our dad, trying to blame him for why he was such a mess, using the opportunity to rewrite history and paint himself the hero. This was the end of my road, too. And in those waning minutes, knowing I was about to leave my son orphaned, the only woman I'd ever love abandoned to raise our child alone, I had prayed to God to get me out of there. Please, give me one more chance. Keep me safe and I swear I'll make it right. And He heard me. I'd been granted a second chance. And I'd fucked that one up, too.

I saw the red-and-blue lights, heard the crunch of footsteps over snowy gravel, authority closing in to take me away.

I woke on Charlie's couch, lights swirling through the window, bouncing off the glass and walls.

Then came the loud knock at the door.

They'd come for me again.

CHAPTER TWENTY-FOUR

CHARLIE SAWED LOGS in the back bedroom. I eyed his car keys in the bowl of waxed fruit on the kitchen table next to my sack of papers. I fantasied a fantastic scenario, where I'd sneak out the back door, slit the cruiser tires with a switchblade, steal a car and speed my way to freedom beneath predawn skies. This is the crazy shit you cook up when you can't fully fall asleep.

At the window, I peeled the curtain as another heavy fist rained down.

"Open up. It's me. Turley."

I cracked the front door, rubbing my eyes like he'd interrupted a wonderful dream. "What the hell time is it?"

"Thought I'd find you here." Turley stepped past, barging inside. He stopped when he heard Charlie raising the roof. "Is that Finn? How you get any sleep?"

"What do you want, Turley?"

"I need you to come down to the station. Some detectives from Longmont been looking for you. Got some questions."

"Detectives?" Like the man sent to execute my brother last year? Those cops on the side of the road weren't detectives. Maybe Turley was willing to double down on that bridge. I sure as hell wasn't.

"They said they'd been out to your place. Truck's there. You're not. I told 'em to head over." Turley looked bored with the conversation. "I said I'd fetch you."

"And take me where?"

"They're gonna meet us at the station."

"Ever hear of calling?"

"Yeah, Jay. Charlie's landline was busy. Neither of you was answering your cell."

"That's because there's no cell reception out here for one, and two, I was fucking sleeping. It's the ass crack of dawn."

I saw the receiver belly up on the nightstand. Must've kicked it over in my thrashing attempts to sleep.

"Which is why I had to drive out here." He reached for my arm.

I pulled away. "The fuck are you doing?"

Turley's hand shot for his holster.

"What? You're going to cuff me? Arrest me? Shoot me?"

The snoring in the backroom stopped.

"No one is arresting anyone. These boys just want to talk to you. Don't be a red-ass."

"What's going on?" Charlie stood in the doorway to his bedroom, pink ham belly more swollen that usual, like the meat had soaked too long in the brine. "What are you doing here, Turley?"

"Hey'ya, Charlie. Sorry to bother you. Got a couple of cops up from Longmont. Need to talk to Jay. Said I'd grab him."

Charlie scratched his head. He didn't understand what was happening. But I did.

"Fine." I grabbed my winter coat, nodding toward the back bathroom. "Okay if I take a piss first?"

"Knock yourself out."

While Charlie and Turley made small talk about ice fishing and elk, I walked into the kitchen, plucking a plastic apple from the fake fruit bowl. I stuffed the evidence inside my coat, double-checking that the blade was still there. I snuck out the side door.

At the back of the house, I pulled the steak knife from my pocket and slit the telephone wire. Then I crept toward Turley's squad car, cracked the driver's side door, and sliced the CB cable, too. Good luck getting a cell signal. I plunged the knife headlong into his tire.

I was turning over Charlie's engine as Turley, the fat fuck, lumbered down the steps, shouting after me.

Speeding out of the foothills, I made for the lowlands. The papers were going to love this one. Another one of the Porter boys embroiled with the law. But I'd fallen for the masquerading cop bit before. Fool me once, not this time. I had to find that reporter Bowman told me about. One objective: Get Jim Case the evidence. After that, I didn't care what happened to me. Without Jenny and my son, nothing mattered.

Nicki still refused to pick up. I kept driving, hitting the Turnpike south, checking my phone every six seconds like a girl waiting on her prom date. The dark winter skies churned, tractor-trailers zipping by, gas stations glowing with the promise of free coffee with every fill-up. I watched the rearview, anticipating the fleet of squad cars that never materialized. I wished I had the complete package to give to the reporter, but waiting wasn't a luxury I had. I decided to forgo getting it right for getting it right now.

I needed to give Nicki time to call me back. The farther from Ashton I got, the better I felt about my decision.

One eye on the road, the other on my cell trying to follow the squiggly GPS instructions, I chain-smoked, jittery, shaky, break-of-day surreal, ears ringing, pulsating, pounding with blood flow, an old Subaru's rumbling gut underfoot.

Pittsfield wasn't far, a few counties south. At this hour, with little traffic, I knew if I got there fast enough I could catch Jim Case before he left for work, which beat all hell out of having to trek down to Concord and trying to talk my way onto a newsroom floor.

Seemed like only minutes ticked by before I was parked outside the turquoise house on the subdivision's street, wondering if it could really be this easy. I checked the mirror, licked my palm to smooth the tangled mop atop my head. My hair looked like I'd shampooed it in a deep fryer, and with the sprouting beard I resembled a crackhead. Unshaven, gaunt, black circles under my eyes, unrecognizable even to myself. I grabbed my papers and rang the bell. The world kept going faster and faster, spinning like a bottle top I couldn't make stop.

A man answered the door. Glasses, limp hair swept to the side, already dressed and prepared to conquer the day, he held a novelty coffee mug, which read: Never Bury the Lead. I thought I recognized his face from his Facebook picture. I also knew from social media that he wasn't much older than me. Somehow he seemed a lot older. I had to be sure.

"Are you Jim Case? Reporter for the *Monitor*?"

He didn't respond, but his eyes told me I had the right man.

I presented my wadded-up paper bag.

Case peered past the weirdo on his porch. No one else on the street, everything serene, another pleasant valley suburban morning. How did I expect him to respond?

"That's everything you need on the Lombardis and Roberts," I said. "Well, almost everything." I thrust the bag forward, my offering.

He didn't take my bag.

"You're Jim Case, right?"

Maybe I had the wrong guy. Maybe he didn't care. I was operating on a few newspaper bylines, a couple thumbnail pics, what Bowman had told me, which for all I knew was spoon-fed bullshit, and very little sleep. If I was wrong, the slammed door would come next.

Instead Case stepped aside, opening his home to let me inside.

Had I been thinking right, I would've asked the right questions, like why he was letting a man as disheveled as me into his home, why he hadn't asked my name yet. Only I wasn't thinking right. I was as far from right as you get. I stood inside the vestibule, on the mud mat, brain all jumbled, doing nothing to help my own cause. Jim Case carefully pried the bag from my clutches. At the breakfast nook, he removed my photocopies and charts, stacking them on the counter beneath a cupboard, going through them, one by one, not unlike Bowman, glancing over at me every few turns.

"Where did you get this?" he asked. It was the first time he'd spoken.

"Friends of mine. Copies from the courthouse. Internet research. Some parents I spoke to. Judge Roberts is selling kids to the North River Institute."

"What'd you say your name was?"

"Jay. Jay Porter."

Jim Case continued to scan through the pages.

"It's not everything you need," I said. "I'm waiting on something else."

"Something else?"

"A report on interstate extradition. I think UpStart is bankrolling the project, trying to inflate numbers to get that new private prison built on the grounds of the old TC Truck Stop. Y'know, in Ashton?"

"Can you wait here a minute?"

His landline rang. And suddenly I knew I had to get out of there.

We both looked at the phone.

Jim Case held up his hands, letting the phone keep ringing. "It's okay, Jay."

"How do you know my name?"

"You just told me."

He was right. I had.

Jim Case swung open an arm, guiding safe passage to a small kitchen table, where he sat down first. "Please. Have a seat."

I could only guess what had to be going through this guy's head. I could smell myself. I stank like that bum inside the Dunkin' Donuts. I didn't know why was he even talking to me. How was explaining Bowman going to help?

But Bowman had said he was next on the list. I had to warn him. I was having that problem where I could formulate cogent points in my head, but when I tried to articulate a coherent sentence, my tongue got all thick, and I couldn't pluck the right word, resulting in a lot of starting and stumbling. I sounded retarded. "Why are you talking to me?" With those words, I knew I only sounded crazier.

"Excuse me?"

"You don't know me. I'm just some guy who knocked on your door at seven in the morning. You shouldn't let strangers in your house. You're in danger."

"Are you here to hurt me?"

"No!"

"I didn't think so. I trust my instincts. It's why I'm a reporter." He pointed at the documents stacked in front of him. "I think we are on the same side. I rely on sources from all walks of life."

"I'm not a bum. I've had a rough few days."

Jim Case held up his hands, the way you do when you agree to disagree.

"I know what I'm doing," he said. "How serious it is. I've been looking into North River for a while. Roberts too. Now why don't you tell me what you know?"

The phone rang again, and I jolted, startled. He made no move to answer it, gesturing for me to stay calm. "It's just the phone. People call me for work. It's okay. You seem really jumpy. Relax. Can I get you some water?"

"I'm fine."

"Talk to me."

"I just told you. Judge Roberts is shipping kids to the North River Institute in exchange for kickbacks. I know the parents are . . . "

"Parents are what?"

"Receiving kickbacks! Housing repairs getting pushed through HUD. Big fat stacks. Payoffs, man." I pointed at the paper trail. "It's all in there. Well, not all of it. You're missing something."

"Sorry, Jay. I'm having a hard time following you. What exactly am I missing?"

"I told you. The out-of-state stuff. I don't know, exactly. But I know where to get it. I'll get it, okay?"

When the phone rang again, I stood up, shoving in the chair.

"Hold on. Where are you going?"

"To prove it. You got a business card or something? How I can reach you?"

He plucked a business card from his pocket, passing it along, wary, like you do meat scraps a feral dog.

I snatched the business card. "Watch your back." I bolted out the front door as the phone started up again.

Back in the car, I popped the battery from my cell. Which I knew would make it tough for Nicki to return my call. There's a fine line between preparation and paranoia. Charlie's was my safe house. I couldn't go home. I realized I was headed back to

Ashton without consciously making the decision to do so. Like a moth drawn to the firelight. Or bug zapper. I needed off the grid. Somewhere with a secure line. I had to talk to Nicki. How hard was it to return a goddamn phone call? Where do the invisible go when they have to disappear?

* * *

When I was young, we used to tease the poorer kids. Anytime the school bus took the Turnpike, we'd point at the fleabag motels, say, "This is where you'll end up living someday." Because kids are mean little shits. And karma is one vengeful bitch.

I needed to dump Charlie's Subaru. I was driving a stolen car. I shouldn't have risked taking it to Pittsfield. Even if I knew my buddy wouldn't press charges, Turley had the license plate, which meant those Longmont cops did too. I had to buy a few hours, long enough to reach Nicki.

Racing north along the Turnpike, I took the Duncan Pond exit, hopped the access road down a dirt path, abandoning the stolen car behind a patch of cattail. I scattered dead branches, bulrush and sedge over the roof and hood. Then I started walking. Pond swamp mucked my shoes. I kept hearing helicopters overhead, but when I'd look up, I'd find nothing but the same churning mountain skies. *This is what skipping sleep does, little brother. Turns your brain to mush. Can't think straight. Goops your oatmeal, bogs you down in a slog of maple. Try stirring that shit with a spoon.*

I weaved through woodland until I hit the string of cheap motels. Despite the early hour, the welfare cases were already out, pushing their shopping carts along icy shoulders. Bums with cardboard signs touting patriotic service in fictitious wars. I spotted a pair of junkies, frighteningly malnourished, about a hundred pounds between them, flightless birds in search of a morning meal. I pulled my collar, hunched my shoulders, and joined the hobo parade.

No one asks for an ID at these motels; that's the beauty of Turnpike living. I paid my thirty bucks and change with crumpled bills and coins sifted from lint, got my oversized key, and locked myself away in a tiny room choked with B.O., fast food, and stale cigarette smoke.

I flicked on a lamp. Low wattage revealed streaks of red and black shooting across the walls and ceiling. The impressionistic artwork felt out of place with the rest of the sparse, pawnshop décor. I remembered overhearing a pair of junkies talking once while I waited to admit Chris into rehab. They were bitching about bad veins, how after so many misfires, the needle would clog with sludge. To clear the line, they'd have to push the plunger extra hard. Drugs and bodily fluids would spit out, spraying everything. That's what I was looking at. Dried blood and wasted lives.

I sat on the edge of a lumpy bed and pulled the janky parts of the cell phone from my pocket. I didn't know how long service providers required to pinpoint location from a tower, whether that was even a real concern or some drug addict urban legend, a plot device employed by lazy TV show writers. But I couldn't afford to test theories. I fitted the battery, retrieved Nicki's number, scribbled it down, and popped the battery back out. I wasn't taking any chances. I called her again from the motel phone. Another voice mail. I left as polite a message as I could, considering the rage burning inside me. I laid out everything Bowman had told me, again, spelling it out in slow, small words. I trusted her with everything—the stakes, how indispensable she was, because what other choice did I have? She'd call back. Or she wouldn't. I couldn't do a goddamn thing but wait.

I peeled off my clothes, sniffed my shirt, which stank worse than my days laboring on the cow farm. I brought the shirt with me into the shower and scrubbed it clean with the complimentary sliver of soap. Rang the tee out, threw it over the radiator to dry. I brushed my teeth without toothpaste, using my finger.

Stepping from the fog, I cleared the mirror with my hand and studied the man standing before me, the guy who was usually clean-shaven, good looking, put together. My left eye twitched. An honest-to-God facial tick. My bottom lid quivered, like teeny tiny worms had burrowed beneath the lashes and were staking claim. I remained transfixed, fascinated by my own eye's squirming involuntarily. The parasites had taken over.

I combed back my wet hair with my fingers, stepped into the next room. Just had the one. The motel didn't offer the option of a suite upgrade. I could smell trap grease from the KFC/Taco Bell combo next door. Peeling the curtain, I watched my new neighbors hoof it across the parking lot, broken men with sagging guts and receding hairlines, six-packs in hand, the day's first already cracked. It wasn't even nine a.m. A beer sounded pretty good about now.

I checked the progress of my tee shirt drying in the bathroom. Still damp. If I tried walking outside with a wet shirt in this weather I'd end up with walking pneumonia. I wrapped the winter coat around me and bundled up shirtless. I could use food. I needed a beer.

I was about to head outside when the telephone rang.

CHAPTER TWENTY-FIVE

"JESUS, JAY, YOU'RE worse than an ex-boyfriend. How many times are you going to call until you get the hint?"

"As many times as it takes for you to call me back!" I tried to keep the anxiety at bay and not sound like a complete psycho. We hadn't parted on the best terms, I knew, conflicting emotions warring inside me, but I needed Nicki on my side. What I said next didn't help my cause. "Where have you been sleeping?"

"What the fuck business is it of yours?"

"That came out wrong."

"I'm busy. What do you want?"

I tried explaining the same information I'd already left on her phone half a dozen times. Her reaction told me she hadn't listened to any of those messages. I reiterated about Bowman and how desperate the Lombardis were for that one particular Xerox. I told her about the reporter, Jim Case. How close we were. Then she tried to make me sound crazy.

"I know, Jay. I got the voice mails. All sixty-four of them."

"I didn't leave sixty-four voice mails."

"Where are you? What number is this?"

"My friend said—"

"Your friend is wrong. Everything I copied from Longmont, I gave you."

"The only reason I asked where you're sleeping is because they sent someone to your apartment, house, wherever you live to get it."

"Who?"

"Lombardi!"

"To get what?"

"The photocopy!"

"I don't know what you're talking about."

"The man I met with—he broke into your place. To steal a photocopy. Kids shipped out of state. Think."

"Why are you talking to a guy trying to break into my house?"

"That's Bowman! See! You didn't listen to my messages!"

"For the last time: I don't know what you're talking about, Jay. Have a drink. You sound fucking cracked out."

"Please, Nicki."

Dead silence on the other line.

"Nicki?"

"Go ahead."

I resented the belittling tone but did my best to break down my night, a conversation and circumstance so surreal—meeting my former adversary Bowman at a Dunkin' Donuts on the seldom-used Merrick Parkway, attached to a gas station I'd never seen before, Jim Case and his phone that never stopped ringing—the longer I talked, the more I began wondering if, in my sleep-deprived, neurotic state, I hadn't gone fugue and imagined the whole damn thing, conflating my brother and me, last year and this. I didn't have any lorazepam with me, chest thumping, thrumming, rattling the rib cage. Thank God Nicki finally came around.

"Wait a second. My last day there. When they fired me, yeah . . ."

"Yeah what?"

"I was all hyped up over Judge Roberts, y'know, back when I thought if I helped you out, you might give a shit about me."

What could I say to that?

"I'd gone down to the basement. There was a box. I think it was meant for records. I told you, remember? Kids shipped out of state to Kentucky and Arizona."

"Yes! That's that one."

"It's funny because it barely mentioned Roberts' name. Had other shit on there."

"Like what?"

"I don't know. It was very academic. Like the overview for a study."

"Do you still have it?"

"I don't know."

"Can you check?"

"Jesus, is it that important?"

"Yes!"

"I'll call you back."

I fired up a cigarette and paced around my room. I peeked out tattered curtains. Fissures cracked the clouds. Freezing rain fell. Cars zoomed up and down the Turnpike, spinning mist and mud, miniature oily rainbows shimmering over mounds of dirty snow. Soon as I was done with one smoke, I lit another. The telephone rang.

"The header reads 'Executive Summary,'" Nicki said. "It's like a cost analysis. An abstract. Concerns the juvenile justice populations in Kentucky and Arizona, the states where New Hampshire unloads its overflow. A feasibility prospective. Y'know, for privatization."

"It says New Hampshire?"

"What do you mean?"

"Does it say that New Hampshire is the one shipping the kids out of state, and not, say, Vermont?"

"Why would New Hampshire keep a record of what Vermont does?"

"Never mind."

"I don't see anything here, Jay. Doesn't mention North River at all. Nothing about UpStart. I don't know what good it's going to do you. Unless you need some furniture hauled away."

"Huh?"

"There's the outline of a business card I copied by mistake. Guess it was paper-clipped to the original. Some moving company."

None of this added up. There had to be more.

"How many pages?"

"Just the one. I must've I stuck it in my back pocket. Found it in my car under a pile of garbage. How perfect is that?" I didn't get the joke. She didn't laugh.

"What do you think it means?"

"How the fuck should I know?"

"I need it." I caught myself. "Wait. Where was it?"

"In my car. Wadded up in a pair of dirty jeans with the rest of the junk."

I remembered her car, which had been spotless. "Nicki, you have the cleanest car I've ever seen. Especially for a girl."

"That's because before I picked you up, I stopped at the car wash and vacuumed the hell out of it, shoved everything in the trunk."

"You didn't have to clean up for me." What would I care?

"I didn't want you knowing I live in my car."

"What do you mean 'you live in your car'?"

"Um, I live in my car."

"Where?"

"In. My. Car."

"I mean, where do you park it?"

"What do you care?"

"We're almost in Canada. It's cold as hell out there."

"No shit."

"I don't understand. I thought you were staying with an uncle? On break from college?"

"I'm not on break. I flunked out. I'm broke. I owe about a hundred grand in student loans. And I *was* staying with my uncle—who's not even my uncle, he's my aunt's husband, and she's dead. I got tired of Uncle Bob getting drunk and playing grab-hands."

"You're homeless?"

"I can go back to New York, crawl home to my parents and admit I can't make it on my own, but until then, yeah. I park at rest stops, shower in sinks, eat my breakfast from a vending machine and why do you give a shit, Jay? You want that photocopy? Fine. You can have it. Then leave me alone."

"Why didn't you tell me?"

"I didn't even know I had the goddamn thing!"

"No, I mean, that you have nowhere to live."

"Why? So I can move into your house with your wife and kid? Rent a spare bedroom. Gonna save me from the streets?" She scoffed. "Just tell me where you want to meet."

I felt like an asshole. How could I have known?

"Jay?"

"Remember the diner from last night? Meet me there. How long?"

"Give me an hour."

"See you then."

"Wonderful. Can't wait."

I lay on the filthy bed, flipping through stations on a tiny TV, settling on a rerun of *My Three Sons*, killing time until I had to meet my connection. How many times had my brother done the same thing? Maybe even in this same room. I almost climbed a chair to search for initials carved in the rafters.

The Olympic Diner rested down the Turnpike, in the opposite direction of Duncan Pond. I hadn't broken any laws. No major ones, anyway. I'd popped the tire of the town sheriff, and taken Charlie's car without permission. My friend would never file a stolen car report. No one was scouring Ashton looking for me, my frantic flight at dawn the by-product of an overactive imagination and sleep deprivation. But those Longmont cops . . . If they *did* find Charlie's car, they'd start to check the motels on the strip. Given personal histories, the Olympic might not have been the smartest choice, either. But Charlie wouldn't tip off Turley. Would he?

Waiting for grass to grow, time dragged. When everything you want is right in front of you, perspective skews, objectivity wanes. I ached to pay back the hurt.

Hour almost up, I put on my tee shirt, now crispy from overcooking on the radiator. I was about to walk out the door when Nicki rang back and said she needed more time.

"Loose distributor cap. I got it fixed. Leaving now. Give me another sixty."

"No problem." I wanted to scream.

After a few minutes, I couldn't take the solitude any longer. I decided to walk over to the Olympic early. If they were looking for me I wasn't any safer inside the motel room than I was at the diner. Besides, I'd take my chances with Turley and Longmont PD before I suffered another hour alone with my thoughts.

The diner was ten minutes away on foot. Fifteen, tops. I didn't sprint there, but I didn't drag ass either. Slushing through the parking lot, I could see Nicki already waiting in a booth by the window. How much time had I lost?

When I stepped inside the diner, the front bell dinged. For some reason, I flashed on *It's a Wonderful Life*, that queer bit about an angel earning his wings. A bizarre connection at the strangest time, which made me laugh out loud. Nicki stared up from her seat, along with the pair of factory boys perched at the counter, all eyeing me like I was about to ask for change because I'd run out of gas with my family freezing in the car. I grew hyper-paranoid, scanning blind spots. What did I expect? Someone to spring from the shadows and throw a black hood over my head? *Pull it together, little brother.*

"You look like shit," Nicki said when I sat down.

"Long night."

The waitress—Greek, gorgeous, eighteen if she was a day—asked if I wanted coffee. I nodded. She filled my cup. I waited until she left before I spoke.

"You bring it?" I whispered.

Nicki leaned over. "Why are you whispering?" She nodded out the window at her car, butted against a telephone pole in the farthest corner of the parking lot. I must've looked nervous, because she added, "It's not going anywhere. Chill."

Cold rains blunted the boulevard, cheap eats and chain retail obscured.

"Did it make any more sense?" I asked.

"The Xerox? No. I told you. It's just a tally of the underage offenders New Hampshire sends out of state."

"Drugs?"

"Maybe. Didn't list specific crimes or names even. Only totals." She paused. "Y'know—nothing you do fixes the past, right?"

"Huh?"

"All this shit you're doing, it won't bring your brother back. Nothing you do will ever bring him back." Nicki caught my eye.

She didn't seem angry with me anymore. "When all this is over, you should call your wife, do whatever you have to do to make things right."

"You didn't seem too concerned about my wife last night."

"No. But you did." She stopped. "I'm not a bad person."

"Didn't say you were."

"I mean, I'm better than this. You met me at a weird time."

How long had it been since that afternoon in Longmont? My timeline jumbled, nothing in order, I inserted Nicki into memories that weren't possible. I had us hanging out together by the reservoir, at parties in the summertime, drinking beers on the hoods of cars. Jean shorts and bikini tops. Soft kisses in setting suns. Springsteen on the radio. I'd known her less than a week.

"The day I met you," she said, "that was the day I'd decided not to go back to my uncle's."

I didn't grasp the relevance right away.

"I would've been at the house, y'know? When whoever came looking for me. Your friend, Bowman. Whatever."

"He's not my friend."

"But I would've been there, see?"

"Not really."

"I called home. My uncle's in the hospital. Slipped on a patch of ice and cracked his skull open. More like shattered. Doctors are calling it 'blunt head trauma.'" Nicki wrapped her fingers around the coffee mug, glimpsing out the glass. "Pretty much brain dead."

"What are you saying?"

"Nothing. Uncle Bob drank a lot. Maybe he tripped over the steps getting the morning paper."

She didn't bother mentioning the next part, that those injuries were also consistent with a good jackboot stomping.

The waitress returned and asked if we were ready to order. I

grabbed the menu, prepared to make up for days of dietary ne-
glect, but Nicki glanced at her phone, and asked for the bill.

"You in a hurry?"

Nicki tucked the phone in her purse. "I'm going back to New
York."

"Just like that?"

"Just like that." She paused and tilted her head so. "Unless you
want to try and make this work between us."

In that split second I ran through the possibility, wondering
what a different future might look like, the separate narrative less
about a specific woman and more about the rotating doors of
parallel realities. Who would I be there? Would I be any happier,
more fulfilled, or the same man, different only in inconsequential
ways, still unsatisfied?

"I'm kidding, Jay. Go home to your wife."

When the waitress slapped down the bill, Nicki snatched it up.

"On me," she said.

I hadn't ordered anything.

We walked out of the diner together. I almost took her hand.
Not like a boyfriend, but because I really did care about her; I
did understand. Behind the tough girl front, someone vulnerable
lurked, someone desperate to be understood, loved like the rest of
us, someone who didn't want to feel alone. But I didn't grab her
hand. I let the moment pass. The walk to her car didn't take long.
I had no time to regret the decision.

"I'm sorry, Jay."

The apology didn't register at first. Hell, I was sorry too.
Another life and things might've been different between us. I
could be honest with myself now, admit the feelings I had for her.
But that's not what she meant. If I'd been paying more attention,
I would've noticed the fresh set of tire tracks and shiny black car

with state plates now parked beside us. Then again if I'd been paying attention, I wouldn't be in this situation in the first place.

The back door pushed opened.

Michael Lombardi patted the seat beside him.

I turned to look for Nicki, but Nicki was already gone.

CHAPTER TWENTY-SIX

ARMS REACHED AROUND me, hands patting me down. They found the steak knife, of course, Charlie's keys, too, my disassembled phone parts and cigarettes. They let me keep the cigarettes.

The man pushed me into the back, before joining the driver up front.

I heard the doors lock.

Through the rear window, I saw Nicki sitting in the front seat of her Jetta. Our eyes met. She waved halfheartedly. The gesture came across as sincere.

Her car pulled away, heading south on the Turnpike. We followed out the parking lot, north, toward the mountain.

"I can't believe I'm back here," Michael Lombardi said. "Want to hear something funny? When I have to campaign up in these parts, I'll hit Berlin, Pittsfield, even Twin Mountain. But I avoid this town like a bad habit. Not sure why. I have pleasant enough memories. Still want to forget them, though." He turned to me. "I remember when your parents died in that car accident. It's not the same, I know, losing a parent at my age, but I had a difficult time when my father passed last year. I can only imagine how rough that had to be for a boy your age. The rumors of your brother's involvement. Even if we weren't close growing up, I felt bad for you."

Not close? This was the first conversation I'd had with Michael Lombardi my entire life.

"But your brother . . ." He let the somber phrase hang there. "Adam and he were such good friends because of the wrestling team. I'd see him around the house often. I could tell then something wasn't right in his head. I didn't learn about Chris' exact troubles until much later." He gazed over the Turnpike, the seedy thoroughfare that disrupted the illusion of quaint mountain living. "Maybe it's not fair to blame this town. Families choose to stay for a reason. I guess I can appreciate the appeal. Country boys, mountain ridges and all of that. Maybe I just hate John Denver."

Five minutes in the back of his car, I had yet to speak. What could I contribute to the conversation anyway? The scenario had already played itself out. I'd lost. Again.

"How do you know her?" I asked.

"Today was the first time we spoke."

"What did Nicki give you?"

"Something I wanted."

"You don't want to tell me what?"

"Why would I? No offense."

"I guess you were able to offer her the right price."

"Any price is better than no price."

"Bowman said—"

"I don't care what Erik—the man you call Bowman—said, but I can tell you this about Erik. He's an angry, spiteful man of limited intelligence. When Adam sold the company to help with my campaign, Erik was left out in the cold. My brother went out of his way—against my counsel—to land Erik a job with Tomassi. That wasn't good enough for Erik, who felt I'd forced him out. Which I suppose I had. But you know politics. I couldn't justify ex-gang members on the payroll. I wouldn't put much stock in the words of a convicted felon."

The car split off the Turnpike, spiriting along the frontage access of Orchard Road, pressing farther into the forest, swallowed by the dense thicket of rocky evergreen.

"Where are we going?"

No one answered. They didn't need to. I knew where we were headed.

The mountain loomed large on the horizon. The driver hooked a left, angling up meandering dirt roads toward Lamentation Bridge and the treacherous Ragged Pass.

Michael caught my eye. "You know this is business, right? It isn't personal."

I wondered if the men up front were the same two cops who'd beat me senseless last week in Longmont. I decided they were not. Even though I hadn't gotten a good look at any faces, these men carried themselves as a different kind of security. Whatever waited for me up on Lamentation would not be good, regardless of who sat in the driver's seat.

The car motored along the rocky terrain, expensive shocks absorbing unpaved roads as we closed in on the southern rim of the mountain and thin ice of Echo Lake.

"We stopped by your motel room," Michael said. "Didn't find much. Looked like a transient had been staying there."

"Didn't you get what you needed from Nicki?"

"Let's say I like to be thorough."

I could feel the air turn thin and cold with the altitude, clouds sinking, skies darkening, heavy curtains drawing on the closing act. For a long time no one spoke, no one made a sound, the only noise the elegant purr of a finely tuned engine hardly inconvenienced by a hostile environment. Higher and higher we rose, until soon we sat parked on the water's edge, slick sheen glistening off the surface.

The two men in front did not exit the car. This was bad. No secrets needed guarding. Nothing I said would be admissible. Because I wouldn't be around later to corroborate. There would be no witnesses left behind.

"So those photocopies, Jay?"

"I gave everything I had to the press."

"Really? You're going with that one?"

"It's the truth." If this was game over, I had nothing to lose. Or hide. "Spoke to Jim Case this morning. Reporter for the *Monitor*? Went to his house in Pittsfield. Talked over coffee. He has it all. Selling kids to North River. Paying off Judge Roberts. The HUD projects your office pushed through. Shipping kids out of state. Inflating numbers. UpStart's stake in erecting a new private prison. Everything. You and your brother are done."

Michael smirked. But it wasn't mean or filled with hate. I couldn't place the emotion behind it until he shook his head, as if in admiration. "I told Adam he was wrong about you."

I wasn't sure which of the two had been defending my honor.

Michael stared out the window. I followed his gaze over the thin ice. This time of year, no one had to cut a hole. You walk far enough out on the ice and the ice would break, swallow you up, swirling black waters bringing you home.

"Your folks had their accident around here, didn't they? And wasn't this where you ran your brother and his drug dealer off the road?"

"Don't you think it'll look a little funny? I speak with a reporter at the *Monitor*, then go missing later that morning?"

"I have no idea what you're talking about, Jay. I'm on good terms with everyone on the *Monitor* staff. Including Jim Case. Nice guy. Solid reporter. You want to go around repeating the hearsay of a disgruntled former employee with confirmed gangland ties and a long criminal record? No one is taking that seriously." He stared back out the window, casually carrying on pleasant conversation. "After what you went through last winter, would anyone really be surprised if, in your distraught state, you wandered up to this particular spot to grieve? I'm sure your doctor will confirm the pills, how much you'd been drinking, your wife leaving you, the final straw. Wandered too far from the safety of the shore. Misgauged the danger. Happens all the time."

A car pulled behind us. Michael craned over his shoulder. I knew the news was only getting worse.

Doors opened. Arms reached in. I was pulled out. Michael Lombardi didn't bother with goodbye. Like a slab of meat passed off at the butcher's. I wouldn't be around to vote in November.

The men who walked toward me now did not wear uniforms, dressed in regular civilian clothes, expressionless. Though I hadn't gotten a good look that night in Longmont, hadn't logged a single distinguishing characteristic, I knew those cops had returned to finish the job. I remembered Chris telling me about waiting for "the Man." How he'd keep looking, checking every pair of headlights, measuring the weight of footsteps. Pointless. When the Man comes around, you know.

Transaction completed, Michael's security detail slipped back in the car, and the black, state-issued vehicle U-turned, exiting the way it'd come. Like they'd never been there at all.

"You're all kinds of stupid, ain't you, boy?" one of Longmont cops said.

"You don't have to do this," I said. "You can drive away, forget you ever saw me. I won't say a word."

"No. You won't."

"You guys are cops. You can't just kill a man in cold blood."

"Yeah. We can. Don't you watch the news? And besides, we

aren't cops anymore. Not after today. This settles a debt. Then me and Bernstein here take a long trip out of state."

"Seems to be a reoccurring theme," I muttered.

The other one, Bernstein I guessed, told his partner to shut the fuck up. Or maybe that was meant for me. Not like anyone was bothering with introductions.

"He doesn't need to know our travel plans."

"Who's he gonna tell?"

Bernstein appeared to be in charge, so I'd direct my plea to him. Soon as I opened my mouth, though, he unleashed a quick rabbit punch, short, compact, concentrated, just below the rib cage, a precision shot to the kidneys. My legs buckled, forcing me to a knee, gasping.

"Don't waste your breath," Bernstein said. "We told you to drop this. You didn't listen. That's on you. Let's go."

I winced up from the ground, wicked stitch in my side, sucking air. The sonofabitch had managed to find the same exact spot, reopening whatever internal wound he'd ruptured the first time. Just trying to breathe hurt.

"You have two choices," Bernstein said. "One, you walk out onto the ice. Voluntarily. Like a man. Two, you stay on your knees like a chickenshit and I shoot you in the stomach. Then I drag you out on the ice, let you bleed out. No one's coming up here. The ice will break. Eventually. You ever get shot in the stomach? You know what that feels like? You won't die right away. But you'll wish you did."

"Michael said no guns—"

"I don't give a shit what Michael said. He's not here, is he? And in a few minutes neither will we." Bernstein pulled his gun, pointed it at my gut. "What's it gonna be, smart guy."

Didn't take long to decide. Wasn't much choice. A nudge

encouraged me to hurry. The glint of a barrel added to the urgency.

The first step onto the ice, I felt the buckle. The second, I heard the crack. By the third, I accepted my fate was no longer in my hands or beneath my feet. The Universe, God, some other Great Decider would cast judgment and let me know soon enough. By the fifth, twelfth, twentieth steps, I began feeling better, almost confident. This was out of my control. I let go of caring. That surrender, coupled with sleeplessness and rarefied air, conspired to create an almost dizzying euphoria.

"Hurry up!"

"What the hell's taking so long?"

"Just put a bullet in the back of his head."

"Harder to explain a bullet hole than bloated body that floats up with the spring thaw."

"The lake never gives up her dead."

"True to a bone to be chewed—"

I couldn't really hear what they were saying, words receding into the howling ravine, nothing discernable above the echo of the canyon. Deep cracks rivered the ice, kaleidoscopic trees branching out, cold water burbling to the surface. I eyed the beach on the other side. I decided then to take back my fate and make a run for it. I'd outrun splintering floes and escape this watery grave. I took off, pumping my legs. I looked down and saw I hadn't moved an inch. I'd been running in place.

I felt the pain in my leg before I heard the gunshot, teeth clamping to the bone, like I'd stepped into a bear trap. I dropped to the ice and saw the long shard that had torn through my jeans and punctured my flesh. The muscle shredded, deep tissue flayed, blood gushing from a primed spigot. I hadn't been shot. The surface had split open before the undercurrent slammed it back shut, trapping my lower leg, hermetically sealed. A jagged spike impaled my calf, rupturing a vessel, which hemorrhaged, shellacking the ice red.

A captive audience, I watched the gunfight erupt on the shore behind me. Turley crouched behind his police car. Exposed on the banks, the Longmont cops, without cover, marched forward, unloading clips, peppering the cruiser's doors, window, and roof. Turley waited out the attack, timing his moment. As the cops refitted their clips, Turley popped over the hood. Two quick shots, like distant firecrackers on the 4th of July. Both men dropped to the ground.

The ice fractured all around me, spreading outward.

"Hold on, Jay!" Turley shouted from the strand. "I'm coming."

Water bubbled up through the cracks. I tried to pry my leg free, but the more I tugged, the deeper the blade plunged, slicing ligament and sinew, cold lake water rising, me sinking.

Turley scrounged around the brush and pond detritus, wrenching free a frozen, fallen branch, stepping onto the ice. I was a good forty yards away.

"You won't make it, Turley. You're too . . . heavy."

He kept coming at me, forked branch extended like some mystic searching for the spring. I tugged on my knee, tried to wriggle free, retrace the grain of the hook back through the meat, but the pain was excruciating. I'd lost a lot of blood. I felt like I was going to lose consciousness.

Turley wouldn't heed my warning, undeterred, relentless. He'd gotten within twenty feet when I saw the man behind him stagger to his feet and train an unsteady gun. I tried to hold up a hand to make him stop, scream for Turley to turn around, but I couldn't do either fast enough.

The bullet tore through Turley's shoulder, blood blowing out the other side. Pistol pulled, Turley spun, report reverberating with a perfect response between the eyes. The man fell. And so did Turley. Into a hole in the ice, sucked down into the swirling black waters.

CHAPTER TWENTY-SEVEN

I WRAPPED BOTH hands around my knee and, fist over fist, jerked and yanked until the razor sawed through the muscle, exacting a sizeable chunk of circulatory and sinew, a glob of honeybee guts sacrificed to the stinger. But I was free.

The cold air cauterized the wound, or at least stopped the worst of the bleeding. Some of the pain abated, mostly because I couldn't feel my leg anymore. Not like my leg was dead or asleep. It wasn't working. It wouldn't move on its own, flopping like a boneless chicken. But I still had the other one. I hopped toward the hole, dragging the dead weight of my useless appendage behind me.

Staring into the abyss, I couldn't see Turley. Nothing moved below in the murky depths. I grabbed the branch he'd been carrying and jabbed it into the hole, poking around, blind. The shore was right there. Both Longmont cops were dead. Two cars sat with keys in the ignition. I could get to the hospital. Maybe save my leg. I could get out of here. But I wasn't leaving without Turley.

I screamed into the darkness for him to grab hold, even though I knew he couldn't hear me in the deep.

He's gone. Let's go. You're hemorrhaging. You won't last much longer out here. You'll get hypothermia. If you don't bleed out first—

I'm not leaving without him!

I jabbed the stick farther into the void, poking, shaking, stabbing. At first I thought I'd snagged some milfoil or that the branch was tangled in coontail. But when I tugged and felt the tug back, I knew I'd hooked something much larger. Hobbled on one leg, with no way to gain traction on the ice, I twisted my torso, all arms and upper body, drawing on my days baling hay on the farm. A bloody hand broke the surface, followed by a gasp for air. Then Turley lost his grip on the stick and slipped back underwater. I dropped the branch and flopped to the ground, reaching in the cold lake, sweeping for his hand. I pushed my arm far as it would go, and then I pushed farther, past elbow and shoulder, frigid waves slapping against my neck. I swallowed water. I hadn't been fast enough.

It's too late! He's gone. You can't save him!

Shut up! Turley! Turley! I extended farther, submerging half my body until I was in danger of drowning too. I felt fingertips, and then a hand close around mine. I gripped the ice edge, arched my back and pulled. Turley bobbed out of the water gulping air like a trout in a shallow bucket. I grabbed the back of his sheriff's coat. He yelped when my thumb found the bullet hole. He splashed and flailed, a drowning man pulling me down too. I didn't let go.

Drifting in and out, present, cognizant, knocked out, awake, asleep, water, sky, hard earth. Turley's arm wrapped around me, carrying me past the dead cops. Black, blue, solid blocks of gray. Wound tied off, still no feeling in my leg. Next thing I know I'm staring up at the interior roof of a police car as Turley whisked us off the mountain. I propped myself up. He told me to lie back down. He was soaking wet, shivering, his skin an unnatural shade of purple.

I padded my coat for my cigarettes. "Hey, man, you got a light?"

"What are you talking about? You can't smoke, Jay. What the hell is going on? What were you doing out on the ice? Why were those men trying to kill you?"

My Marlboros were drenched anyway. "The Lombardis don't like me any more than I like them."

"Huh?"

I stared at my leg, which was wrapped in Turley's sheriff's coat. I fumbled to untie it.

"Let that alone. You need a tourniquet. You cut something pretty bad in there."

I saw why Turley was shivering. He'd wrapped my leg in his shirt, too. He wore only the wet tee. "You'll get hypothermia."

"I got the heat on full blast. I'll be fine. Are you going to tell me who those men were?"

"You talked to them." I was getting lightheaded. I'd lost a lot of blood. "Cops."

"Cops?"

"You said a couple Longmont cops. Looking for me."

"Yeah. A pair from IA. I had to leave them at the station when I got the call."

"IA?"

"Internal Affairs."

"I know what it stands for. I mean why does Internal Affairs want me?"

"How the hell should I know? You're the one running all over town, half-cocked, causing trouble, acting like a wackadoodle."

"We have to get Charlie's car."

"Don't worry about Finn's car. Highway patrol spotted it behind Duncan Pond. Already sent one of my men to retrieve it. We have bigger problems. There are two dead men on the banks of Echo Lake. Two men I had to put down because they were trying to kill you *and* me. There is going to be an investigation. Now ain't the time to play cute. I need you to come clean."

I wished I could explain. I tried to coax the words out. Maybe saying them aloud would make this all real, and we'd stumble on the truth together. But my tongue swelled, gray matter sopped up. I could feel myself slipping. I was going under, consciousness surrendered to the white noise of the car's heater.

*   *   *

I woke in a white room. White lights. White walls. White dressing gown and sheets. Took me a second to appreciate I wasn't dead and only laid up in a hospital bed, the sweet relief of morphine pumped direct into my vein. Turley stood over me.

"IA filled me in," he said. "No wonder you ran. I wish you'd come to me."

"Sorry about your tires," I said, my voice slow, thick as syrup.

"I'll send you the bill. We couldn't find your phone to call Jenny. No one's answering the landline at your house—"

"No," I said. "Don't call her."

"She's your wife, Jay. She needs to know."

"My cell phone's in pieces somewhere on the mountain. I don't want Jenny worrying. She's half a state away. Please. It won't help my cause. Only hurt."

Turley grabbed a chair and slid it beside my bed. I could see where they'd bandaged up his shoulder.

"Got lucky," he said when he caught me staring. "Bullet went right through." He gestured at my leg, which I now saw was suspended in traction. "In addition to puncturing your saphenous vein, a shard of ice severed a nerve in your calf. Which is why your leg went numb. Doc says the sensation should return. Eventually. Until then, it'll feel like your leg's asleep."

"How'd you know I was on Lamentation?"

"A woman called the station. Anonymous tip. Said you were in trouble."

"And you just knew to look on the mountain?"

"I know you find this hard to believe, Jay, but I'm actually good at my job." He made sure he had my full attention. "Thank you."

I brushed him off.

"I was a goner. Shot. Under the ice. Left for dead. You were wounded. The car was there. You needed to get your ass to the hospital. Doc was shocked when I told her you were able to pull me from the lake with the amount of blood you lost. Shouldn't have been possible. But you stuck around, risked your life to save mine. I know we've had our issues—"

"Let's not get too sentimental. If you didn't show when you did, I'd be on the bottom of Echo Lake right now."

"I guess we'll call it even, then." Turley extended his hand. The shake meant more than evening a score.

Turley pushed himself up out of the chair. "You sure you don't want someone calling Jenny—"

I shook my head.

"Well, Charlie's on his way here now. And those two IA cops are sticking around. Those boys from Longmont were a couple real bad apples. You're lucky to be alive. Been investigating them for a while. IA's insistent on talking to you. You'll need to do that eventually. But if you need more rest, I can have them come back later—"

"Send in the clowns." I realized I was slurring my words, the morphine making me loopy.

A few minutes later, Turley returned with two men wearing suits off the rack. Pencil pushers with soft bodies, gray at the temples, this pair hadn't seen the front lines in a long time. Turley introduced them as Investigators Ludko and Lotko with Internal Affairs, which might've been funnier had I been in the mood to laugh. I quickly lost track of who was who.

"Are you up to give a statement?" Ludko or Lotko said.

"About what?"

"The police officers who assaulted you in Longmont," the other one said.

That *did* make me laugh.

"Morphine," Turley whispered to them.

"Aren't they both dead?"

"Yes."

"Then what's the point?"

"This goes deeper than two dead cops. Snelling and Bernstein had a long track record of this kind of violence. We think it may be connected to something bigger."

"Like what?"

"A bounty program. Carrying out the orders."

The other investigator cut his partner off. "That's what we're here to find out."

Charlie and Fisher walked in the room.

Turley turned to them. "You guys mind waiting outside a moment."

"Let them stay," I said. "We're all in this together."

Turley looked to the two investigators, who nodded it was okay.

"Roberts," I said.

"Judge Roberts?"

"Longmont County judge."

"We know who he is."

"Kids are being shipped to diversion programs, padding numbers. Out of state. North River. It's all about trying to get that new private prison built." I was too tired to reiterate the rest. "Talk to Jim Case," I said. "He's a reporter with the *Monitor*. He'll fill you in on the details."

"Would you mind answering a few more—"

"Look at him, man," Charlie said. "I think he's had enough for now."

"Finn's right," Turley said. "Jay's been through the wringer. He can probably use some rest."

Just then the doctor walked in, a young Asian woman half my age. "Yes," she agreed. "Jay needs to sleep. I'm going to have to ask you all to leave and come back later." Then to me: "How are you feeling?"

I shrugged through a dopey smile, feeling blissed out and stoned.

"Morphine will do that." The doctor tapped the tube running from an IV bag to the crook of my elbow, before reading blips on a machine. "Vitals look good. But you really should rest."

Everyone turned to go.

"Hey," I called out to Charlie and Fisher, the doc. "Can I get a minute with my friends?"

"Sure," she said. "But make it quick."

Ludko or Lotko gave me their business card and said they'd be in touch.

Soon as they left, Charlie asked what happened.

"First," I said. "I need to apologize." I made sure Fisher saw I was looking at him too. "These last few days. This last week. I don't know. I mean, I'm hooked up to this machine, my leg is shredded cheese, I'm pumped full of painkillers, so this could be the drugs talking. But I finally feel like myself again."

Charlie pointed at my leg. "What happened out there?"

I gave them an abridged version of the events that transpired after I borrowed Charlie's car without permission—the reporter Jim Case, Nicki's betrayal, Michael Lombardi's surprise visit, the two Longmont cops dead on the mountain.

"Holy hell," Charlie said. "Michael Lombardi?" He looked toward the door, where no one stood. "Why didn't you tell those two investigators?"

"Because it would sound nuts. Especially now. After how I've been acting. A state senator? I gave that reporter everything we had. When they read those papers, they'll glean what's really going on. It'll make more sense if they see it with their own two eyes."

"Except Nicki sold us out."

"Only on the smoking gun. If those two IA cops are serious, there's plenty else to get started. They'll have UpStart dead to rights."

"How much money did Lombardi pay her?" Fisher asked.

"No idea," I said. "I'm guessing a lot. Can't blame her."

"You mean that?" Charlie asked.

"Sure. Why not?"

I knew it was Nicki who had placed that anonymous tip to Turley, saving my life. Since she'd been the one to jeopardize it in the first place, we were talking sideways move, at best. She'd chosen to cash out instead of pursuing a dead-end cause. I had no interest in excuses or apologies. But I understood the decision.

"I wish we knew why Lombardi wanted that photocopy so bad," Charlie said.

Fisher slapped his shoulder. "Let Jay sleep. This will still be here tomorrow."

I tried to wave goodbye but could feel that morphine dream pulling me back under.

I proceeded to pass out for the next nineteen hours.

* * *

It was all over the news the next day. Soon as I woke in the hospital bed, something told me to click on the TV set.

The Kids for Cash Scandal raged across every station, footage of Judge Roberts being led out of the courthouse, shackled, head hung in shame. Details tickered across the bottom of the screen. Roberts' attorneys offered neither steadfast denial nor ten-cent words to obfuscate the facts. I waited for allegations of baseless, egregious, politically motivated witch hunts. Something. But there was nothing. From the looks of it, Roberts was willing to hang himself out to dry all by his lonesome.

I caught glimpses of Michael Lombardi milling about with the rest of the talking heads in the background, glad-handing, mugging for the cameras, milking the photo ops.

My hospital phone rang.

"You watching this?" Charlie asked.

"Got it on now."

"You see Michael Lombardi? What the fuck?"

"I don't know, Charlie."

"You catch the interview?"

"What interview?"

"Lombardi's taking credit for the whole thing."

"What?"

"Claims his office put a task force together to investigate. Been months in the making. All his doing."

"How is that possible?"

"You tell me."

"I'll call you back."

A nurse came in, all smiles and perky cheer, inquiring whether I was hungry. I told her to leave me alone.

How had Michael Lombardi been able to get in front of this? His office, far from getting blamed, was being lauded. And the press gobbled up the bullshit. A special task force assigned? Were you kidding me? In less than twenty-four hours, fallout occurring in my sleep.

When I saw Jim Case laughing alongside Michael Lombardi on top of the courthouse steps, I understood the fix was in, a lone gunman sacrificed. I scrolled through other stations. More of the same. Nobody connected obvious A to blatant B. No one hinted at impropriety by UpStart. Two independent bad guys, Judge Roberts and North River, spurred by individual greed, had done wrong, everyone else in the clear.

I plucked the card left by IA off the nightstand. I grabbed the phone but stopped short. If Jim Case was standing up there with Lombardi, what was I going to do? Report Michael Lombardi for giving me an unsolicited ride? I had no concrete proof of anything. I buzzed the nurse back, apologized for my rude behavior, and asked if I could get something to eat. "Is there a copy of today's *Herald* lying around?"

She returned a little later with runny oatmeal and the day's early edition. There was nothing on the shoot-out by the lake. I rang Turley.

"How you feeling, Jay? Doc says you're on the mend."

"I'm fine. Listen, Turley. What happened? Up on the mountain?"

"What do you mean?"

"The aftermath with those two cops—"

"You were right."

"Huh?"

"About the diversion center. Snelling and Bernstein were working on orders from that judge they arrested. You asked the right questions. Set the wheels in motion."

"Where'd you hear that?"

"Those IA boys. Ludko and Lotko. You're a hero, Jay. You've seen the news, right? Roberts confessed. You helped expose a scandal. The scope of this is huge—"

"I got to go."

I hung up.

Why was Roberts agreeing to take the fall alone? Everything's for sale, I supposed. For the right price. Wire enough cash into an offshore account, and Roberts retires on the Fed's dime, doing soft time in a country club, kids and grandkids inheriting a windfall. One thing was clear: Lombardi wasn't going down with this ship.

I spent the rest of the morning watching the news and reading the paper. There was a silver lining. News reports had sentences at North River overturned, arrangements rescinded, prisoners released. My going to Jim Case had stirred shit up, forcing Lombardi's hand. Even if no one was interviewing me for the evening news, I knew I should feel proud of myself. Brian Olisky, Wendy Shaw, all the other teenagers wrongfully imprisoned would be set free because of me. I didn't need the glory. I knew what I'd done. Except I wasn't interested in helping kids like Brian Olisky and Wendy Shaw. At least not as much as I was in nailing Lombardi's ass to the wall. I loathed admitting that.

I was about to switch off the TV when I heard the bubbly blonde reporter mention the moving company. Blue Belle. Owned by Judge Roberts' brother. A brief mention, passing reference. But it clicked. I recalled those big trucks Charlie and I had seen up at North River. I went to turn up the volume but by then the pretty blonde had already moved onto the next hot-button topic. Today's viewer has a short attention span.

I thought about Xeroxes and unauthorized copies, the mundane details of conflicting reports and tallies for out-of-state penal colonies, how the quickest route can sometimes be the hardest to find amidst all the misdirection. The outline of a business card suddenly didn't seem so random. A contact's name or routing number could make such a business card very valuable; a vendor like that would be the perfect front to launder cash.

I wondered if I should reach out to Fisher and Charlie, see how frequently UpStart used Blue Belle to move freight. How about Tomassi? Michael's friends in the state Senate? Something told me the answer would be a lot. We didn't need the actual photo-copy to get started. Jim Case might be for sale, but we could keep going. We had the name, a start. The rest would be the tough part. Coincidences, hunches, and guts don't add up to much without the hard work. If payoffs had been laundered through this Blue Belle, I'd still have to prove that, and I doubted Michael or Adam had grown careless overnight.

And just as fast, I lost heart. I was finally on the mend. Was I really thinking about lacing up the gloves again? After all this fight had cost me? For what? I remembered what Nicki said our last morning together—the same thing Jenny, Charlie, and Dr. Shapiro-Weiss had been trying to pound into my thick skull ever since Chris died. Nothing I did could ever bring my brother back. Of course I knew that. In my head. But I always found ways to circumvent the irrefutable, convince myself of some greater cause, another injustice that needed my intervention. Which was all bullshit. No matter what lies I told myself, I'd been chasing the impossible. I could never resurrect the dead.

I knew I should take the small victories where I could find them. But when I viewed these meager gains in a different light, what had really changed? Even with North River stripped of its accred-itation, its doors forced closed in the wake of a scandal, the new Coos County Center would open its doors soon enough, grand opening slated by year's end. More a stay of execution than any permanent solution. Everyone was a winner. Except, of course, the ones who'd lost.

CHAPTER TWENTY-EIGHT

"THAT'S THE LAST of it," I said, setting the final unopened box of wedding dishes on the hardwood floor.

"What's wrong with your leg?" my wife asked. "You're limping."

"Banged it on something. No big deal."

"Well, what do you think?"

Jenny's new apartment in Burlington, like her mom's, sat on the picturesque shores of Lake Champlain, with plenty of natural light and open, airy space.

"Nice view."

Out the window, the April rains fell slow through brighter skies, splatting off the water, green grass poking through stubborn white snow. The new place would be nice for Aiden. Driving into the condo complex, I'd seen a small play area with a swing set, twisty slide, and jungle gym. A quaint gated community in a good school district. I wanted the best for my boy. Even if I couldn't be the one to give it to him.

Aiden ran in the room and tried to jump on my back, missing the mark. I spun around and caught him before he fell, carrying him like a football into the living room and flinging him on the couch, tickling his belly until he was hyperventilating.

"Please, Jay," Jenny said. "Do not get him all riled up. He's got to take a nap."

On cue Lynne stepped in from the other room. "I think you

should hang that picture—" She stopped, eyeing me coolly with her silent victory. "Oh, hi, Jay. Didn't hear you come in."

"Just bringing up the rest of Jenny's stuff."

"That was very nice of you," my mother-in-law, soon to be ex, said.

I winced a smile. Like I wouldn't help Jenny get her things. This was the mother of my kid. We'd be together forever, one way or another.

"Mom?" Jenny said. "Would you mind getting Aiden down for his nap?"

My son gave me a tight hug around the knees.

"I'll be up next weekend," I told him. "We'll get pizza and ice cream."

Aiden toddled after his grandmother, stopping in the doorway to wave goodbye to his father.

Jenny and I walked out to the landing of her new apartment. The rains came down harder now, drumming off parked cars, splatting down stories. I lit a cigarette, leaning over the railing.

"What are you going to do?" she said.

"I'm moving back home."

"Home? You mean Ashton?"

"I can't stay in Plasterville. Lease is up on our house, and it's more space than I can use." I didn't need to tell her the dull ache of painful memories were more than I could live with. "I called Hank Miller to see if I could rent my old apartment above the garage. Said it's been empty since I moved out. Couldn't bring himself to get another tenant. All mine if I want it."

"What about your job?"

"I'm going to start working for Tom Gable again. He says estate clearing ain't been the same without me."

I tried to laugh. Jenny pretended to smile.

"I miss being outdoors. I'm not cut out for the nine-to-five grind."

"You gave it a year, Jay."

"About as long as you gave our marriage." I caught myself. "Sorry. That was a rotten thing to say."

My wife took my hand, gave it a squeeze, and we both gazed out into the squall.

Over a month had passed since my breakdown. That's what Dr. Shapiro-Weiss called it. The seasons had started to change. This far north, temps remained cold, but if you thought about it hard enough you could almost smell the new grass, the maple and tree sap, flower buds fighting to come alive.

"Y'know, this move," my wife said, searching for encouragement. "We'll just see where this goes."

I nodded, keeping my stare fixed straight ahead.

"For right now, this is a good place for me to be. For Aiden, too. With my mom here, she can watch him during the day while I work."

"How's that going?"

"Turns out I *am* cut out for nine-to-five."

She smiled. I didn't.

"He's just a friend, Jay." Jenny was talking about Stephen, who'd helped get her an administrative assistant position with his bank downtown. "No college degree, no experience, I'm hardly qualified. Without his help, I'm tending bar. I can't keep doing that at my age."

Jenny was making more money at the investment firm than I'd been at NEI, and for the first time in a long time she seemed happy, like she had a purpose. I tried not to connect good fortunes as the natural result of getting away from me. But I knew the kindest thing I could do was stay the hell out of her way. When someone stands on a chair and tries to pull you up and you try to pull them down, the gutter wins every time.

"When do you move back?" she asked.

"Just about done. Only have a few boxes left." After we'd separated our possessions, with Aiden's toys and clothes, the good furniture and bedroom set going to my wife, I was left with a couch, coffeemaker, and photograph book. Which was fine by me. I wanted the transition to be as seamless for my son as possible. And I didn't need the reminders.

"Are you going to be okay?"

"I'll be fine. Dr. Shapiro-Weiss referred me to a psychiatrist near Ashton. I'm glad to be back there. It's where I belong."

Neither of us said anything for a while.

"I'm sorry we ran out of time, Jay."

I put my arm around my wife, and she laid her head on my shoulder. We watched the rain fall together.

*　*　*

I'd been working all week up at the old farmhouse on Old Farms Drive. On the other side of Ashton, an old farmer named Joe had died in his sleep, alone.

I got back from the foothills around seven, rosy eve succumbing to darker purple night. I scrubbed my fingers with gritty soap beneath the spigot, and headed upstairs to catch the Red Sox game starting in a few minutes. I'd popped my leftover Chinese chicken in the microwave when I heard a soft knock.

I opened the door. A woman and small boy stood there. I figured they must be lost. Either that or some religious fruitcake wanted to convert me. Why else would a forty-something woman and little kid be standing on my stoop at this hour?

"Jay?" the woman said. I didn't know her.

The microwave bell dinged.

I stared at the boy, who possessed a vague familiarity, a fleeting thought flying in my head and then out just as quick. All boys that age look the same. I didn't grasp anything tenable because tenable wasn't possible.

She waited for an invitation. I couldn't shake the sense I'd met them both before. Even though I was certain I hadn't.

"Do I know you?" I asked the woman.

"It's been a while," she said, trying to keep a smile. "Katherine. Kitty? I knew your brother. We spoke on the phone last winter when he went missing?"

"I thought you lived in California now?"

"We do."

I looked at the boy again and understood now why I thought I'd seen him before. Because I had. My whole life. They had the same eyes, the same scraggled bedhead. Even when he squinted up at me, eye half-cocked suspicious, the same stubbornness lingered.

Kitty didn't need to confirm what I suspected. It was obvious as the rising sun.

"Can we come in?" she asked.

"Yes. Of course." I scrambled to collect the tees and flannels hung to dry on the backs of chairs. Unwashed dishes and empty beer bottles cluttered my bachelor pad. I swept last week's dinner plates and cups into the sink, ran some water, tried to scrape the spackle with a spoon. "Sorry for the mess. Wasn't expecting company." I left the dishes to soak.

Kitty and I spoke last winter when Chris went missing but I hadn't seen her in years. The last time I had, she'd been fifty pounds lighter, with bright orange sores lining her lips and black circles ringing her eyes. Not that I spent much time in her company. I avoided my brother's druggie pals like they all had Hep C.

"You're not easy to get ahold of," Kitty said, the boy sticking close by.

"My number changed. New phone."

Kitty stroked the boy's mop-top, working up the courage. "I finally told myself, 'Kat, hop on a plane. You have to do this. Face to face.' I wish I hadn't taken so long."

"You're lucky you waited. I just got back."

"Vacation?"

I shook my head. I didn't need to explain my failed experiment in day jobs or marriage. She wasn't here for that. Most of life relies on timing anyway, which is just another form of luck.

Kitty glanced around my apartment. I studied her movements, her new appearance. She retained that ex-junkie look. Not that she was unattractive or haggard. She was pretty. Mom pretty. But pretty. She'd filled out since I'd seen her last, and was dressed like an adult instead of an angry teenager all in black, her dark hair blown dry. It was her eyes, which held onto some of the horror. Kitty had survived a life most will never see.

I stared down at the boy. "What's his name?"

"That's Jackson," she said, hugging him near.

I recalled our brief conversation from last year. Not the best time, my attention wandering. But I distinctly remembered her saying she had a girl, whose birth coincided with her clean date.

"I thought you had a daughter?"

Kitty dabbed at her eyes, fighting the tears. I said I was sorry. Jackson glowered at me. He had the same fiery indignation, too.

"No," she said. "I'm the one who should apologize. I don't even know where to start."

I crouched down, meeting Jackson on his own level. "Y'know,

I have a son as well. About your age. He's not here right now, he's with his mom in Vermont, but he left some toys. Would you like to play with them?"

Jackson checked with his mother, who nodded it was okay. I brought him into the living room and showed him Aiden's collection of Transformers and superheroes, Batman coloring books and cars, crayons, assorted building blocks to construct better worlds, his own corner for when he'd come visit.

My fat cat wandered in the room, curious about the new visitor.

"Don't worry," I said over my shoulder. "She's declawed. Big puffball."

When I walked back in the kitchen, I asked Kitty if I could get her anything, coffee, beer? Then I remembered the whole sobriety thing.

"I'm good," she said.

"You want to sit down?"

We both sat at the kitchen table, lost for words, while Jackson buzzed spaceships and cowboys in the next room.

"When you called looking for your brother . . ." Kitty stopped herself. I could see her recalibrating direction, stumbling for footing, adjusting on the fly. The pained expression on her face betrayed the guilt eating away at her.

"It's okay," I said. "Chris wasn't the easiest guy to deal with."

"I loved your brother, Jay. I did. And I wanted him to be a part of Jackson's life. Someday. When he got his shit together. I wrestled with whether to tell him. Maybe knowing he had a responsibility to something other than himself would've spurred him on to make some changes. Truth is, I didn't know for sure if it even *was* his until I was out in California. That time was so crazy. I'd been on the streets for years, chemicals messing my brain up, all out of whack, and here was my chance—probably my last chance—to clean up, get my life back. I was so sick and tired of being sick and tired. My sister . . . What I'd put her and my mom through . . ." Kitty stopped again, holding off the waterworks.

"It's okay."

"No, it's not. I had no right keeping that information from him. I knew who Jackson's father was. I mean, look at him. After you and I spoke, I talked to my sponsor. I was grappling with what to do. I prayed on it, asked my Higher Power for help. I finally decided to do it. I was secure enough in my sobriety—your brother deserved to know. Then I read on the Internet he'd died. Suicide by cop. Felt like a part of me died, too. You have to understand, your brother had a real hero complex. I couldn't have him showing up in Joshua Tree on the heels of a three-day Greyhound ride, strung out, jonseing, saying he was ready to be a dad and asking for fifty bucks and a ride downtown. And that is what would've happened. I couldn't risk it. I had to be there for Jackson."

"So you don't have a daughter?"

"When you called, I was scared. I don't know why I thought saying I had a daughter would make any difference. I guess I wanted a cover story as far from the truth as I could get, so you couldn't put two and two together. Maybe the lie made the fantasy easier for me to believe. Ridiculous, I know. Daughter, son, what would it matter? I'd been dreading that call from your brother. When I left here, I was showing. Chris had to suspect the truth. At least the possibility. When I called you back last year, I'd been at work and I panicked. I wanted to help you find him but I had a thousand thoughts racing through my brain, wrestling with what to tell you, editing out information in real time. I didn't know if it was already too late, and I—" Kitty started crying again.

I got up from my chair and hugged her.

"I always held out hope he'd get straight."

"We all did."

The nauseous stench of microwaved leftovers swamped the kitchen. I got up and dumped my dinner in the trash. Gave her a moment to collect herself. I stood at the sink, rewashing the same spot on a dish.

"I had this fantasy," Kitty said. "Your brother would call me up one day and he'd sound like the Chris I used to know, back before we both got so fucked up. There had been a time when we were regular people, y'know—maybe 'regular' isn't the right word—but we weren't what we became. And he'd tell me he figured it out, had gotten straight, kicked for good and was ready to start living again. I'd be able to hear it in his voice, and I'd say he should fly out for a visit, and he'd say he'd love that. I don't know how he'd get to my house from the airport—that wasn't part of the fantasy—but he'd knock on the door of our house in Joshua Tree. The sun would've just set, and the sky out there, you have to see it, the way horizons wash rosy pink, how pretty saguaros and pepperbushes can be, the desert sky like nothing you've ever seen, and I'd let Jackson answer the door, and Chris would be able to tell right away. Like you did."

Jackson ran back in the room. Now comfortable with the surroundings, he was grinning, happy, a well-adjusted little boy. The way Kitty cradled him, the warm, protective smile, you could feel the bond, the love. I couldn't comment on the morals involved, whether or not telling my brother was unethical. But she'd done the right thing. If Chris found out, he *would've* hopped a Greyhound and shown up at her door, strung out, deluded, wanting to play the hero. And if Kitty tried standing on that chair to pull him up, two more lives would be ruined.

Kitty stood to leave. "I've got to get him to bed. We fly back tomorrow afternoon. Out of Boston. Cheapest flight, y'know?"

"Where are you staying?"

"I figured we'd grab a motel on the Turnpike."

"Don't. Stay here."

"I don't want to be a bother—"

"It's no bother."

With my invitation Jackson had already run off into the other room to play with the toys.

"Are you sure?" she said. "We show up out of the blue. I dump all this on you. You probably need time to process—"

"It's not a problem."

I turned around and watched Jackson playing on the floor. When he glanced up at me, our eyes met, and I got to stare into my brother's eyes once more.

"I have plenty of nights to spend alone."

"Well, if you're sure—"

"Please. We're family."

"Okay, let me get Jackson ready."

"You guys take the bedroom."

"Jay, you don't have to—"

"You take the bedroom. I sleep on that couch half the time anyway." I wasn't lying. Most nights, whenever the movie or ballgame would end, I'd pull the blanket down and crash there.

I fetched their bags from the rental car. While she readied Jackson for bed, putting on pajamas and brushing teeth, I fitted the mattress with clean sheets and brought out fresh towels. I told my nephew how nice it was to meet him. I gave him a hug and kiss goodnight, and left them to their bedtime stories.

After she'd finished tucking him in, Kitty joined me on the porch, where I leaned over the railing smoking cigarettes. Above the mountain, a giant white moon lit up the night sky, exposing farming flats and stone walls, the cow fields of my hometown.

"Thank you," she said.

"Told you. Not a problem. My pleasure."

"I mean more than just letting us sleep here."

I nodded I understood, and we remained still, looking out over the valley, listening to the soft winds of Lamentation.

"Can you do me a favor?" I asked.

"Anything."

"Tell me more about my brother."